Marley

Marley

a novel

JON CLINCH

ATRIA BOOKS

new york   london   toronto   sydney   new delhi

An Imprint of Simon & Schuster, Inc.
1230 Avenue of the Americas
New York, NY 10020

First Atria Books hardcover edition October 2019

ATRIA BOOKS and colophon are
trademarks of Simon & Schuster, Inc.

For information about special discounts for bulk purchases, please contact Simon & Schuster
Special Sales at 1-866-506-1949 or business@simonandschuster.com.

The Simon & Schuster Speakers Bureau can bring authors to your live event.
For more information or to book an event, contact the Simon & Schuster Speakers Bureau
at 1-866-248-3049 or visit our website at www.simonspeakers.com.

Interior design by Alexis Minieri

Manufactured in the United States of America

1   3   5   7   9   10   8   6   4   2

Library of Congress Cataloging-in-Publication Data has been applied for.

ISBN 978-1-9821-2970-5
ISBN 978-1-9821-2972-9 (ebook)

For Wendy. Forever.

Marley was dead, to begin with.

—CHARLES DICKENS, *A CHRISTMAS CAROL*

Marley

1807

Prelude

One

Sunrise, but no sun.

The merchant ship *Marie* tied up at the Liverpool docks hours ago, beneath an overcast sufficient to obliterate the moon and the stars—and now that dawn has arrived conditions have not improved. The fog over the Mersey is so thick that a careless man might step off the pier and vanish forever, straight down.

But Jacob Marley is not a careless man.

The *Marie* belongs to him, every plank of her hull and every cable of her rigging and every thread of her sails. Every *other* plank and every *other* cable and every *other* thread, to be precise. The rest are the property of his business partner, Ebenezer Scrooge. Scrooge could tell you exactly which plank and which cable and which thread, because that is how his peculiar and peculiarly focused mind works. Marley relies upon him for that. The two have been shackled together in business for exactly eight years now, although it seems like a thousand. They may as well have emerged together from the womb.

Scrooge lies abed at this cruel hour, rigid as a corpse behind his curtains, sorting his dreams into stately columns and rows. Marley is out

3

here, dockside in the damp, to oversee the unloading of the *Marie* and the modifying of her identity to accommodate a modified world.

The ship's crew, weary from their journey but invigorated by landfall, have dispersed to tavern and knocking-shop, where their arrival has the routine and rhythmic quality of a changing of the watch. Whether standing at a brass rail or stretching out upon some ghastly damp cot, each man assumes a position only recently vacated by a recently satisfied customer. These previous are not merchant seamen like the men of the *Marie* but Royal Navy men instead, just now reporting back for duty upon a moored ship known to Marley by reputation. She is the HMS *Derwent*, recently in from Plymouth on her maiden voyage, although the newspapers have been full of her for months. A newly christened brig-sloop of nearly four hundred tons, she is slated to sail for the African coast at the turn of the year—and there to begin interdicting the heretofore perfectly legal slave trade. The *Derwent* is but the first of many ships set to engage in this devilish work, under the oversight of His Majesty's newly constituted West Africa Squadron. To Marley's way of thinking, it is all a great waste of iron and men and shipping capacity.

He watches the sailors as they strut and stagger past, youngsters sharp and gay and confident of their place in the world despite their recent immersions in grog shop and whorehouse. And once the *Derwent* has swallowed them whole he turns his attention to the unloading of the *Marie*. Armed with a fistful of negotiables, he enlists a rough band of longshoremen from alleyway and flophouse. Man after man they squint into the daylight with a cough or a groan or a regretful shake of an aching head, and then they fall to emptying her decks and purging her hold like an army of half-crippled insects, bearing away bales of fragrant tobacco and white cotton, barrels slowly aslosh with molasses, and hogshead after hogshead of refined sugar—a pharaoh's ransom heaved in teetering pyramids upon the quayside. Marley observes them closely, keeping watch upon the forward hatchway for the emergence of a set of heavy strongboxes. In all truth he cares little for the *Marie*'s legally manifested cargo, as long as these particular boxes—chained each to each like prisoners, labeled *Scrooge & Marley* in a fierce and florid hand—remain secure. The ordinary goods are but passing through his clutches on the way to their true owners, while the strongboxes belong to him. And partly to Scrooge, of course. The instant he spots them he orders them borne straight to his carriage, their weight sufficient to set the weary springs groaning. The customs agent, in exchange for a secret handful of Spanish dollars, fails as usual to notice them.

His most important mission accomplished, Marley turns his back upon the laboring men and strides up the gangway and proceeds belowdecks. He seeks Captain Grommet, master of the *Marie* for longer than anyone can say, and he finds him sharing a ration of rum with Mr. Flee, her first mate. The two have been allied far longer than Scrooge and Marley, although to less cumulative financial effect. Grommet, clad all in black, is a hatchet-faced skeleton thin enough to conceal himself in the *Marie*'s rigging. Flee, discounting the jut of his evil-smelling corncob pipe, is as square and solid as a sea chest stood on end. This present tot of rum is clearly not their first of the morning.

"Ahoy there," Flee hiccups, not grasping their visitor's identity in this chamber whose only light drips from a waterous green deck prism mounted overhead.

Grommet silences him with a baleful glance. He brings himself to his feet, unfolding like a conjured specter. "*Good morning, Mr. Nemo,*" he says, in the oily tones of an undertaker hopeful of finding work.

Marley clamps his thin lips into a razor-cut line but does not correct him, for it is his custom in all matters relating to the *Marie* and her various cargoes to do business under that name. "Grommet," he says. "Flee." His eye is on the jug.

"I know, I know," confesses Grommet. "It is a bit early."

Marley offers the hint of a smile. "That's nothing to me."

"Very good, Mr. Nemo," says Flee, hoisting his cup. "Very good indeed. You're a true gentleman and a kind master."

"I am not so true," says Marley, reaching into the depths of his over-coat to withdraw a pair of envelopes—one marked "G.," the other "F." He holds them close to his vest, as if deciding whether or not he should provide these two with their pay after all. "Nor am I so kind. The simple fact is that I shall no longer *be* your master, although whether or not you stay on with the ship will likely be your decision."

Grommet's black eyes flare. "You're selling her?"

"So it would appear." Marley reaches out and tucks an envelope into each man's pocket, with a tenderness prompted more by the negotiables within than by the individuals under his employ.

"It's that damned Slave Trade Act, ain't it?"

"That and certain other concerns." For Marley never tells anyone his entire business.

Grommet's mind begins working. "Perhaps we could arrange to haul some other cargo on that leg."

"Some other cargo?"

"Anything you wish."

Marley scoffs. "What I wish, Captain Grommet, is that you could name for me some other cargo whose value equals that of a hold packed with men."

Grommet cogitates. Flee chews his lip. They can think of nothing.

"In the absence of such miraculous cargo," Marley goes on, "Mr. Hawdon and I have elected to sell the *Marie* and leave the business of slaving to the Americans."

"Americans."

"Just so. I'm certain that you'll get along famously. The new owners are a pair of Quaker gentlemen: a Mr. Bildad and a Mr. Peleg."

Grommet makes a mental note, the gears within his bony head grind-ing almost audibly. The names seem to ring a very old and rusty bell.

Marley turns on his heel and makes for the companionway. "By the sound of it, they're Old Testament fellows. Believers in the Almighty and so forth. If I were you, I'd mind the rum."

→→

Marley follows the last few men down the gangplank to the quay, where he enlists a brace of them to help rig a long plank across the *Marie*'s stern. Together—Marley is as willing to bark his knuckles as the next fellow— they suspend it from the quarterdeck rail, just below the wooden plate that bears the ship's name. That sorry panel is as disreputable-looking as the rest of the ship, having like the balance of her endured two or three decades of nautical abuse with little in the way of cosmetic or even mechanical attention. Under close examination, it would seem to have begun life either a shiny black or a deep oceanic blue, with incised letters done up in gold leaf, the letters themselves surrounded by nosegays of stylized flowers similarly executed. Marley studies it from every perspective, noting with satisfaction that the fog has begun to burn off and the sun to emerge at a favorable angle. Then he scrambles down and strides toward his carriage.

He returns bearing a folding table in one hand and an ancient portmanteau in the other. Regaining the scaffold, he sets up the table and opens the portmanteau wide. A single glance reveals within its depths a collection of rags filthy and filthier, burnt candle ends, slender vials containing traces of pigments everywhere along the spectrum from earthy to brilliant, iron nails gone mostly to rust, a much-used wooden mallet, the broken stubs of a score of Conté crayons, a stoppered vial of some clear solvent, an array of mysterious hand-built tools that resemble medical instruments or devices of torture, at least one corroded knife, various lengths of string, graphite powder leaking through the weave of a rough cotton bag, straightedges straight and otherwise, a set of cold chisels in various sizes, a dozen lucifers bound up with twine, quantities of bear grease and whale oil sealed up in little tin tubs bearing carefully lettered labels, paintbrushes of the highest quality and the lowest, and atop it all a single plover egg, painstakingly wrapped in cotton wool.

With these implements he works a miracle, for although Marley possesses many talents, the greatest of them is forgery.

Within an hour's time the *Marie* has been rechristened the *Mariel*. No observer should ever guess that the new painted letter was not incised and gilded thirty years prior, right alongside its fellows. Even the floral sprays around the name have been shifted and augmented, balancing the design and fooling the eye. Marley is satisfied, and Marley's standards are the very highest. As he dismantles his works and regains the carriage he congratulates himself upon having committed an act almost godlike, for back in his locked desk at Scrooge & Marley are official papers documenting the tragic loss of the *Marie* somewhere in the Atlantic, one week ago today. They will prove useful with the insurers.

1787

Two

Professor Drabb's Academy for Boys has all the qualities of a prison but the warmth, all the qualities of a graveyard but the fresh air, all the qualities of a slave ship but the view. It is no place to make friends, but young Ebenezer Scrooge has been friendless before and he shall be friendless again and so his time here marks no particular loss.

The Academy occupies a mansion of dull red brick, grand at one time but diminished now by years of neglect. All barriers between the indoors and out have grown permeable, and the dank chambers packed tight with row upon row of desks and tables and beds exhale the stink of earth and rot and decay. The professor keeps some wretched livestock (a few grizzled sheep, a flock of mangy chickens, two or three gouty pigs), which roam as freely in the building as in the yard. The breezes stalking the halls via broken or missing windowpanes and crooked doors that won't close properly if at all do little to mitigate the stink, and can be counted upon only to provide certain seasonal variations upon it—summer means acrid chicken droppings tracked from dooryard to dining hall to sagging cot, winter means starved rats decaying behind the walls.

Professor Drabb patterns his management of the operation upon the methods of God Himself, which is to say that he acts capriciously and at great remove. Entire days have been known to pass—weeks, in the more extreme cases—during which he has gone completely unseen except by one or two boys who are privileged to wait upon him in his lofty room, high in the windy cupola, just below the creaking weathercock. From time to time he issues commands by means of these worthies, although in the end it's impossible to say how accurately or completely his meaning makes its way down the stairs.

This year, one of those fortunate boys is Jacob Marley. His origins are unknown and his presence within these halls is unexplained, neither of which is cause for singling him out. Here at the Academy, every boy has secrets. Secrets are their refuge and their currency and their stock in trade, and in this respect Jacob is no different from the rest. Rumor has it that his father is a diplomat of immeasurable wealth and his mother is a lifelong intimate of Queen Charlotte. Rumor has it that his father is a spy for either the Prussians or the French or both, and that his mother is a mystic who, having blinded herself with a poker, now resides alone in a mossy dungeon where she is attended to by a loyal army of nuns who do nothing but read her the book of Psalms from morning till night. Rumor has it that Jacob poisoned his twelve older brothers so as to guarantee himself a more satisfactory inheritance.

No one knows for sure.

Jacob Marley is about the same age as Ebenezer Scrooge, although he has the advantage in seniority. He has been a student at Professor Drabb's for many years, while Ebenezer is new. Scrooge arrived at the close of the summer perched upon the box of a wagon driven by an anonymous individual in his father's employ, and when the horses passed beneath the crumbling archway and drew to a halt upon the weedy courtyard he let himself down without assistance, trunk and all. He entered the main hall as the wagon clattered off, only to find it echoing and empty. Along various winding passages he wandered like a drop of mercury in a maze, following channels worn into the ancient planking by the passage of generations of ill-used boys. He found Professor Drabb's office but no Professor Drabb. He found classrooms presided over by great looming monstrous boys and narrow beady-eyed devilish boys and no boys whatsoever. He found laundries and workshops and underground manufactories where children toiled like the damned.

Undaunted, he exited into the courtyard and scoured the property from margin to margin. To the north was a dry riverbed, to the west was a half-burnt forest, to the south was a scrubby hedgerow marking the limit of a neighboring farmyard, and to the east was the lane via which he had gained this paradise. Every inch of it was unpopulated. He returned to the mansion and dragged his trunk up to the second floor, where he deposited his belongings at the foot of a sagging and apparently unclaimed bed. Then he headed back down the stairs to join one of the classes he'd seen in progress. The other children—they seemed about his age, although they looked like old men long denied nourishment— ignored him vigorously. Thus began his lessons at Professor Drabb's Academy for Boys.

As far as Ebenezer can determine, the business of Professor Drabb's Academy for Boys is carried out entirely by the boys themselves. They teach the classes and they cook the meals and they fend off the creditors. They mete out discipline and they enforce policy and when the sheriff comes knocking they pay the bills. It is all according to a principle that Drabb calls Manly Self-Determination, whose tenets are explained in a framed broadsheet hanging upon the wall of each public room. The language employed by that disquisition is so archaic as to be very nearly Anglo-Frisian, and the logic wielded in its coils would mystify a scholar of the Talmud, and the type in which it is set is cruelly microscopic. There is every chance that no party on earth, not even its ostensible author, has read it all the way through and survived.

The details do not matter, though, for the principle is the thing. All the rest is interpretation, a task at which generations of boys have proven themselves remarkably expert.

Ebenezer waits the better part of a week before Drabb himself finally makes an appearance. Unannounced and unanticipated, he comes floating down the stairs from his aerie, soft and vague and aimless, the very dreamlike picture of a careless and benevolent god. He is clad in some kind of shabby academic gown or formal sleeping garment, and atop his very round head is a stocking cap pulled tight to his eyebrows. He yawns as he comes, and he makes straight for the kitchen where preparations for supper, such as it shall be, are under way.

If any boys but Scrooge notice him, they give no sign. Ebenezer, on the other hand, puts down his work and follows the professor straight into the kitchen. "Excuse me, sir," he says, hoping to introduce himself, but Drabb makes no response. Two or three of the boys look up from feeding the iron stove or hacking away at withered carrots to give their new classmate steely looks. Another, hard by, touches his sleeve in warning.

Drabb adjusts something within the folds of his robe and gives an imperious sniff. "Chicken tonight, is it?" he asks no one and everyone.

"Soup," says the largest of the youngsters present, a surly-looking villain who has taken upon himself the run of the kitchen.

"Chicken soup?"

"Just soup, sir."

"What sort?"

"Vegetable." Meaning carrot peelings and tepid water.

"I would prefer chicken."

"As would we all, sir."

"I would prefer *roast* chicken, actually."

"We're down to a half dozen, sir."

"A half dozen what, boy?"

"Chickens, sir. Like you was asking about."

"No matter. I shall require no more than one."

"But the boys, sir . . ."

"What boys?"

"Our boys, sir. *Your* boys."

Drabb surveys the hungry looks of the children gathered round-about. "These preening, privileged rapscallions?" he says. "Do they think their fees should cover not just the most prized and practical education in all of England, but luxurious dining as well?"

"I don't know, sir. You would have to ask them."

"Instead of pining away for roast chicken, they should be remembering their lessons. Pythagoras ate no meat, and he gave us mathematics."

"Pythagoras, sir?"

Blood rushes to Drabb's face. "Do you boys retain nothing of your education?"

"No more than we're taught, sir."

The professor selects a child at random, a small one, harmless and half-starved, and he takes him by the neck with one meaty hand. Were he to lift him into the air and shake him as a cat shakes a mouse in its final throes these silent children would be unsurprised, for all of them but Scrooge have witnessed such violence before. But he only draws him close, studying him through bulging eyes and breathing upon him the hot and fetid breath of one who has just risen from a week in bed. The child seems prepared to withstand anything, suffer anything, confess anything. If he were made of wax, he would melt.

Overcome with disgust, Drabb flings the innocent toward the boy in charge. "Have this ungrateful little ruffian go out and slaughter my supper," he says. "Perhaps he'll remember *that*."

Ebenezer's instinct is toward anonymity, and it proves to be his best defense. At least a dozen other boys claim to have never crossed paths with Drabb at all—there are legends of some who spent entire careers here, arriving as little more than babes and exiting as fully fledged members of the criminal class—without the professor ever learning their names. These few, along with the occasional child who might sicken or die or otherwise wash out early, are the lucky ones.

Young Ebenezer is seated alone in what passes for the library one December afternoon, working out a long series of sums in the dying light, when his comfortable invisibility threatens to collapse around him. The development comes at the hands of Jacob Marley.

"You won't like this," says the boy, closing the door behind him and thrusting an official-looking document between Ebenezer and his calculations. The top of the page reads *Sweedlepipe & Steerforth, Solicitors*, and the scrawl at the bottom would seem to be the signature of that same Sweedlepipe himself. Everything in between is the work of a professional scribe with a hand far superior to his employer's, and both its penmanship and its intent are terrifyingly clear. Sweedlepipe and Steerforth, acting on behalf of Mr. Elias Stump, the farmer whose acreage lies beyond the hedgerow to the south of the Academy, are filing a lawsuit against Professor Drabb "for damages committed upon Stump's property including but not limited to the breaking of six (6) windows, the destruction of one (1) outbuilding by fire, and the loss of two (2) prize geese through means unknown—such damages having been committed in person by a youth in Drabb's charge, one Ebenezer Scrooge."

Ebenezer is speechless.

"Be glad the professor hasn't seen this yet," says Jacob. "He'd have your skin."

"But I had nothing to do with—"

"Of course not. No one did. Stump does this every now and then. Hires a lawyer, makes up a charge."

"Why?"

"He hates Drabb like poison. He'd see the place closed down if he could."

"But he can't think he'll win."

"He lives to torment the professor, that's all."

Ebenezer shakes his head, marveling at the pig-headed meanness of some people. He feels positively vindicated.

"Still, the problem remains," says Jacob, running one finger along the text of the letter. "Your name is on the suit."

"I cannot imagine why."

"No one knows how Stump chooses his targets. He works in mysterious ways. He does like to go after the weak, though—and you happen to be new."

"Just my luck."

"The trouble is, there's not a single boy left here who's ever been named in one of Stump's lawsuits."

"Sent home, were they? I'd be happy to be sent home."

"Oh, they weren't all sent home." He picks up the letter and folds it and restores it to its envelope. "They're just not here anymore."

"What became of them?"

Jacob carries the envelope to the grate and puts a flame to it. It bursts alight and dies without warming the chamber the slightest fraction of a degree.

"What was their fate, Jacob? The other boys?"

"Never mind them," says Jacob. "Just be glad that we keep watch for these letters. Those of us with more experience owe it to the rest of you."

Naturally, he has a plan. He assures Ebenezer that it has worked many times before, saving the skin of any number of boys imperiled by Stump's phony charges.

"We must settle the case," he says.

"Settle?" says Ebenezer.

"Settle."

"How?"

"The usual way. With money."

"Six windows," says Ebenezer, working the damages out in his head, "plus an outbuilding, plus two geese . . ."

"Two *prize* geese, at that."

"It would come to a fortune!"

"We must make every effort. Your life depends upon it."

"No." Ebenezer sags. "It's impossible."

Jacob presses a steadying hand upon his shoulder. "Your father must have resources."

"He employs most of them to keep me here."

"Then you shall write to him, and plead to be brought home at once. I shall cover your tracks with Stump and Drabb and the solicitors until you are well beyond their reach."

"No," says Ebenezer. "Father would think me at fault."

"Well, his punishment surely would be lighter than Drabb's."

"Perhaps. But in the end he would send me off someplace even worse than this."

Jacob sighs a long sigh as he taps his forehead with a finger. "Do you receive some small monthly stipend? Some kind of allowance?"

"It is but a pitiful amount."

"Then we shall make an offer. We shall work out terms."

"Repayment could take years."

"Consider the alternative," says Jacob, opening the library door to let himself out. "Now, you must leave it all to me. I shall handle the correspondence in my role as Professor Drabb's secretary, and we shall have you off the hook in no time—God willing."

The post is slow and erratic. Weeks pass with no word from Marley beyond the occasional report that negotiations are under way or temporarily stalled or pressing forward against all odds. Ebenezer ducks when he encounters Drabb in the hallway and seethes when he spies Stump at work upon his squalid acreage.

If only those two would settle their differences without involving me, he thinks. The situation is unendurable, and yet he endures. When his spirits are at their lowest, he permits the thought that Jacob Marley is working on his behalf to cheer him a bit. Perhaps he has made a friend here after all.

He finds himself in just such a funk one gray afternoon in the late spring, when Jacob descends from Drabb's aerie with a thick envelope in his hand. "Success," says Jacob, taking him by the shoulder and aiming him into Drabb's disused office.

The terms agreed upon in the covering letter seem like something less than success to Ebenezer, but Jacob assures him that they are the very best possible. "You'll have a ha'penny left over each and every month," he says, "free and clear. I'd count that as a victory."

Ebenezer looks unconvinced.

"These fellows would have had your scalp if we hadn't taken things in hand."

"I suppose you're right," says Ebenezer. "And I don't mean to seem ungrateful."

"We'll find a way for you to make it up to me, if you insist." He smiles and withdraws from the envelope a set of contracts written in duplicate, already signed by Sweedlepipe and Stump. He rummages in the desk to locate a bottle of ink and the stub of a quill pen and hands everything over to Ebenezer. "Sign here," he says, indicating the spot. "And here as well. Yes. That's right. *Well done*."

Three

Belle Fairchild has always found Ebenezer Scrooge interesting—charmingly distracted in his manner and surprisingly puckish in his observations—at least when she can capture and keep his attention. Teasing him out of his shell was one of her favorite activities when they worked for old Mr. Fezziwig, but now that they have gone their separate ways she encounters him less often. She does see his sister, though, Fan, one of her oldest and dearest friends.

By means of that connection she has invited Ebenezer to join the church choir, in which her own bright and soaring soprano contrasts nicely with Fan's deep and passionate alto. Thus it is with these two, always and ever: Belle a creature of spirit and air, Fan steady and earthbound. The choir happens to be short a second bass at the moment, and although Ebenezer's voice falls a good bit higher than that—closer to a baritone—he accedes to her wishes and promises to attend Thursday evening's rehearsal. Belle thinks she might detect a twinkle in his eye as he does so, as if he knows what she's about and is making himself a willing party to it. But as she smiles back he looks away, distracted by some invisible thing a few degrees beyond her left shoulder, and that's the end of it.

She is not an avid husband-seeker, not yet, although it pays to keep an open mind. She has watched while her own sister—older than she, about Scrooge's age—has bloomed and faded faster than anyone with an ounce of kindness in his heart might have thought possible, and so she is not entirely unwary as she looks toward the future. Belle is not, after all, a girl with financial or social prospects. Scrooge, on the other hand, would seem to have prospects aplenty. He's engaged in a business partnership with another striver, one Jacob Marley from out in the countryside somewhere. Two eager lads merging their fates and their fortunes, although to look at them you'd think neither would have two pennies to rub together. "That's the secret," Scrooge would say if she were bold enough to ask. "Economy in all things." He and Marley have other secrets, too, ones not so easily prized loose.

He will arrive in the choir loft late, having lost track of the hour as his workday came to a close. Whether one ought to call this concentration or distraction makes little difference, for either way it will prove to be an enduring asset to both Scrooge and his partner. Right now it is a mere inconvenience, cause for a missed supper and a breathless run to the church through London's darkened lanes. The fog has crept in and the lanterns are not yet lit, and although he could hire a boy with a torch to accompany him he would no more waste money in that fashion than he would throw it away on a carriage. So this lanky scarecrow in his ill-fitting black waist-coat and his rolled-up shirtsleeves and his oft-darned tights accommodates himself to the darkness in his favorite way: He turns it into an exercise in memory and computation. Scrooge keeps within his mind a detailed map of the city built up from earliest childhood, and he holds in some secret compartment of his heart or his lungs or perhaps his liver a compass of unerring accuracy. Let some angel or devil or ghost intent upon abduction drop him from a terrible height into the least of the city's lanes, and he will know instantly which direction he faces down to the degree. So even as he snuffs his candle and passes through the warehouse door and fastens the lock upon its rusty hasp behind him, he is busy making calculations. Three blocks north, then five blocks east, then north-northeast along a curving lane through one, two, three, no, make it four intersections, and then a sharp turn due west at the fifth down a narrow courtyard—and there's the church. He's running before he's finished making his mental chart, and he's halfway to his destination before he begins breathing hard. In no time at all—no false turns, no dead ends—he skids to a clattering halt at the church door. Upon his lips he bears the smile of a victorious Olympian.

The sanctuary is dark save a candle sputtering here and there, most of the available light warmly gathered in the loft where the director has begun running the sopranos through their scales. *The sopranos being the high ones*, he thinks. Should choir or director or pianist detect his footstep on the winding stair, no one makes any audible response, which gives him hope that he may be able to slip in unnoticed. That hope rises right along with him until he gains the loft at last and spies there in the glimmering candlelight Belle herself, seated at the end of the row closest to the head of the stair, glancing up from her hymnal to greet him with a bright gleam in her eye and a smile as subtle as it is inscrutable.

Scrooge coughs.

The piano stops.

The sopranos strangle.

Belle rises and sets down her hymnal. "Miss Percival," she says to the director, "may I present Mr. Scrooge?"

"This is your bass?" says the old woman, glowering from behind her music stand.

"Yes, ma'am."

Miss Percival squints at Scrooge with hopelessness written upon her narrow face. "He don't look like a bass. Not at all."

Scrooge wrings his hands and offers a pleading smile that by daylight would terrify even the bravest of children.

"Ain't enough meat on his bones."

"Madam," Scrooge puts in, "I can assure you . . ." but his voice cracks into a register startling even to him, and he abandons the cause.

Miss Percival scoffs and turns her attention to Belle, the source of this disappointment. "A fellow that skinny just don't resonate," she says, as if Scrooge were not even present.

From the other end of the front row, from her place down among the altos, Fan comes to his aid. She says, "I'll have you know that my brother was always the true singer in the family," which makes Scrooge swallow hard. "You should have heard us on Sunday evenings, the whole family gathered around the piano. Mother sang soprano and father sang tenor. More than once we had to put Ebenezer in the butler's pantry and lock the door rather than let him overwhelm us with that powerful basso of his."

"Oh, really?" says Miss Percival, not believing a word.

"This was before he learned to control his breathing, of course. These days he's as harmonious a chorister as you'll find short of the choir at St. Martin-in-the-Fields. I mean the ones on the payroll."

Which Scrooge sees for the cover that she intends it to be. He resolves that henceforth his singing shall be a mumble, a wheeze, a vague and timid muttering meant to suggest great power under tight rein. Just that much and no more, which suits his untested abilities perfectly. *God bless Fan*. He gives Miss Percival a little bow and smiles cautiously at no one in particular and sidles toward the lone empty chair in the back row, where a hymnbook is waiting. The gentlemen to his left and right—a Mr. Carstone and a Mr. Gradgrind—welcome him as if he is cavalry arrived for last-minute reinforcement.

"Now we'll give them a run for it," says Mr. Gradgrind, beaming. Even at a whisper, his voice rumbles like distant cannon fire. Mr. Carstone agrees, in tones that might be more audible to the larger members of the cetaceous family—the finback, perhaps, or the mighty blue.

Miss Percival taps her baton on the music stand and glares at the basses. Mr. Gradgrind and Mr. Carstone straighten their posture and Scrooge follows suit, as if he is strung between them on a line. His voice cracks and crumbles as she propels them through their scales, but his presence encourages the men on either side to such an extent that as a group they have never sounded better.

Miss Percival's ear is discerning, though, and she is a hard one to get the better of. "Now I should like to hear Mr. Scrooge alone," she says, lifting her whalebone baton, narrowing her eyes.

"Am I to be a soloist, then?"

The cunning Miss Percival is not to be outsmarted. "To judge from your sister's recommendation . . ." she begins.

Scrooge interrupts, aghast or feigning it. "Begging your pardon—I came here not to elevate myself, but to praise the Almighty."

Miss Percival puckers her lips and draws her narrow chin into a tense knot.

"I am quite certain," he goes on, "that I can accomplish such praise in fellowship with these gentlemen far better than I ever could alone."

Suffused with delight and solidarity, Mr. Carstone and Mr. Gradgrind clap him on his jutting knees, one to each. Miss Percival, crestfallen, moves on to torment the tenors. And Scrooge's place here is made fast.

The anthem this week is to be the Reverend John Newton's "Amazing Grace." A favorite of seamen and other desperate types the world over, the hymn was the product of a storm-tossed shipboard conversion. Newton lay down one black night a slave trader and arose at dawn transformed, certain that prayer had induced the Almighty to calm the gale on his behalf. *No more kidnapping Africans out of the jungle*, he would decide by and by. *No more hauling cargoes of disease-riddled human beings across treacherous waters to the Promised Land. And no more flogging dark-skinned men and women to within inches of their commercially unacceptable deaths, either.*

"Amazing Grace" is a dirge in three-quarter time, its gloom poorly matched to its hopeful message. The eight-part arrangement that Miss Percival has found is no exception, and the lugubrious tempo that she sets only deepens the effect. Scrooge has time to think as the music trudges forward, though, and between the vocal support of the men to either side and the simplicity of the bass line he is able to get his footing nicely. He has no clue as to what any of the notes are, but that doesn't matter. It's all relative.

Steady on this low one at the bottom for three beats and then up a sizable notch for one and then up a smaller one at the end of the phrase to finish things out. As for interpreting whole notes and half notes and dotted halves and so forth, the familiar melody lets him grasp their coded secrets with little effort. So by the time the choir has finished polishing "Amazing Grace" and moved on to "O Sacred Head, Now Wounded," he understands that he doesn't actually need to read music at all, at least not in the conventional sense. He only needs to see the lines of the bass clef as a kind of map for singing, with rhythms indicated by numbers done in hieroglyphs. Nothing could be simpler. As his confidence grows he even begins to sing out a little—not much, but a little—and bit by bit he grows happy.

When the rehearsal is over, Belle goes to sit alongside Fan and wait for Scrooge to come by.

"The bass section has never sounded better," Fan says when he does.

"It was a group effort," Scrooge demurs. "All I did was give them confidence."

Belle stifles a tinkling laugh. "Oh, I believe Fan is the one who did that."

He stops and thinks for a moment and has to allow that she's correct, the trumped-up story of his remarkable musicality having been his sister's idea. "At least I didn't disappoint them," he says.

Belle rises. "Oh, Ebenezer," she says, "you did marvelously."

Scrooge blushes and studies his feet.

"So—can we look for you on Sunday?"

"I shall be here."

"And the next Sunday, too?"

"I suppose." Whatever enthusiasm he has developed for the music seems to be slipping away under the assault of commitment.

"You *suppose?*"

"Never mind our Ebenezer," says Fan from out of nowhere. "I'll see to it that he comes." She stands alongside her brother and puts a hand on his forearm, which gives him a start.

"And every Sunday after that?"

"Don't."

Belle leaves off with a pout. Hope still glows in her flashing gray eyes, though, and the halo of her golden hair gleams like possibility in the candle-lit loft. "There'll be a reception after the service. With tea and cakes."

Scrooge tugs at his sister's hand. "If I can spare the time away from my desk," he says. After all, he has even now begun to adopt the work habits that will serve the enterprise of Scrooge & Marley so very well and for so very long.

"On the Lord's day?" She is incredulous. Truly.

"As far as I know, the Lord has never balanced the accounts without my assistance."

If he means this as charming or ironic or even merely clever, it misfires. Belle turns away and attends to her hymnal. Fan pats her on the shoulder and watches dully as her brother vanishes down the dark stairs. "He'll warm up," she reassures her friend. "Just not quickly." And with that she too is gone.

A summer chill has coalesced in the night air, and the fog that blooms in the streets is damp but not dense. Lanterns glow within it like dandelion heads gone to seed. Belle hugs herself and moves from one pool of light to the next, all alone in the universe except for certain distant and muffled sounds: the clopping of horses' hooves, the grinding of iron wheels, the disconcerting laughter of unknown men. She lives with her parents and her sister in modest rooms above a stable, behind a house so grand as to be nearly invisible. Her grandmother served in that house and lived in these selfsame rooms a long time ago, and she was so beloved that when she fell ill the owner of the house, a gentleman called Liveright, granted her and her son permission to stay there in perpetuity. The incautious naming of Belle's father in the paperwork, capitalized upon by a young barrister called Tulkinghorn interested more in establishing his reputation than in achieving any immediate profit, kept him ensconced there even after his mother joined the heavenly choir—a condition which still brings endless delight to him and endless torment to Mr. Liveright. "There are limits to all things," Liveright likes to say, "even kindness"—although he cannot prove it to be true.

Belle's father is a clerk, skilled and loyal and well trusted by an employer of some generosity, and the effect of his good income upon these poor premises is considerable. The walls are freshly painted and the furniture, although not of the latest fashion, is clean and sturdy. The dishes are unchipped and the utensils are untarnished. Fresh fruits and vegetables abound in the larder during the warmer months, and in the winter a fire blazes in every hearth with no regard to the cost. In short, funds that ordinarily would have gone to merely getting by have been freed to be lavished upon the niceties.

Such conditions are agreeable in the present but precarious in the long term. Upon many occasions Fairchild has warned his daughters, "Beware of getting too comfortable, my dears, and never forget that these premises are not mine for you to inherit. When I pass away, it will be Mr. Liveright's duty and no doubt his pleasure to cast you both out into the street—and your mother, too, provided she fails to predecease me." He swears that he takes no special pleasure in limning this tragic scenario, but he rehearses it so often and so vividly that it's impossible to say for certain. Either way, with the passage of time Belle has begun to see the prospect of a life on the streets or in the poorhouse as a genuine possibility. Thus as she climbs the narrow stair and lets herself into her family's quarters she finds herself reflecting upon the qualities and possibilities of young Mr. Scrooge.

"Did he appear?" her sister, Daphne, asks from over by the hearth. Daphne is the mirror image of Belle, with the burden of eight additional years heaped upon her. She has not yet given up on her marital prospects but is beginning to weaken in that regard. Failing the arrival of some spontaneous good fortune, she shall soon resign herself to being no more than a spectator in matters of the heart, and it is a spectator she seems to

Belle just now, alone in the lamplight, squinting over her needlework, inquiring hopefully as to Mr. Scrooge's presence in the choir loft.

"Oh, he most certainly appeared," says Belle.

"And?"

"I'm afraid he is not much of a singer."

"Too bad." Daphne frowns, almost sympathetically. "But I can't say I'm surprised."

"Miss Percival says he's too thin. Not enough resonance."

"She's being kind," says Daphne.

"Miss Percival? Kind? Have you made her acquaintance?" This last is pure irony, for Daphne studied the piano under Miss Percival for many of her childhood years. She has forgotten most of her lessons now, but under close inspection her knuckles still bear the marks of Miss Percival's application of that long whalebone baton.

"She's always had an eye for a handsome gentleman," Daphne says, "although it does not become her any longer."

"Are you saying that you find Mr. Scrooge to be handsome?"

Daphne lowers her lashes. "When we were in school together, he was quite admired—by some."

"By you?"

"By some."

"Was this before he was sent away, or after he was brought home?"

"After."

Belle's face takes on a faraway look. "The return of the conquering hero."

"You could say that. I'm sure there were some who did."

"But you weren't among them."

"No. I always found him . . . cold."

"Cold?"

"It's why I'm not surprised that he isn't much of a singer. He doesn't lack *resonance*—he lacks *feeling*. And how is a person to sing without feeling?"

"You're being cruel."

"I have experience."

"Because you're *older*." She says it like the slight that it is.

Their father's voice comes from the makeshift parlor. "Ladies, ladies," he says.

Daphne whispers, "I'm only as old as your Ebenezer."

"He is not *my Ebenezer*."

"You're interested in him."

"I find him interesting. That's different."

"Not very."

Again, from the parlor: "*Ladies*."

Belle tries a different tactic. "Perhaps you don't know that Fan's heart was broken when he was sent away."

"She was not much more than an infant."

"She was old enough to know that her brother had been wronged."

"She was young enough to idolize him for no reason other than the difference in their ages. Ebenezer was difficult even then. Everyone knew it."

"So you don't blame the father for shipping him off like some criminal transported to Australia for life?"

"It wasn't Australia, it was a boarding school. And it wasn't life, it was three or four years."

"Did he improve, then? Is that why his father had him brought home?"

"His father relented. Ebenezer came back unchanged."

"According to Fan, he came back broken."

"Humbug," says Daphne. "And even if he is broken, you'll never fix him. You're interested only in his finances."

In the parlor, their father groans as he hoists himself from his chair. "*That's enough, ladies!*" With a shuffling of slippered feet he heaves into view, his waistcoat buttoned crosswise and his hair on end and his pipe-stem clenched between his back teeth. He has just now gotten a full charge of Virginia tobacco going, and he squints through the smoke with a look suggesting that he mistrusts the entire world. "I'll have you know that the finances of your fascinating Mr. Scrooge simply will not endure scrutiny."

"Daphne is the one who brought up his finances."

"More blessings upon her, then. Mr. Scrooge is, after all, not to be separated from his finances, as anyone with knowledge of the Exchange will tell you. Nor is he to be separated from his partner, Mr. Marley." He says this last as if the two businessmen are doomed to be joined together not just in this world but forever and ever, even into the afterlife, even unto the extinguishing of the last sulfurous ember of the last burning chunk of brimstone mustered up by Old Scratch himself. "The *disreputable* Mr. Marley, if I may make myself abundantly clear."

If Belle desires to offer up a word in defense of Scrooge, or if Daphne desires to offer up further condemnation of the man and his business connections, the wrath upon their father's face prevents them. He takes the pipe from between his teeth and studies the little inferno within it as if he'd like to try its heat upon Mr. Marley's immortal soul, and then he jams it back into his mouth and goes on around it. "You know what line those two are in, do you not?"

A shrug from Belle.

"You know why the sign over their warehouse door reads simply 'Scrooge & Marley'?"

Another shrug from Belle.

"Because those two gentlemen like to keep things mysterious. Vague. Nebulous. *Hazy*." From behind the fog of his pipe, he would seem to know what he's talking about.

"I assume they're in shipping," says Daphne, thinking to put an end to this interrogation by means of her superior knowledge of the world.

"Yes," agrees Belle. "Import and export."

"Oh," nods Fairchild. "They're in import and export all right. And do you know exactly *what* they import and export? Hmm?"

"Tobacco, sugar, rum?" offers Belle. And then she has an idea. "Is it the rum you object to?"

"No. And certainly neither the tobacco nor the sugar." Patting his little round stomach.

"What then?"

Fairchild sighs theatrically. How shall these innocents survive without him? He wrests his pipe from between his teeth and fastens upon his daughters a penetrating look. "I object, children, to the *slaves*."

Belle stiffens. Daphne cringes. Every atom of breathable air evacuates itself from the room.

"Slaves?" inquires Mrs. Fairchild from the parlor. "Do I hear that Mr. Scrooge is keeping slaves?"

"He's not keeping them, Mother. He's transporting them."

"Transporting them?"

"Yes, Mother. That's where the profit is."

"Oh my."

"*Oh my*, indeed."

"That nice young Mr. Scrooge, of all people."

"Yes, Mother. That nice young Mr. Scrooge."

"A churchgoing man."

"He is that. In fact, I hear that he's recently joined the choir." He shoots Belle an even darker glare than he has already been maintaining.

"Perhaps it will do him good."

Fairchild scoffs. "It will do little enough good for those poor savages whose blood taints every farthing in his pocket."

"I wonder, though—do you suppose he tithes?"

"I wouldn't know, Mother."

"That would be blood money, then, wouldn't it?"

"Indeed it would." He turns and makes as if to regain the parlor, but before he goes he favors Belle with a parting glance. "On the other hand," he says, "the church has relied upon worse. And besides—when I've crossed the Jordan at last, blood money could be the only hope of those I've left behind."

Whether that's a tear in his eye or a twinkle is impossible to know.

Four

Scrooge is no Marley, and Marley is no Scrooge, and their partnership is the better for it. A matched pair of oars may propel your boat nicely across a placid country pond, but real navigation on the perilous waters of the world, be they aquatic or financial, requires resources more sophisticated and diverse.

Ebenezer Scrooge does the ciphering and is himself something of a cipher. Tall but not overly so, slender but not exceptionally so, he is remarkable mainly in his unremarkableness. Time will work its changes upon him, of course. Unrelenting labor will crook his back and a stubbornly suppressed appetite will waste his flesh and a narrowness of mind will twist his features into a perpetual scowl—but for now he is undistinguished and undistinguishable from the general run of young men of his class and position. When he emerges from his countinghouse he goes garbed in a rusty suit and a threadbare collar and raveled stockings, all of which serve as unconscious concealment for the dreams of avarice that flare unsummoned within his heart.

He is happy at his desk if he is happy anywhere, for in the progression of inked digits along closely ruled lines he detects something close to the music of the spheres. The numbers sing to him, and he attends with an open heart. In their rising and falling, in their entries and omissions, in their conflicts and resolutions he hears symphonies—complex and vast and endlessly beautiful. This is nature's gift to him, and in turn it is his gift to Marley.

For Marley has no patience for numbers. His gift is for a different sort of complexity altogether, a theatrical one constructed of fantasy and façade. Down to his very blood and bones he is the man for the job, as suited to this role as Scrooge is to his. Not that he differs from Scrooge to any significant physical degree. Should they be laid out side by side upon a mortuary table, measured for their shrouds and fitted for their coffins, they would not seem so very different. Marley might be a shade broader in the shoulder and more narrow at the hip, Scrooge a bit scrawnier in the leg and a trifle less deep in the chest, Marley a bit squarer of jaw and Scrooge a trace weaker of chin, but otherwise they differ little—so long as they are spread out inanimate upon our imaginary slab.

For it is *movement* that makes the difference. In motion, Jacob Marley possesses a grace that his partner lacks and may not even perceive, so fixed upon the numerical is the automatic counting machine known as Ebenezer Scrooge. Utterly in command of himself and finely attuned to the perceptions of others, Marley gives up nothing to the resourceful cuttlefish in the matter of camouflage. His coloration, his appearance, good God his very dimensions, seem amenable to modification in service of the moment's need. A rough giant when some thieving miscreant requires intimidation, a wise counselor when some wealthy young widow knows not where to invest her inheritance, Jacob Marley can be all things to all men. And especially to all women.

As for the specific nature and fruits of his work, consider the good ship *Seahawk*, sister to the *Marie*, of which the chartered joint-stock company known as Scrooge & Marley is sole owner. Scrooge & Marley paid not a crown toward her purchase, having gained ownership through a long and cloudy sequence of transactions involving shell companies and false fronts registered in places as distant as the Polynesian islands and as close as the lockbox beneath Mr. Marley's own bed. If any actual funds changed hands anywhere along the line, they did so without his knowledge or intent. The *Seahawk*'s last-known quasi-legitimate owner, a certain Sr. Giovanni Cavalletto, whose only reported address was a room in a broken-down *pensione* on a flooded street in Venice, is surely still awaiting payment from someone or other.

Marley has all the paperwork, though. All the charters and forms and licenses and documents of transfer, signed and witnessed by a dozen hands in a dozen languages, sealed with the waxy impressions of officialdom from a dozen faraway territories. All of it indisputable, and all of it false.

While Scrooge is in the countinghouse, then, Marley is to be found either at home among his forger's tools or at large in the world, sniffing the air for possibilities. He lives by himself in a lowering pile of a great gloomy house set alone up a deep yard behind an iron fence, and although his own suite of rooms is modest, he keeps the rest to himself rather than renting it out. He shall have a use for each of these empty rooms, by and by. Marley has a use for everything.

There are funds coming in, of course. That's the essential thing. A certain amount unavoidably arrives in bank drafts and other traceable legal transfers, a fact that Marley has accepted as an unfortunate cost of doing business. The remainder, to such an extent as he can arrange it, comes in cash. Scrooge & Marley will accept the currency of most any nation, provided a favorable exchange rate can be negotiated and a means of conversion found. In a pinch they have been known to accept gold and silver bars and even the occasional velvet bag of uncut gemstones, although in Marley's mind such transactions smell a bit too much of actual high-seas piracy of the old sort, treasure chests and desert islands and all.

It is he who physically handles negotiables of this kind, secreting them about the empty chambers and hidden passages of his crumbling house, and it is he who oversees their metamorphosis from one form into another. He has established a large undercover network for these purposes. An assistant sub-clerk in the Liverpool Custom House, for example, will turn Spanish pieces of eight into British pounds sterling for a modest fee. A dustman off Regent Street has anonymous connections that can do the same with Dutch guilders, no questions asked. Only a few of these individuals are privileged to know him as Mr. Marley. He rarely signs the same name twice, or in the same way.

The business of recording these varied transactions falls to Scrooge, as does the work of transforming them into something that an outside observer—an officer of the court, for example—would understand as the records of a modest importing business of the sort they seem to operate. He keeps two detailed sets of books, along with various other ledgers and listings that serve as guides to interpreting them. Piled around him as he works, and growing day by day like underbrush, are cross-references and codices, scribbled notes and coded entries. It is his obsession and his joy. Five-year-old Wolfgang Amadeus Mozart, rising from his little bed with the strains of some symphony bursting within his brain, was never more thrilled by the spontaneous act of creation than is Scrooge by these enchanting numbers. The realities they represent—casks of rum, bolts of cloth, the hides of enslaved men—are nothing to him. He cares only for their music.

The street beyond Scrooge's door, like most streets in London, is a thing of monstrous filth and decay. Almost a quarter-million horses are abroad these days in the bustling city, carriage horses and dray horses and riding horses, too, and moment by moment they do exactly as horses will. One dare not grow too complacent upon the muddy streets.

It is down this treacherous avenue that Scrooge's sister, Fan, makes her way one evening. She lives with her mother, her father having passed on some years before, and today being Friday it is her custom to drop by toward closing time and drag her brother home for supper. It is his one decent meal of the week, at least in the opinion of his mother. Surely a periodic examination of his narrowing frame would not suggest otherwise. He seems to live on nothing but tea and calculation.

She finds him bent as usual over his desk. A single dying candle flickers at his elbow, meager defense against the gloom that the advancing day has ushered into his grim little chamber, but he neither notices the failing light nor minds it. His pen scratches away automatically, seemingly under its own power, suggesting that he could work in utter darkness should conditions require him to, the virgin expanse of his ledgers lit only by the fires of his imagination. "Ebenezer?" she inquires when he fails to look up. She has never found a way to shorten her brother's Christian name, some easy equivalent of everyone's "Fan" for her "Fanny." So "Ebenezer" it is, and "Ebenezer" again, this time accompanied by a rap of her knuckles against the top of his desk.

He startles, and his pen goes skittering across the page, the nib tearing a little furrow into the paper and the ink filling that furrow with a long black blot. "Damn," says Scrooge. He lays down his pen and reaches for some blotting paper and tries to minimize the damage, muttering something about an entire afternoon's work being lost, lost, lost.

"It's just a little smudge," says his sister, dabbing at it with her handkerchief.

He shoos her as he would shoo a fly.

"There's no real harm done." She's aware, of course, that any efforts at comfort or distraction will prove useless. As long as she's been on this earth, she's known her brother to be a perfectionist through and through. She steps back and restores her handkerchief to her sleeve and scans the rows and columns of numbers arrayed before her. They are sufficiently regular in their arrangement to have been stamped and set out by a machine, with only that single ugly black stain marring their order.

He burrows in a drawer and finds a straightedge, which he positions along the ledger's central fold. "I shall have to write this entire page out again," he says, "and the page on its reverse as well." But before he can make the tear she stays him.

"Not now, Ebenezer. Mother has supper waiting for us."

He resists, relents, studies the ledger with a sorrowful eye.

"Perhaps things will look different in the morning."

"Perhaps I won't sleep a wink all night."

"If you eat enough supper, you'll sleep well indeed." She closes the ledger and snuffs the candle.

Mother Scrooge lives under modest circumstances in modest rooms down a modest lane in a modest neighborhood. She saves and scrimps the whole week long to lay out the most extravagant meal possible when Ebenezer comes on Friday, and tonight is no exception. There will be roast goose, preceded by onion soup and served alongside boiled potatoes with lots of butter, freshly baked bread, and pastries both savory and sweet. The meal will be accompanied by a bottle of claret and followed by thimblefuls of a rich Spanish port that the Scrooge family has been conserving for years. The various scents in the air are both marvelous and deeply comforting, but Ebenezer instantly detects something amiss.

"Four seats at the table?" he says. "Four?" His mother has had to borrow that last chair from a neighbor, three being the most she has required upon these premises for a long while.

"You're a keen observer," says she, trundling out of the kitchen and presenting a floury cheek for the application of her son's birdlike kiss. "Tonight we are to have a dinner companion." She looks from Ebenezer to Fan and back again, impish.

"Oh, Mother," says Fan. "Have you acquired a gentleman friend?"

"Hardly," she says.

"Is it a gentleman at all, then, or a lady?" says Fan.

"A gentleman," admits Mother Scrooge.

"Known to us?" says Ebenezer, joining in the guessing game.

"Very much so," says his mother, her look going from mischievous to quizzical. "In fact," she goes on, "I'm a bit surprised that he didn't arrive right along with you."

Two identical knit brows from Fran and Ebenezer demonstrate their shared lineage.

"I sent a note to his office today. I received no reply, but then I hadn't requested one."

"The gentleman must be away," says Ebenezer. "Yes, there's no doubt of it. He's away on business, and he didn't receive your message."

"Perhaps I should have requested a reply after all."

"Certainly. Certainly. Always the practical thing to do. Then again, you would think someone in his office . . ."

"You would think," says his mother.

"If it were a well-run sort of place . . ."

"A well-run sort of place. With proper management and oversight. Staffed by decent and professional gentlemen."

Ebenezer sighs and shakes his head like the most jaded old veteran. "I fear that such offices are difficult to find, Mother. Standards have fallen off everywhere."

She allows the subtlest hint of a twinkle to gleam in her eye. "Even at Scrooge & Marley?" she asks.

Her son stiffens as if someone has thrust an icicle down his shirt collar. "I should say not."

"Then you would have noticed a messenger boy, had he come by this morning?"

"Most assuredly. I believe one did appear, in fact."

"With something for Mr. Marley, or for you?"

"For Marley, I believe. Yes. I recall setting it upon his desk."

"Without noticing that it was from your own mother?"

Ebenezer cocks his head.

"Standards have indeed fallen off," she says, laughing. "Even at Scrooge & Marley."

"Wait . . ." Ebenezer lifts an inquisitive digit. "Why would you be writing to my business partner?"

"You silly goose," his mother says, taking her daughter by the hand and drawing her toward the kitchen, where there is a bit of work left to be done. "He was to be our fourth. Now we shall have to eat every last bite ourselves!"

The vacant chair is still present, along with its empty place setting, when they sit down to supper. It stands opposite Scrooge's place at the neat little table—his sister is on his right and his mother is on his left—and its persistence seems to him a kind of reproach. He tries to keep from staring at it, saying as he helps himself to a second portion of potatoes, "I don't recall that I've broken bread with Mr. Marley in years, and I'm surprised to have come as close to it as I have this evening. Whatever were you thinking by inviting him?"

"Well," says his mother, "you two are in a partnership after all."

"That doesn't mean we're friendly."

"Perhaps you should be."

"I don't see the value in it. We are business associates, not boon companions." He saws at his portion of goose, methodically slicing it into a grid of little squares to be eaten one after another in sequence.

"Friendly relations have never hurt anyone," says his mother, with a meaningful glance toward his sister. "Isn't that true, Fan?"

He looks up at his sister in time to spy a blush dwindling from her cheek. "Mother," he says, shocked by the woman's audacity. "You would lure Mr. Marley here on behalf of—"

"Oh, Ebenezer—don't be such an old stick."

"It's indecent," he says, cringing. "Why, the man is practically her brother."

"A moment ago you were claiming that you barely know him."

"Her *financial* brother, I mean. His fortune and mine are closely joined, after all. If Fan cannot rely upon me for support, then she cannot rely upon him."

His mother purses her lips.

"She must have prospects other than Mr. Marley."

Fan speaks up. "But I think him very fascinating."

Her brother scoffs.

"And he was terribly solicitous when I encountered him on the street the other day."

"Fascinating and solicitous do not make a match."

"I'm not *marrying* him, Ebenezer."

"Good."

"At least not yet," she teases, and her mother gasps.

Ebenezer puts down his knife and fork and lays a steadying hand upon his sister's arm. "What you find fascinating about Mr. Marley," he says, "is no doubt related to an aspect of his character that I would describe as *mysterious*. His intentions and his whereabouts are often unknowable, even to me. His opinions—on everything but finance—are so flexible as to be practically nonexistent. He is in effect something of a chameleon. I have seen him become ten different men before ten different people, altering his language and his manner and even his ideas so as to serve his immediate aims."

"And yet you chose him for your business partner," says Fan.

"I did."

"You have never been a good judge of character, Ebenezer."

"Now, Fan . . ." says Mother Scrooge.

"A fair point," he says. "But Mr. Marley is irreplaceably skilled at his particular work. And I am the one who looks after the books."

The map of London built up within Scrooge's mind does have a gap or two, for he has not been everywhere. The portion of the East End known as Spitalfields, for example, is but an amorphous blot. Ever since the Revocation of the Edict of Nantes, the parish has been home to Huguenot silk weavers, a group with whom Scrooge has had little contact and about whom he possesses no curiosity—although a careful reading of his ledgers would reveal that the firm of Scrooge & Marley does indeed have certain commercial interests among them. The weavers of Spitalfields have, after all, overtaken their French forebears in the world market for high-quality satins, velvets, and brocades, for silks figured and watered, for exotic paduasoys, and even for the most sought-after ducapes. There are fortunes to be made.

So it is down the lanes of Spitalfields that Jacob Marley treads. The houses lining Dorset Street are grand indeed, proclaiming the wealth and position of their inhabitants. Looming high on either side, blotting out the weak sun, they seem eternal, immutable. Marley knows the lie behind that illusion, however, for these great houses have sprung up almost entirely within his lifetime. The earth upon which they stand yielded up the fruits of agriculture until the very instant the first French spade pierced the soil. So it is with the rise of any civilized thing, he reflects, and so it will be with its fall. Nothing lasts.

He has been negotiating today with a certain Antoine Bernière, leader of a cabal of Huguenot craftsmen seemingly bent on impoverishing Scrooge & Marley at all costs. They believe they're succeeding—a misapprehension that Marley has worked hard to sustain and that suits his intentions nicely. Bearing in his pocket a renewed contract signed just now under much feigned protest, he slinks away from Bernière's door with the look of a beaten dog, but the spring returns to his step the moment he rounds the corner. He is bound for an ancient and low-slung building well known to him, a place that sulks miserably in the shadows of the grander buildings that surround it. Reaching it will require several unlikely turns down crooked lanes and up soot-stained alleyways and along the shabby edges of vacant courtyards. The house he seeks, a thing of wattle and daub and shabby repute, is a relic of a time when mansions like Bernière's were only the most distant of dreams, and it will likely remain here when they have been reduced to memories. It was a farmhouse to begin with, squatting for generations upon its forlorn parcel of land, but now that London has swallowed it up, it has found a different use.

Cemented inside the front window by a paste made from spiderwebs and the crumbling remains of various winged insects is a sign promising ROOMS TO LET. How more than one or two such rooms could fit behind this hunched façade is a mystery, but once he is inside, the place begins to reveal its true dimensions. The ceiling is lower than might be considered practical, but its nearness makes possible a set of rickety stairs to the left, leading upward to something that by all the laws of physics should not be much more than a loft, despite a sign directing patrons to the (unlikely) second and (incredible) third floors. A different set of stairs leads down into what must be some sort of ghastly catacomb, perhaps a former root cellar. To the right a handful of ratty chairs huddle around a dead hearth, two or three of them occupied at the moment by sleeping men of questionable vitality. The nearest of these figures rouses at Marley's entrance, yawning and reaching out to consult the contents of an empty mug.

Marley steps around the men and raps on the rough wooden plank that passes for a bar. "Mrs. McCullough?" he calls.

In a trice the lady emerges. She is massive, catlike, and languidly aggressive, and her entrance is preceded by the dizzying scent of some perfume most likely sold by the hogshead. "Welcome back, Inspector Bucket."

"Who's in?"

"Ain't they all the same in the eyes of the law?" She bats her lashes, habitually but perversely coquettish.

"Who's in?"

"Lizzie," confesses the lady, with a trace of regret.

"Just Lizzie? Not Madeline?"

"It's early, Inspector. Come back this evening, why don't ye?"

"I keep a very busy schedule, Mrs. McCullough."

"No doubt of that, Inspector, but I'd hate for our relations to suffer on account of her. Next thing ye know, ye'll be talking to the magistrate."

"I have better things to do than talk with the magistrate," says Marley. He nods gravely and turns toward the stairs. "Lizzie will suffice."

1805

Five

"Your brother is painfully slow in courting," says Belle.

She and Fan pause at a muddy crossroads to let a carriage thunder past, and in its wake they lift the hems of their skirts and proceed. They are walking nowhere in particular. Their real errand, as usual, is the communion of their thoughts.

"My brother is painfully slow in most things," says Fan. "Other than calculation."

"Then he must calculate the progress of our courtship."

"If he were to do *that*," Fan replies, "you'd be marching to the altar right now. And where would I be?"

"At my side."

"And the next morning? When you and Ebenezer began married life?"

"Perhaps you'd be dreaming of how you danced the night away with that devastating Mr. Marley. Surely he'd be invited to his partner's wedding."

Fan's look turns dark and pensive. "No matter what I say, no matter how poor my opportunities with other gentlemen, no matter how grim my future, Ebenezer's opinion remains fixed."

"What if I were to speak with him on your behalf?"

"He won't concede."

"He might."

"He won't even listen."

"He might listen to me."

"No. Not where Jacob is concerned." She pauses and makes a show of pretending to examine the contents of a shop window, and after a moment she gathers herself and states to Belle's reflection: "Ebenezer has a heart of stone."

"Fan! That isn't true."

"It is. You may as well know it."

"I *don't* know it. And neither do you."

"I've known him my entire life, Belle. He never changes. You can hope for transformation if you like, you can swear that you detect little increments of improvement on his part, but in the end he never changes. He never will."

"So *we* must change *him*."

"I've tried. I've failed. I've given up."

"Then I shall take it upon myself," says Belle. "Both for your sake and for my own."

The deliveryman has a wooden leg that belongs to him, and a horse and wagon that don't. His name is Mr. Wegg, and he has taken possession of his employer's implements in order to deliver a lot of used furniture to the offices of a certain Mr. Krook. The horse is lame and the wagon has one wobbly wheel and altogether they complement Mr. Wegg nicely. They are three broken Musketeers, out seeking fortune and adventure.

The furniture heaped up in the wagon bed is wretched in the extreme, having been repeatedly discarded from the houses of various London families, passed down from one to the next like misfortune or disease.

That anyone would desire a stick of it is beyond even Mr. Wegg's imagining, and he's the one who found it in the first place, half-buried in the great ash heap at his employer's place of business. He had pulled it out to be set aside for burning, when a passerby—that same Krook—spied it and expressed interest. Warmth is one thing. Money is another.

Contrary to all expectation, Mr. Krook's office is located in a mainly residential part of the city. The building that houses it stands alone behind an iron fence at the top of a deep and dreary yard, its solitariness suggesting that it has been shunned by other human habitation and sent up here to do penance in isolation. The gate is ajar when Wegg pulls up, and with much clacking of his wooden limb he clambers down and swings it wide. The yard before the house is steep, paved with a sticky soup of mud and lichen and horse manure, so rather than risk a direct assault on the front door he drives his rig upward from side to side in a long series of switchbacks. Mr. Wegg will have trouble enough returning the horse and wagon before his employer discovers them gone; he does not require the additional trouble of pulling them from some mucky half grave—an exercise in which his wooden leg would surely be an impediment. Mr. Wegg is a circumspect individual, after all. Especially since the accident that took his leg.

The door is an ordinary household portal; a bit larger perhaps than most, adorned in its center with a massive knocker of old brass. He tries it to no avail. There is no indication of commercial activity here—no listing of business occupants, no set of bellpulls, and in particular no sign of his customers, the firm of Krook and Someone-or-Other. He waits. He tries the knocker again. He waits. Out of sheer boredom he does an undignified pirouette upon that wooden leg of his, and then he gives the knocker one more go. Nothing. So he tries the door. It opens onto a dim hall and a stairway so broad that a hearse might fit sideways across it—an unearthly vision that gives Mr. Wegg a shiver as the portal behind him claps shut.

He calls upward into the dimness. "Halloo! Mr. Krook, sir? Halloo!" Receiving no answer, he tries the first step, which produces a ghastly squeak and yields ever so slightly beneath his tread. The wood is rotten for sure. This place could be the death of him, and all for the price of some hard-used furnishings not strictly his own to sell. He tests the next one, which seems a trifle more solid, but he is rapidly losing faith in the enterprise. It was not a good idea at all. His employer will be returning in an hour or two, and poor old Mr. Wegg will be caught out here on a fruitless frolic of his own. *This will come to no good end*, he decides, and he turns to abandon the project while he still can.

"Mr. Wegg?" echoes a voice from above. "Is that you, sir?"

"The very same," he says, encouraged but not entirely.

"Excellent," says the voice. "Come up, then, why don't you? You're just in time."

"I'll not come empty-handed," says Wegg. "Send down the boy."

"The boy?"

"The boy to help with the carting."

"There's no boy," says the voice from upstairs. "There's never been a boy."

"You promised a boy."

"I have no boy, Mr. Wegg, so I doubt very much I would have promised you one."

"I have a wooden leg, Mr. Krook, so I doubt very much I would have come without the promise of a boy."

"We have a bargain, Mr. Wegg."

"The bargain called for a boy."

Footsteps sound from above, and a gentlemen that Wegg recognizes as Mr. Krook peers over the third-story railing. "If it suits you, then," says the gentleman, "you may return your wares to the dust pile. You'll have no payment from me—and no further trade, come to that." Just as suddenly as he appeared, he vanishes.

Payment. The delightful sonority of the word alters Mr. Wegg's way of thinking. He tries the third step and finds it sturdy, quite sturdy indeed. He considers the content of the wagon—a desk in three pieces, four ladder-back chairs, a pair of modest cabinets—and decides that if he is quick, he can have everything up the stairs and stowed away in the offices of Krook and Someone-or-Other within a half hour's time, boy or no boy. He sighs, salivates over the prospect of a piping-hot supper at his favorite tavern, and sets to work.

It's a noisy business, accompanied by extravagant curses and punctuated by the irregular hammering of that wooden leg on the open stairs, but it's over quickly enough. *Not a moment too soon*, thinks the irritable and ostensible Mr. Krook, who, thanks to Mr. Wegg's racket, can barely concentrate upon his own affairs. He has set up a worktable in the hall, over which he has spread a sheet of heavy sailcloth and upon which he has arranged the supplies of a calligrapher and sign painter. Brushes of various sizes, pots of ink and paint, a set of ship's curves, a flexible lead rule, and a supply of gold leaf. He is nearly finished executing upon the door to the room in question a sign reading KROOK & FLITE, LTD.

"Is this your specialty?" says Wegg, jutting out a finger. "Sign painting?" He's finished with the furniture and stands awaiting his pay. "You've done a fair job of it."

"Thank you," says Marley, drawing a few coins from some hidden spot on his person. "The truth is, Mr. Flite and I are in tinware. But I have always found it wise to be flexible."

"Aye, sir. Flexibility in all things—that's the ticket."

"Amen, Mr. Wegg," says Marley, but Wegg has already vanished down the stairs, pockets ajingle and wooden limb stamping furiously away, with the aim of restoring his employer's horse and wagon before his own flexibility gets the better of him. That, and then a well-deserved hot supper.

What sort of Englishman is forever too busy for tea? The nose-to-the-grindstone sort, to begin with. The sort who gets ahead without connections, who makes something of himself without benefit of small talk or social lubrication or the seeking of personal kindnesses. The Englishman too busy for tea is also likely to be solitary, perhaps even lonely. In other words, Ebenezer Scrooge.

A small fire is burning in the stove when Belle bursts in from the windy street. "Oh, thank goodness," she says upon detecting its faint warmth.

Scrooge looks at her from over the top of his glasses, one finger marking his place and the nib of his pen hovering wasplike. "Cold?"

"Oh, yes. A cup of tea would be nice, don't you think?" She makes the suggestion herself, for it would never occur to him.

He nods toward the cupboard where she'll find what she requires—a kettle and spoons and cups and all the rest of it, left behind by whatever tenant occupied these rooms prior to the arrival of Scrooge & Marley. She sees that the supply of tea is nearly gone, and makes a mental note to replenish it when next she visits. She fills the kettle and places it upon the stove while Ebenezer continues scratching away. By the time the steam has begun to rise, she finds herself warm enough to remove her coat. She pokes her head into Mr. Marley's chilly office and sees that, as usual, he's absent. This will make her mission easier. Encouraged, she returns and makes the tea and presents herself at Ebenezer's desk, a steaming cup in each hand, leaving no opportunity for him to object. She hovers until he clears a place. Closing his ledger seems to provide him a stab of actual pain.

"I suppose," she says, tilting her head toward the doorway that gives onto Marley's chamber, "that you're happier in his absence."

"I almost think I wouldn't know," says Ebenezer. "He is on the premises so very little."

"So perhaps you don't mind his company?"

"I have hardly experienced his company. In the six years that we have been yoked to each other, we have passed no more than a hundred working days in each other's presence."

She sips her tea, and nods at Ebenezer to suggest that he do likewise before it cools. "But you do have opinions as to his character."

"Certainly."

She lifts an eyebrow.

"I fear that I find him . . . coarse."

"But he presents himself as quite the sophisticate."

"Mr. Marley presents himself in many ways." He sips his tea and looks wistfully at his ledger.

"Don't we all?"

A shrug from Scrooge. He purses his thin lips, angles his teacup to consider the leaves that have collected at the bottom, and sets it down carefully. "By the way," he says, "I know perfectly well why you're asking about Mr. Marley."

"You do?"

"I do. You're asking on behalf of Fan. I have made my opinion known to her on many occasions, more clearly and in more detail than I ought to make it known to you."

"So I have heard."

"What has she told you?"

"That you disapprove. That's enough."

"It ought to be."

"And yet she persists."

"My sister has a stubborn streak."

"As do I, Ebenezer."

He smiles. "Does this mean that you intend to plague me on her account until I give in?"

She laughs. "Hardly."

"Good."

"It means I have held out for certain concessions of my own. In my case, from my father."

"Concessions?"

"Just so."

"Having to do with . . . ?"

"With *you*, Ebenezer."

He could not be more fully dumbstruck if a spirit had materialized before him.

"He doesn't approve of your . . . work."

Ebenezer places a hand upon his ledger, as if he's been required to swear upon a holy book. "My work is beyond criticism."

"Your bookkeeping, certainly. That isn't what troubles father."

"Then I am at a loss."

She rises and begins to gather up the tea things. "He objects to certain of your cargo."

Ebenezer thinks.

"Frankly, I object as well."

"You mean the leg from Africa to America." He puts it this way, rather than name the sin outright.

"Yes."

"It is all perfectly legitimate. It is all perfectly profitable."

"And it's all perfectly vile. Yet I care for you, and so I attempt to see past it."

"And your father?"

"He knows me. He knows I have faith in you."

"To do what?"

"To see the light, by and by, without his insistence upon it."

Ebenezer sniffs.

"One day everyone will come around to the side of right—including you and Mr. Marley. The trade will die of its own wickedness, or it will be outlawed."

"And then what?"

"You will find other cargoes, and you will wonder why you waited so long."

"Finding other cargoes would be Jacob's department."

"Your name is over the door."

"As is Jacob's."

"Yours is in the first position."

"We are equals."

She hesitates. "I think not."

He scoffs.

"I think you are the better man."

He looks into her eyes for just an instant but it makes him uncomfortable, and he looks away just as quickly. "But what has all of this to do with Fan and Jacob?"

"Do you care for your sister?"

"Of course."

"Then stop frustrating her. Show faith in her judgment, as my father has shown faith in mine."

Ebenezer, whose brain always trades in equivalencies, grasps the parallel at once. He chafes beneath the implications just a trifle—having stated that he is a better man than Jacob, is she further suggesting that her father is a better man than he?—but there is something about the depth of feeling that has brought her here, a great humanitarian reaching out not just to him but to shiploads of Africans who are clearly more to her than tonnage in a hold, clearly more than tally marks upon a ledger, that moves him. "Very well," he says.

"Thank you."

"I shall put some thought into that African cargo."

"I trust that you will follow your heart," she says. "Particularly now that you know mine."

Six

In Marley's house there are many mansions.

Besides his own living quarters, the building holds multiple separate apartments of one, two, or three rooms each, a cavernous attic, a vast and echoing basement, a vile and damp subbasement below that, and a cartographically unchartable array of closets, cubbyholes, passageways, chimneys, crawlspaces, and hidden chambers. Thanks to Marley's efforts at filling its various long-vacant rooms, the occupancy of the place is nearly complete. The tin merchants Krook & Flite—third floor, last on the left—now rub shoulders with a Mr. Pecksniff (international investments) and the firm of Nemo & Hawdon (import/export specialists). A freshly minted lease even now awaits the signatures of Squeers & Trotter (purveyors of specialty foodstuffs)—second floor, first on the right— but it will have to wait until the men from Grimby & Murdstone's wine- bottling operation finish wrangling their last wagonload of casks down the long, steep stairs into the basement. The *upper* basement, that is. No one, not even one of Marley's fictional entities, could tolerate the lower.

As for why he is wasting this perfectly fine space upon an actual flesh-and-blood tenant when he could be filling it with credible alibis and hard currency, Marley has his reasons. First, the wine merchants will provide visible activity sufficient for a houseful of false fronts, which will help the place appear legitimate from the street. Second, should any curious authority come sniffing about, the presence of the wine merchants and their ranks of warehoused casks should serve as convincing evidence that everything is on the up and up. Third, beginning this very night, his private quarters will be only a few steps from a limitless supply of the very finest tawny port in England.

Once the men have gone, Marley retreats to his workshop, which is accessible both from his bedroom and through a hidden stairway behind a sliding panel in the offices of Krook & Flite. Beyond the accumulation of dust, little has changed within the tin merchants' premises since the afternoon a few months before when Mr. Wegg dropped off the furniture. The desk still stands in its three component pieces, and the chairs still cluster together at a vacant nexus like a gathering of spirits convened to discuss the afterlife. The two cabinets are no longer empty, however. They are filled with bundled bills and various other treasure, too precious and fungible and anonymous to be entrusted to any banker.

One day Marley will get around to assembling the desk and arranging the chairs and otherwise making the place look occupied, but for now the lettering that camouflages the door will have to suffice. He has employed Wegg to obtain furnishings for the other offices, always maintaining the fiction that he is the selfsame Krook and always paying in cash. Wegg has been cooperative and solicitous to a fault, and knowing an opportunity when he sees one he now keeps an eye open for any such appurtenances as might befit Krook's growing community of fellow tenants. He winks and says, "Remaining flexible, I see," whenever the two meet on the stairs. Should Marley spy him on the street, however, he will slip to the other side rather than risk being called by the wrong name in public.

Seated at his worktable, he dips a pen and warms up his wrist. His *left* wrist, for he has decided that his left hand will provide the signature of

Mr. Squeers. It is to be filigreed, ornamental, bombastic. His right hand will supply the signature of Mr. Trotter, which by contrast will be meticulous and regular, the sort of timid and bookish penmanship that a young fellow might have acquired at boarding school and never shaken. The lease itself is a marvel, stamped and witnessed and dated five years prior so as to agree with certain other manufactured records he has passed on to Scrooge for incorporation into the narrative of their business life. He holds it up to the candlelight and smiles a smile of great personal satisfaction. No element is amiss, no detail unpersuasive. Which is not by any means to say that a single aspect of the document is perfect. The paper, dog-eared in one corner, is slightly embrittled by means of an arcane process known only to Marley and a handful of other specialists. The wax seal is unevenly centered and the stamp pressed into it is irregular, deeper on one side than the other. It looks hastily done but its offhandedness is a matter of much consideration. Such is art.

Marley dips his pen and describes Squeers's signature in a series of loose calligraphic extravagancies. While the ink spreads and dries he warms up his right fist, and when he is ready he executes the contrasting signature of the fictional Trotter. *Just so*, he thinks as he blots it clean. *The mark of a man who believes he knows exactly what he is about in this world*. The sober Mr. Trotter, set alongside the immoderate Mr. Squeers. It occurs to him as he slips the lease into a drawer that to an untrained eye, Trotter's signature might look very much like that of his partner, Ebenezer Scrooge.

Leave it to the French.

Scrooge & Marley's Huguenot contacts in Spitalfields are determined to hold a Christmas ball, and they are further determined that Scrooge and Marley should attend. The invitation arrives in the company of another envelope, larger and containing a statement of accounts that

Scrooge studies with his usual avidity. He has no interest in the smaller one, which would seem to be of a nature more personal than commercial, so it sits unmolested in the entry for several days.

Marley, on one of his rare visits, discovers it and slits it open at his desk.

"The Huguenots desire the pleasure of our company," he calls out with a whoop.

"Is it a summons of some kind?" asks Scrooge.

"Of some kind," says Marley. "It's an invitation to a grand ball. At the home our own Monsieur Antoine Bernière. On the evening of December 24."

"Oh dear," says Scrooge.

"Have you other plans?"

"I . . ."

"You cannot *possibly* have other plans."

"I . . ."

"Cancel them." He leaves his desk to stand in the doorway between their two offices. "Ebenezer, just imagine the feast that those Frenchmen will put on. Imagine the wine alone! This is our chance to recover some of what they've stolen from us over the years."

"We do quite well by the Huguenots."

"Not so far as *they* know. They believe they're pauperizing us and starving our children."

"We have no children."

"Never mind the facts, Ebenezer. This will be a most memorable affair."

A sniff from Scrooge. "I don't care for fancy balls."

"You've never attended one."

"Because I don't care for them."

"Ebenezer."

Scrooge puts down his pen. "The church choir is to go caroling that night. Belle would have my head."

"Not if you bring her to the ball."

"Then Fan would have Belle's head."

"Not if I bring Fan."

Scrooge harrumphs. Not even the notion of the three of them arrayed together against his position is enough to change his mind.

Marley alters his course. "Think of the contacts we shall make," he says. "Men of business from throughout Europe. Men involved not only in textiles but in shipping and manufacturing and wholesaling of every kind. The most wealthy and elevated in the world—and they will be ours for the acquaintance."

The idea warms Scrooge's heart, and he gives in.

Were the magi abroad upon this Christmas Eve, they would never find the holy child—certainly not in London, where the streets are choked with a fog thick enough to render anything from carriage to cathedral invisible at five paces. Strain as they might, Balthasar, Melchior, and Gaspar would seek illumination in vain.

Dorset Street, however, is a hard-fought exception. Down either side the lanterns burn with a ferocious festivity, lighting the way not for followers of any star but for acolytes of a different kind of gleaming majesty. The pound sterling. The piece of eight. The krone. The Hamburg mark and the mark kopparmynt. The dollar. They arrive, these believers, one by one and two by two in magnificent carriages drawn by magnificent horses, and their finery is in turn magnificence itself. One does not enter the precincts of the Huguenot silk magnates ill-clad. Especially not on Christmas Eve.

Even Scrooge & Marley have hired a carriage, an expense that pleases neither of them. It does not gleam, and the horse that draws it is swaybacked, and the driver seated on its box is hunched and grim, but a carriage it is, and it's costing them money and they make the most of it. It is definitely superior to walking.

They draw to a stop at the curb and wait for Bernière's footman, who is occupied with more elevated patrons than they. Belle parts the window curtain and gazes out at the brilliant throng surging in the glow of the lanterns, and a dire thought blooms in her mind. "We shall never fit in," she says, reaching with her other hand to clutch Ebenezer's fist.

Of the half dozen encouraging responses he could make, he utters none. He does not so much as offer a denial.

"Fear not," Marley puts in at last. "You two ladies would be an ornament to any occasion, even one as exotic as this."

Fan blushes in the shadowy chill of the carriage, but Belle is not encouraged.

"And I do mean 'exotic,' " he adds. "No doubt many of these grandees will speak nary a word of English. That should make fitting in easier."

"How so?" asks Fan.

"Unhindered by the handicap of words—or even accents, with which we Englishmen measure everything—we shall be on equal footing with all comers. And I put our ability to present a smile and a hand of friendship alongside that of any party on earth."

"It's not a competition," says Fan.

"Everything's a competition," says Marley. "And even a stick in the mud like our Ebenezer can manage a smile if he must. As for the rest, leave it to me." He gives Scrooge's knee a little shake that's meant to be encouraging.

Fan looks out the window and gasps. "But look at those gowns."

"Precisely!" says Marley. "That's exactly what those ladies will be doing—studying one another's gowns. They'll pay no mind to yours."

"But—"

"Yours has the advantage of being unobtrusive."

"No woman desires to be unobtrusive."

"The spotlight is a demanding place, Fan. I have always found the shadows to be much more amenable. You'll see."

—➤—

Within the palatial home of Antoine Bernière, atop a grand double staircase that unfurls itself on either side of the reception hall, a twelve-piece
orchestra is playing. At the sight of them Ebenezer takes Belle's hand and
leans close to whisper in her ear. "Quite a change from that mad fiddler
of Mr. Fezziwig's!" he says. And right on cue the orchestra strikes up a
rendition of "Sir Roger de Coverley," the selfsame piece that Fezziwig's
man played on that fondly remembered Christmas Eve. The tune being
that of an old country dance, a certain percentage of the foreigners do not
know it and a certain percentage of the highly placed Londoners actively
disdain it. The musical performance itself lacks the vigor and spark of the
solo fiddler's rendition, but despite its being overdecorated and under-
cooked Belle takes Ebenezer's hand and tugs him toward the dance floor.

"You are full of surprises, Ebenezer," she says when they've found
their place and joined in the swirl of movement, for the skeletal Scrooge
can still dance after all. He is a bit wooden, and a close observer might
detect the calculations going on within his brain as the music ratchets
along from one part to the next, but music is just mathematics made audible and he finds himself right at home within it. "We should have done
this long ago," she tells him, and she means it.

The dance proceeds around and around and their cheeks grow
ruddy. From time to time Belle catches Fan's eye, but instead of joining
in, she and Marley linger upon the periphery. He is scanning the crowd,
making calculations of his own. At one point she gives him a pleading
look but he stands firm, offering by way of explanation only a small but
wicked smile that suggests he's planning something far more interesting than a mere country dance. The music concludes to a merry burst of
applause and the orchestra slides into a waltz—a much-needed chance
for the dancers to catch their breath, perhaps even an opportunity for the
whispering of urgent secrets and tender promises—but by now Marley

and Fan are off winding their way through the crowd. He travels like a huntsman, sharply vigilant, unseen unless he chooses to be, seeking some prey beyond Fan's perception.

Just as dancers move according to fixed and long-established symmetries, so those on the periphery behave according to certain principles and patterns. They swirl, gather, separate, and coalesce again and again, following eddies and currents imperceptible to any but the most observant. Marley rapidly develops a sense for it all, detecting by signifiers as small as a woman's sigh or a man's wandering look which conversations might be worth joining and which are merely a waste of valuable time. He is not long in finding Bernière himself, master of the ball and founder of the feast, locked in conversation with an individual whose appearance suggests a small but ferocious animal. The fellow is sleekly groomed, his mustache clipped thin as a dueling scar and his jet-black hair greased into submission. The clothing in which he has attired himself for the evening is so understated as to be overwhelming, meticulously though invisibly tailored, with not a thread out of place. To Marley he smells of pomade and money.

Marley draws close but keeps his shoulder angled to Bernière and the elegant little animal, making small talk with Fan but listening in on their conversation. It seems that the gentleman comes from Rome, has made his fortune in the North American fur trade, and believes he knows everything. To Marley's mind these are all excellent qualities. He adjusts his position relative to Fan and the two men and briefly fastens upon Bernière a gaze sufficiently magnetic to draw his attention.

"Marley!" says Bernière. "I am delighted you could come!"

"Bernière," says Marley with a little bow. "Permit me to introduce Miss Scrooge."

Fan's smile and extended hand work as promised, but it is the little Italian upon whom they have their most profound effect. He beams, bows, awaits his turn.

"May I present Sr. Monteverdi," says Bernière.

"Charmed," says Fan.

"Please," says Monteverdi, displaying his teeth. "You must call me Valentino."

"Can it be?" says Marley. "Valentino Monteverdi? Of the fur trade?"

Monteverdi beams even more brightly, for although he warms to the subject of a beautiful woman, he warms even more to the subject of himself.

"Monteverdi in the flesh," says Marley. "I am honored."

The Italian nearly bursts.

"Mr. Marley is in import and export," says Bernière.

"Transportation! It is the greatest of my expenses," says Monteverdi. "The trappers, they ask little. The tanners, they ask less. But the men who own the boats! Such villains they are! Nothing is sufficient to fill their pocketbooks!"

"And so it is with Mr. Marley's firm," says Bernière. "They are the veriest predators, I assure you."

"Now, now," says Marley, his little smile hinting that Bernière may be correct.

"Yet you invite this, this *predator* into your home," says Monteverdi.

"I am a generous man."

"Ha-ha-ha! Too generous, I think! You must count your silver when he vacates!"

"I'll have his partner do the counting. Scrooge has a reputation of being incapable of making a mistake, even if it would be to the firm's advantage."

"Scrooge?" His eyes go wide. "The lovely Miss Scrooge is this villain's associate in business?"

"Oh no," says Marley. "She is my companion this evening. Her brother is my partner."

It takes Monteverdi a moment, but he catches on.

"Her considerably *older* brother," adds Marley, which causes Fan to blush.

"That so lovely a creature should possess a brother of such perfect repute . . . it seems too marvelous."

"Mr. Marley acts as his counterweight," says Bernière. "It's all we can do to escape his clutches with our skin."

Monteverdi sweeps his little hands around to indicate the room, the house, all of it. He looks like an imported timepiece. "And yet you seem to squeak by."

A smile of confession from Bernière.

"So it is determined, Mr. Marley," says Monteverdi with an impish look. "We must discuss business."

"I shall be in your office on the day after tomorrow."

"So be it," says Monteverdi. "And now, perhaps Miss Scrooge would favor me with a dance."

How could she possibly refuse?

The line of carriages stretches down the block and around the corner, so rather than wait for their own to arrive, they resolve to walk to it. "I know this district well," Marley says. "The footing will be sure and the street void of assailants, for the most part." It is cold, though, frigid in fact, and the moisture in the air seems to have coalesced in pulsating halos around the lanterns.

Scrooge breathes deeply and coughs. On the corner is a church, its tower invisible in the darkness and fog, and at their approach its gruff old bell awakens and strikes the hour. "Merry Christmas," says Scrooge.

"Merry Christmas," says Belle, leaning her head upon his shoulder.

And so the greeting goes from one of them to the next as they round the corner. The new street upon which they find themselves is comparatively dim, and the buildings are closer together, but the presence of the carriages and the drivers and the stamping horses provides a certain civilizing warmth.

As the last stroke of twelve dies in the darkness overhead, Marley takes Fan's arm and leans in. "I feared that I should never get to dance with you," he says.

She laughs, the sound of a bell very different from that of the rusted old monstrosity in the tower. "Mr. Monteverdi *was* insistent."

"And you were an excellent sport."

"He was charming, really."

"We ought to put you on the payroll."

"Jacob! How dare you suggest . . ."

"Oh, Fan," he says. "I don't mean a word of it."

Shadows pool in doorways and recesses and the mouths of alleys, and they move from the darkness cast by one carriage to the darkness cast by the next. Fan pulls herself tighter to Marley. "Where *is* the carriage?" she asks.

"Just ahead," he says, as if he knows for certain.

From the shadows comes a woman's voice. "Inspector?"

Marley winces, at least inwardly.

"Inspector Bucket, is that you?"

Marley makes no answer, biding his time.

"Inspector?"

"You've the wrong man," says Scrooge.

"Yer not the one I mean," comes the voice. "I'm speaking to yer friend." The shape of the woman resolves from the shadows, one ghastly accusatory hand thrust toward Marley. "I'd know ye anywhere, Inspector."

"Madam," says Marley, "if madam you are, and not some evil spirit abroad on Christmas Eve—I assure you that I am not your Inspector . . . Docket."

"Bucket," says Mrs. McCullough.

"Bucket."

"The girls have the night off, Inspector," says Mrs. McCullough, stinking of gin, commencing a slow collapse back into her pile of rags and shadows. "Just so ye know."

"We are reassured, madam." He steps over her fallen shape and thrusts out an indicative hand of his own, joyous as the whale-spotting inhabitant of some teetering crow's nest. "Just there, ladies. Our carriage awaits."

And so it does, just in time.

1806

Seven

Word having arrived on December twenty-sixth that Monteverdi has given his staff their freedom until the new year—how silly of him to have forgotten! how intoxicated by the presence of the lovely Miss Scrooge he must have been!—Marley's visit to his office has been postponed. Even the alternate date that they set proves impossible as well, since all the furnishings have been moved, and many of them discarded altogether (perhaps, imagines the resourceful Marley, to the dust pile of Mr. Wegg's employer), so as to permit a top-to-bottom redecoration of the facilities. Everything shall be redone in marble and gold leaf and the most sumptuous of fabrics. Nothing is too elegant or too dear for Sr. Monteverdi.

Marley writes back that perhaps they should meet in a coffee shop known to him, but Monteverdi insists that the only coffee that shall pass his lips comes from a tiny Roman *caffetteria* just across from the Pantheon, where the water still trickles in via one of the very last functioning aqueducts. *Tea, then*, suggests Marley, an affront that causes Monteverdi to go silent for nearly a week. Marley stalks about, clenching his teeth the entire time. So easily could a big fish be lost.

In the end they resolve to meet within the modest premises of Scrooge & Marley.

"Welcome to our humble quarters," says Marley as they pass through the warehouse door.

"Not so humble," says Monteverdi, with a twist of his lips that indicates he believes the opposite. "Not so humble at all." He is wearing the very same clothing he wore at Bernière's Christmas Eve ball, or else an exact duplicate of it. *Most likely he owns a dozen*, thinks Marley, *each one worth a month's income and more.*

Rather than follow his lead around the perimeter of the warehouse and directly into the office, Monteverdi begins prowling the aisles. "Hmm!" he says, and "Most interesting," and "Just so!" He trails a stubby finger along each shelf, leaving his mark on every single thing. There is a suggestion of claiming about it that troubles Marley's mind but not enough to ask him to stop—not now that he very nearly has him. By and by the little man comes to a bin containing a dozen magnums of tawny port, not technically the property of Scrooge & Marley but belonging instead to Marley himself, who has appropriated them from the wine merchants located in the basement of his house.

"Any good?" asks Monteverdi.

"Quite."

Monteverdi stands on his tiptoes and levers a bottle free. He examines its label, pursing his lips and squinting. "We shall see," he says at last. "Let us drink to our negotiations! And then let us drink to our agreement! And finally let us drain the bottle to our mutual good health!" Off-balance and weighted down by the cumbersome thing, he scuttles off.

They must pass by Scrooge's office to enter Marley's, and he glances up from his ledgers to acknowledge this avid little figure.

"Sr. Monteverdi," says Marley, "may I present Mr. Scrooge."

Monteverdi switches the bottle to his left hand so as to greet Scrooge with his right. "I regret that we did not make the acquaintance of one another at the home of Bernière!" he says. "I did, however, discover that sister of yours!"

"Then you've already gotten to know the better part of the family," says Scrooge, with a beseeching look. If Monteverdi would only release his hand, he could get back to work.

But Monteverdi is either oblivious to nuance or above it. "We shall see if you are correct!" he says. "Perhaps you are the lady's equal! Perhaps even her superior!"

"Well . . ." says Scrooge.

"Time will tell!"

"I suppose it will."

Monteverdi waves the bottle with his left hand. "Perhaps you will join us for a toast?"

Marley comes to his partner's rescue at last. "I'm afraid Mr. Scrooge does not care to imbibe."

"Additional for us, then!" says Monteverdi, letting go of Scrooge's hand. And then, recovering himself and fixing a glower upon Marley, "Provided your bottle is of sufficient quality, I mean."

"You may be the judge of that," says Marley, ushering his victim through the door.

Monteverdi can hardly begin to estimate the number of beaver pelts waiting in his Fort Albany warehouse. Their quantity increases by the minute, he says, thanks to his close and friendly relations with trappers and Indians alike. The shipping agents that he has employed, on the other hand, are quite a different story. They have long been deep in the pockets of various French and British and American interests, each of which has been only too happy to siphon off a portion of his profit. Thieves they are, one and all, and he is counting upon Mr. Marley to deliver him from their clutches.

"I have my own people," Marley says.

"And are they known to me?"

"You've surely heard of them, but doing business with them is beyond your reach. Without my assistance, that is."

Monteverdi sniffs. "I know everyone in the Americas. Everyone up to Mr. Washington himself, and he is president."

"Jefferson is president now."

"I likewise know him well." His eye drifts toward the wine bottle.

"That's all very fine, but Jefferson isn't your man. He has other things on his mind. The people I'm talking about, my people, stand ready to help you."

"And the names of your people?"

Marley has been anticipating this question, and in inventing their names he has gone for the biblical. "Bildad and Peleg," he says.

"Ah," says Monteverdi. "I have heard reports of them, and yet I have somehow not made their acquaintance."

Marley nods. "And the reports that you've heard?"

"Sir, they are without flaw!"

"As I'd imagined. Their reputations are pure sterling. Untarnished."

Monteverdi nods, as proud of the fictional Bildad and Peleg as if he'd invented them himself. "Tell me, are these men located in Fort Albany?"

"Never," says Marley. "They aren't some newly arrived northern opportunists. They're staunch colonial gentlemen of the Quaker faith, believers in God and champions of fair commerce, and their base of operations is within the Commonwealth of Massachusetts. Upon the island of Nantucket, to be precise."

Monteverdi gawps. "The Nantucket Quakers are very brave men. They hunt the sperm whale, no?"

"Indeed they do. And many of them work aboard ships that are owned and run by that selfsame Bildad and Peleg. My men. Our men. *Your men.*"

Monteverdi beams. "Have you perhaps a corkscrew at the ready?"

Eight

Taking full advantage of Sr. Monteverdi will require a network of greater complexity and scale than any that Marley has previously constructed. He could go through the old channels, of course—the shadow companies he's already established, the various flesh-and-blood customs agents and harbormasters and maritime insurers he's co-opted in both London and Liverpool. But this is to be an international operation, expansive in reach and impenetrable in nature, and it demands the very best of him. He warms to its possibilities.

He does wish, though, that he could involve Scrooge from the start. The man would be a great help in this sort of work, had he an ounce of imagination. Old Scrooge could surely tie arithmetical knots that no one—be he auditor or deckhand—could ever untangle, if only he weren't so damned practical about everything. But each man has his limitations, and confinement by the facts—whether real or manufactured—is chief among Scrooge's. It will be best for Marley to concoct the whole affair as usual, to map out the entire labyrinth, and then turn it over to Scrooge once the money starts to come in.

Those phantom Quakers, Bildad and Peleg, will be the key to everything. He leases them one of the larger offices at his disposal, purchasing a new suite of ruined furnishings from Wegg and lettering the details upon the door:

BILDAD & PELEG

NANTUCKET, MASS

INT'L CONVEYANCE & MARITIME MGMT

LONDON OFFICE

Soon enough the firm is equipped with bank accounts and legal representation and a full complement of the required licenses. Some of the banks and law firms involved are actual London establishments where Marley and his fictive companies have done business before, whether or not the institutions retain any record of it. The rest are entirely new inventions, purpose-built in support of the sham known as Bildad & Peleg. If Monteverdi could witness the labor required to establish an operation of this scope and complexity, he might sympathize and make Marley the silent partner that he will make himself before long.

As the days turn into weeks and the edifice of misdirection takes shape, Marley asks himself why he has not previously considered using companies based on foreign soil. They provide a freedom that he has never known before. The barrier of time between England and America alone is a godsend. Anything can happen—anything at all—in the six or eight weeks it takes for information to make the crossing. Cargoes can disappear, inventories can be altered, entire legal entities can come and go. Nonetheless, international trade does impose certain unavoidable realities. There are friends to be made on the ground in the United States, allies to be enlisted, officials to be bribed. And so he resolves to undertake a voyage there himself. He does not consult Monteverdi. On the contrary, his goals require that he slip away without the Italian's knowledge, leaving behind a series of elaborate alibis that Scrooge may employ to account for his long absence.

Fan, however, is another matter. "Take me with you," she says right off. "It will be an adventure."

"Alas," says Marley, "I shall have no time for adventures."

"Then I shall be your secretary."

"I do not require one." For the fewer explanations he must give, the better.

"In that case," she says with a smoky gleam in her eye, "I shall simply be your traveling companion."

The idea tempts Marley and very nearly sways him until he remembers the many kinds of female companions with whom he may arrange to associate in the months ahead. French women and English women and American women, seagoing adventuresses of flexible morality, grieving widows in desperate need of consolation, unattached heiresses green in judgment, dark Indian maidens fresh from the tipi and smelling of earth, woodsmoke, and animal musk.

"Perhaps," he says, catching his breath, "rather than rushing into some ill-conceived ocean voyage together, we should take a longer view. I shall be returning home in May, and at that time I believe we ought to begin planning our lives together." He does not even know himself if he means this—there is so much time between now and then, and so much distance between here and there, and so much possibility roundabout—but it has the desired effect of shocking her out of her momentary insistence.

"Are you—are you proposing marriage?"

Marley conjures a mysterious smile. "I am proposing that we consider whether I ought to propose marriage."

"You make things far too complex."

"All of life is complex."

"Besides," she says, beaming, "I already know the answer."

"Don't rush," he teases.

"Oh, Jacob." She stands on her toes and leans toward him with her eyes closed and her lips parted for a kiss, but he stops her with the touch of a finger.

"You have until May to make up your mind."

"May."

"May. Let us say nothing more of it until then, not to anyone, for I would sooner die than undertake an ocean voyage without my *betrothed*."

Thus he leaves her both uncommitted and entirely content.

Thus he will he be free over the next few months to acquaint himself with the world beyond London and Liverpool. By the time he arrives home, the broad Atlantic will have become to him nothing but a great washtub, within which every kind of sin may be cleansed forever from the record.

Nine

Fort Albany
Hudson's Bay
Canada

March 18, 1806
My dearest Scrooge:

Greetings from the New World!

Our work here proceeds on Schedule and to encouraging Effect. Although Trade in this locale is dominated by the Hudson's Bay Company, I can assure you that there remain many Opportunities for the smaller Enterprise to Profit—a Circumstance that has no doubt been capitalized upon by our Sr. Monteverdi.

He is a bit secretive in his affairs, no question of that, a Tendency which surely goes with operating a profitable Business in the shadow of a Competitor of enormous Size and Influence. Under these Conditions it is wise to maintain but a modest Presence upon the Field of Battle. All in all he is widely if not well known to men in these parts, who consider him Honest if a bit "Sharp"

81

in his dealings. Some have found him too "Sharp" indeed, and have indicated by small Signs that they may be induced to conspire against the Italian so as to recover some of their losses. I have learned from these Gentlemen, and have devised ways to Capitalize upon all matters as fully as possible.

So as to doubly Insulate the firm of Scrooge & Marley from any potential Loss or Legal Action, I have been traveling and conducting Business under the identity of Mr. Wilkins Micawber of Boston, legal representative of a certain Mr. Elijah Peleg of Nantucket. It is to this Micawber—care of the Bank named upon the reverse—that I request you to send an additional £15,000 in notes upon the next reliable ship to make the Crossing. These funds shall go toward unexpected Investment Opportunities as well as the necessary Lubrication of certain Individuals so as to ensure their support of our Interests. Have no Fear: I am keeping careful Records and will provide a full and accurate Accounting upon my return.

You will find a portion of the Resources secured within a Lockbox concealed in the lower drawer of the small desk in the Office of Squeers & Trotter, second floor, number 3. The remainder may be found within the sliding panel just behind the cabinet in the Office of Mr. Pecksniff, third floor, number 5. The keys are located in their usual Spot.

With kind personal Regards, I remain,

Yours truly,

Jacob S. Marley

Ten

Scrooge has his hands full in Marley's absence. In addition to his book-keeping duties, he must each day follow a highly detailed set of instructions inscribed by his partner's hand in a stack of coded notebooks that positively bristle with arcana: currency conversion tables, addresses and transactions both real and fabricated, names and aliases of a sprawling universe of contacts, floor plans of buildings actual and imaginary, time-tables of ships' arrivals and departures, maps as inscrutable as the furtive handiwork of any treasure-hoarding pirate. Certain of the most sensitive data is written in a disappearing ink of Marley's own making, highly flammable yet visible only by the brief but close application of a candle flame. Portions of his March 18 letter have been inscribed in just such ink, and Scrooge barely has time to read them before the entire page goes up, very nearly taking the warehouse with it.

He wishes that he could hire an assistant, some clerk who could take over at least a portion of the record-keeping. But how would he ever explain the twists and turns of the systems upon which Scrooge & Marley's books depend? More to the point, how would he explain the need for any of it? There will, no doubt, come a time for such things—

of this he is certain. He may be full of vigor and sound of memory now, but one day his energy and his mind will begin to falter. Inspired by that notion, he begins in his few idle moments to concoct a means by which he might separate some of the simplest bookkeeping from the most sensitive information. *One day*, he thinks—*one day I shall have a clerk*.

In the meantime, he carries on. Belle sees precious little of him, and when they do meet he is distracted, weary, even snappish. "It's unfair of Jacob to burden you so," she says as she unpacks a picnic hamper upon a cloth spread out upon Marley's desk. If she cannot get Scrooge out into the open air, this will have to do.

Scrooge is still scribbling away at his desk in the other room. "It's all for the good of the partnership," he says.

"Marley gets to enjoy a voyage to America, and you get to take on his work." She comes and stands in the doorway, arms crossed and hip cocked. "To my way of thinking, that's good for only one-half of the partnership."

"Now, now, Belle. It's for a short while only."

There is consolation in his voice, but when he looks up she can see upon his face the markings of his toil. His brow is seamed, his eyes are sunken, and his hair—drawn back into his customary pigtail—has begun a long retreat from his forehead. He looks to her like the very ghost of himself, come back from the future to provide her with a warning.

She goes to him and softly takes the pen from his hand. "Oh, Ebenezer," she says, laying it aside and placing a hand upon his. "There is more to life than bookkeeping."

He harrumphs, that irritable old haunt, armed with his own counsel about what might lie ahead.

"There is, in fact, more to life than Scrooge & Marley."

He draws his lips into a deep frown. "Scrooge & Marley is a bulwark against the workhouse."

She tightens her grasp upon his hand and draws it toward her, taking a single tentative step back to remind him of the picnic lunch waiting in Marley's office. "Come," she says.

He shakes his head like an old horse. "I have no time."

"Jacob has time to go to America. You have time to eat."

"I dare not let a moment slip past unaccounted for. I certainly have no time for pleasures." He reaches for his pen once more.

"You sound like a Calvinist."

"I am not a religious man."

"I know. You've been absent enough from the choir."

"My apologies to Mr. Carstone and Mr. Gradgrind."

She draws his hand nearer her breast and fastens her eyes upon his. "Also to me, I should hope."

Something within him awakens. His free hand leaves off in its search for the pen and falls abruptly to his side. He rises to his feet. "I am sorry," he says.

"For missing choir practice?"

"For everything."

"That's better. But perhaps you could be more specific."

"I—"

"You're a bookkeeper," she says, a playful glow breaking over her face and illuminating it. "A full enumeration might be in order."

"An enumeration of my sins, you mean."

"Of your regrets. We don't have all day, after all."

They step into Marley's office, where she has laid out a luncheon of cold roast beef and boiled potatoes and pickled beets, with two slices of apple pie for dessert and hot tea to wash it all down.

He halts, stricken as a lost woodsman stumbling into the banquet hall of some monstrous king. "You are altogether too kind to me," he says.

"Is that one of your regrets?"

His eyes brim. "That you are so kind? Not at all. That I have failed to notice it until now? Yes."

"Wonderful," she says. "You've made a fine start." She reaches to pick up a plate but notices as he hesitates, lost in thought and bending back a finger, apparently having come up with another personal shortcoming to add to the list. She laughs and reaches out and enfolds his hand in hers. "That's enough for now, Ebenezer."

And he looks at her, and he sees that it is.

The very next day he visits Belle's father with the aim of requesting her hand in marriage. He is not rebuffed, but neither is he welcomed without hesitation.

"Belle speaks of you often," says old Mr. Fairchild, ensconced in a deep armchair with his pipe going.

"She does," echoes Mrs. Fairchild from the depths of the adjoining parlor. "She surely does."

"*Mother*," says Fairchild with a cough, "Mr. Scrooge has come to speak with me."

"Of course. Don't let me interrupt," she says.

Fairchild sucks at his pipe. "Go on, then, Mr. Scrooge. Finish your thought."

"Oh, I was quite finished," says Scrooge. "In fact, I believe you were saying . . ."

"Was I saying something? I'm afraid I don't recall."

"What you were saying"—from the parlor—"is that Belle speaks of Mr. Scrooge quite often."

"Ah, yes. She does. Often."

Scrooge clears his throat. "I hope that she speaks of me in good terms."

"As good terms as *possible*, I would say." His pipe has failed, and he draws hard upon the stem.

Scrooge waits for clarification. He knows Fairchild's opinion as to the decency of his investments, but he would like to hear it from the man himself.

Fairchild withdraws a tool from his pocket and begins burrowing in the pipe bowl, hot embers showering down onto his upholstered chair.

Scrooge watches, his nose atwitch, awaiting either a sudden catastrophic fire or some further clarification from Fairchild. When neither proves forthcoming and Fairchild's pipe is back in business at last, he finds that he can wait no longer. "You say she speaks of me in terms 'as good as possible.' Has she reservations?"

"Belle? No."

"Have you?"

"Perhaps. I am older than she is, of course. Wiser, and more experienced. And I have her best interests at heart."

"Do you doubt my ability to support her?"

Fairchild scoffs. "You are wealthy enough and getting wealthier, by all accounts."

"I could provide references, if you like. Accounts, holdings, histories . . ."

"You need not. You seem to have heaped up sufficient treasure of the earthly variety, if not the heavenly."

Scrooge pulls at his lip. "Then do you judge my character to be of insufficient quality?"

Fairchild sniffs and waves his pipe in a circuit that takes in his family's rooms, the stables below, the entire doomed arrangement. "A gentleman in my circumstances can make few claims or demands as to quality. I should be fortunate if my daughters can keep a roof over their heads after I have gone to my grave."

"Then it must be the *source* of my funds to which you object."

Fairchild nods.

"The source of *a portion* of my funds, to be precise."

"Let us not quibble."

Scrooge keeps on. "I have heard," he says, "that you disapprove of certain *cargo*."

"Ceasing to call men 'cargo' would be a fine start toward repairing your reputation, Mr. Scrooge."

"I have a reputation for rectitude and probity."

"In many things, but not in all."

"Our work is entirely within the law."

"Man's law, not God's."

Scrooge quietly absorbs the blow.

"And one day," says Fairchild, "man's law will catch up with that of the Almighty."

"I trust that it will, sir."

"You do?"

"I do."

"And what then?"

"Then Mr. Marley will have to comply with both God's law and man's."

"What has Mr. Marley to do with it?"

"The contracts and negotiations are his portion of the business. I only maintain the records."

"A fine excuse that is."

"It is not an excuse, Mr. Fairchild. It is our arrangement."

"And yet you are half owner."

"I am."

"So you must approve of these contracts and negotiations of his?"

"I must not and I do not. Belle awakened me to the unsustainable and unsavory qualities of this business a good while ago. As a result, I have on many occasions entreated Mr. Marley to locate other cargoes, other routes."

"And?"

"I fear he has made but slow progress."

"You *fear*? Do you not *know*?"

"Mr. Marley deals in complexities and entanglements. I deal in innocent sums."

"These are sums of *men*, Mr. Scrooge. These entanglements are forged with *iron chains*."

Scrooge hesitates, the shadow of something not fully incarnate passing before his eyes.

"As long as you are linked to those poor sufferers, Mr. Scrooge, you shall not be linked to my daughter."

"I understand."

"So. You may wait until the passage of the Slave Trade Act, or you may redouble your efforts to convert Mr. Marley in advance. It is up to you."

"I shall not wait, Mr. Fairchild. I shall take it up with him the very moment he returns from America."

Fairchild harrumphs. He takes one last draw on his pipe, finds the bowl cold and the effort fruitless, and sets it down. "Fair enough," he says. "When the work of conversion is fully accomplished—when you and our African brothers have been freed from the wicked ties that bind you all—you shall have my permission to save my daughter from the poverty that shall fall upon this family at my death."

He says the last as if the notion of his own end delights him without limit.

Eleven

"They mean to be married!" shouts Fan before Marley has even reached the gangway. He has not been expecting to see her to begin with, and her impenetrable and contextless greeting disorients him. These last few months his mind has been on anything but the romance between Scrooge and Belle. It has been on anything but romance at all, really, at least not romance of the conventionally approved variety. "Belle and Ebenezer!" she clarifies at the top of her lungs, and it all becomes clear. "They are to be married!"

She bounds up the gangway in a swirl of cornflower blue, the most brilliant display of life and color anywhere upon this dead drab waterside, and she is so delighted to have spied her long-lost Jacob that she does not notice as he palms a scrap of paper handed him by a statuesque woman to his left. The woman smiles and watches as the two embrace and stumble off toward the quay, upon her face the perfectly equable look of a gambler whose card will surface in time. Her contentment fails only when he crumples her note into a pea-sized ball and scuffs it to tatters in the dirt beneath his shoe. So much for her affair with the mysterious and darkly romantic Dr. Payne.

Fan is still going on about the as-yet-unscheduled wedding. "Ebenezer forbade my writing you with the news," she says, "but he could not keep me from checking the listings each day so as to be first when your ship arrived." She positively beams, her expression that of an impish child who's gotten away with some petty mischief.

Marley, having lately seen his share of wickedness, finds himself enchanted by her enthusiasm. "*Naughty Fan*," he says, ever the complicit rogue. Her very youth is sufficient to burst something within his brain. Did they even have girls this young in the Americas? None that spoke any language known to a European. Savages, they were. Nothing at all like Fan. While she chatters away he permits himself to inhale her fresh-bathed scent and touch the crisp shoulder of her dress, and he very nearly swoons. "So the old fellow has agreed to tie the knot," he says when he has collected himself. "Did you ever—?"

"Miracles happen," she says, a manifest miracle herself.

"Perhaps it was my fault. Absent my supervision, the old boy got up to some new tricks."

"Quite the opposite, Jacob. You left him far too busy. Why, we barely saw him for Friday suppers."

"Perhaps he was dining with Miss Fairchild in secret."

Fan shakes her charming head. "He worked until all hours. Mother and I came to fear for his health."

"And yet Cupid still found his opportunity. *Poor old Scrooge*," he laments, one hand going theatrically to his chest. "*Stricken through the heart*."

"There are worse fates," says Fan.

"Name one."

"Never knowing love."

Marley laughs. "You had your answer at the ready."

"I've had ever since you departed to think about it."

"Fair enough," says Marley, taking her hand. "Let us fetch my bags, and then I shall go see about your lovesick brother."

✈

Once he and his partner are alone, Marley gets down to business. "I'm afraid I have brought home more work for you."

"I welcome it," Scrooge answers with an unaccustomed airiness, "provided you resume doing your own share."

"I shall."

"Then we shall be as content as ever."

"You're a changed man, Ebenezer."

Scrooge straightens up, a gleam in his eye. "I am the man I ought to be. The man I should have been from the start."

"Can I still rely upon you?" Marley's question is not entirely idle.

"Absolutely. So long as you do not rely upon me to forfeit my life for the sake of my ledgers."

Marley smiles without entirely meaning it. "God bless you, then. God bless you for a man transformed."

Just here is the moment when Scrooge would ordinarily lower his head so as to return to his bookkeeping, but for once he does not. This alteration from his usual rhythm sets Marley on edge. Apparently they are to continue talking. "Should you have any doubts as to your ability to support your intended . . ." he begins, taking the long way around.

"I do not, or else I would never have asked for her hand."

"Of course, Scrooge. Of course. It was but a figure of speech. A way of introducing the results of my work abroad."

"Ah," says Scrooge, living and learning.

"For we have been most successful in gaining a foothold in the New World."

"Splendid," says Scrooge, establishing upon his face an expression that says he means it. The look puts Marley on the wrong foot again. He feels as if he is talking with a stranger. What magic has Belle worked upon him?

"Our investments are quite secure," he begins.

"I should hope so. We have invested enough in this American adventure. One-third of our capital, if my accounting is correct."

"Which it is, I have no doubt."

"A figure of speech, Jacob." Scrooge chuckles, having caught his partner at his own game. "So what have you done with it?"

"I've diversified."

"Meaning?"

"Multiple accounts, multiple banks, multiple identities." He withdraws from his pocket a sheaf of papers and flattens them upon Scrooge's desk. "This will serve as your map to our dealings in the New World." The pages are crammed with charts, diagrams, arrows, and numbers, all annotated in a hand so small that a mouse would require corrective lenses to make everything out. Scrooge takes it all in over the span of a moment, and his face illuminates.

"'Tis a thing of beauty, *Mr. Micawber.*"

"'Tis an engine for making money, Mr. Scrooge."

"I can see that. And a very powerful one." He unfurls a long finger and indicates one detail in particular. "I do like this," he says, tap-tap-tapping with a hard fingertip. "Interest compounded upon overhead compounded upon interest. That's lovely. It never ends, does it?"

Marley cedes a self-congratulatory smile. "By the time Monteverdi's first shipment arrives here, we shall own it entirely."

"And when will he learn the truth?"

"At the final accounting, I should say."

"By which you mean the Day of Judgment."

"Thereabouts."

Scrooge studies a calendar. "Judgment Day aside, by summer's end our investment will be repaid threefold."

"Guaranteed."

Scrooge straightens the papers, folds them, and secretes them in a drawer. Then he draws a deep breath, comes to his feet, and extends a gracious hand to Marley. "You, sir," he says with perfect delight, "are making yourself the savior of my incipient marriage."

"I'm afraid I don't understand."

"You know Belle's hatred of the slaving business."

"I do." He puzzles, awaiting clarification.

"Her father's, as well."

"Yes, yes. But what has *this* to do with slaving?"

"Good God, man! Your American operation generates four times the profit margin that slaving ever has! Properly developed, it will free us from that wicked trade entirely!"

"Ah," says Marley, just as if he has been doing Scrooge's bidding all along, divesting them little by little of the odious business. "I take your point."

Wordless glee from Scrooge.

"On the other hand," says Marley, full of regret, "we shall still have those empty vessels down along the African coast . . ."

"Then don't send them there in the first place. Concentrate only on east-west crossings. Simplify."

Marley pulls at his chin. "One hates to put all of one's eggs in a single basket."

"So long as we are engaged in slaving, I shall never be wed."

"Poor Ebenezer," says Marley with the lascivious grin of one to whom never being wed might be terribly appealing.

"I am quite serious. Those are the terms."

"Very well. Let us see how things go."

"The threat of abolition is growing serious, too."

"Abolition?" He has not been reading the news, or else the news has not been making the transit to North America.

"The Slave Trade Act. Should it pass, the entire trade will be cut off."

Marley reflects. "Then perhaps we have found our exit just in time. Should the act pass, I mean."

"Even if it doesn't pass," says Scrooge, "the time has come."

➤

Isn't this a fine welcome home? Marley fumes at his desk for as long as he can endure being one room away from his reformed partner, sorting bits of paperwork and reacquainting himself with the slim contents of his desk and looking out the window at passersby having a more pleasant time of it than he is on this lovely spring day. He keeps a smile upon his face and whistles a merry tune that he picked up somewhere in the New World, hoping to drive Scrooge mad but failing. By and by he has had enough and he exits without a word of farewell.

Out on the street, he steams. The *nerve* of Scrooge to instruct him in his business. The *ingratitude* of Scrooge to turn his American triumph into a demand for further labor. The *softness* of Scrooge to let a woman bend him to her will. This is not the man with whom he threw in his lot all those years ago. This is not the Ebenezer Scrooge who minded his own affairs and kept his nose clear of Marley's. This is a changed man, a potentially dangerous man, a man who must be contained if the enterprise of Scrooge & Marley is to move forward.

His mind alive with these thoughts, he plunges through the streets like a ship of war. He juts his chin and leans forward as into a gale, taking long, incautious, oblivious strides that part the crowd without regard to the presence of man, woman, or child. Behind him, the pennant of his pigtail streams out in declaration of his warlike intent.

Thus he roams the city for hours, losing himself several times over and eventually finding his way home without conscious effort, drawn perhaps by the lodestone lure of the riches he has hidden there. At a certain point he simply looks up from the gutter to find himself standing in the darkness outside his own gate. With a screech of old iron he lets himself into the yard and follows the overgrown path to the broad front door. The familiar knocker, an enormous and disused thing of tarnished marine brass, hangs silent as an empty gibbet while he fishes out his key and works it into the lock. All the district roundabout is silent, absent even the nighttime cry of cat or bird or babe. No bell sounds from the pinnacle of some church tower. No toper bellows from the depths of some alehouse. The whole world is dead.

He pulls the door shut behind him and finds his way up the broad staircase in the comfortable and conservative dark. He has long been profligate with candles, but Scrooge's insistence upon meddling in his end of the business instills in him a new caution. He has placed altogether too much trust in the man. He has given away more secrets than may prove healthy. From this day forward he shall need to work in greater darkness, and he must begin now.

Instead of going directly to his quarters he haunts the passages of his deep-shadowed house, creeping from door to door with a ring of keys jangling in his hand, admitting himself one after another to the offices he has established there. Within each he moves from cabinet to desk to closet to secret sliding panel, confirming the presence of every pound note and piece of eight and ducat. All is well, of course, for Scrooge is nothing if not honest. The only funds missing are the fifteen thousand pounds sent to Marley in America, required to facilitate the Monteverdi business. Reassured, he lingers in the last of the offices like some dragon reclining upon his treasure and reflects upon the state of his affairs. Krook & Flite, Squeers & Trotter, Nemo & Hawdon, Mr. Pecksniff, and the remainder of his fictional allies have been true to him as no one else on earth, and from this day forward he shall entrust his fate strictly to them. Scrooge may handle only such harmless calculations as he shall permit him to see. There is already treasure enough behind these false fronts to place Marley—provided he gets his due—within England's more elevated classes. And when poor old swindled Monteverdi's ship comes in—well, on that day he shall be a rich man indeed.

Let Scrooge, with his miserable counting and calculating, settle for a smaller share. He will never be the wiser.

Twelve

As spring turns into summer, Marley's mood brightens. Any day now that enormous cargo of pelts will begin its voyage across the Atlantic, and his fortune will take a turn for the better. Of course he will still bow and scrape to the likes of Bernière, perhaps even more theatrically than ever before, but the charade will acquire an even deeper delight. Imagine it! His wealth will soon rival that of the city's richest merchants, and he will have accomplished it without once soiling his hands with honest labor.

The ship upon which the cargo will arrive is not a part of Scrooge & Marley's secret armada, and so the only word he receives regarding its schedule comes through the network of shippers and financiers that he established in America. They are a charmingly credulous lot—bumpkins really, piteously faithful and forthcoming in their correspondence—and they keep him apprised of their activities on a weekly basis. The *Betsy* has suffered a delay upon her journey from Africa, they say, thanks to a setback involving the loss of a large percentage of its cargo to dysentery and native stubbornness. The ship's resourceful captain, finding his hold lightened and his masters' profits imperiled, has wisely sought additional lading in the West Indies. Thus the delay.

As alive with anticipation as any child on Christmas Eve, he slacks off the pace of his daily work and concentrates on the enjoyment of summer in the great city of London. His thoughts turn to the fairer sex, and they subsequently sort themselves out and settle upon Fan, whom he invites one noontime to share a stroll in Hyde Park. The world, as he has recently seen on an international scale, is crowded with women willing to be partners in whatever adventure he might propose, and for however long his interest might remain aroused. There are always more, and yet there is always Fan. He must seek a middle way of some kind. *Good God*, he thinks, *even her brother, the native calculating machine, would be sorely tried to strike such a balance.*

"I thought you would never write," she says as she hurries breathless to the gate.

His only response is an inscrutable half smile.

"After all, Jacob—you said that I should have until May to decide upon our future."

He cocks an eyebrow.

"And now it's the middle of June."

He squints. "When did I speak of our future? Or of your deciding upon it?"

"*Jacob.*" She says his name as if he might be teasing. "You promised it before you sailed to America."

"Oh my," says Marley, offering her his arm. "That was so very long ago, I fear I cannot properly remember." He sweeps her along the walk like a man sweeping away the past, setting in motion by sheer will some newly minted replacement that suits him better.

"You remember *everything*, Jacob. I know your mind."

"You do?"

"I wanted to run off with you, but you proposed marriage instead. You proposed a *potential* marriage, but marriage still."

He stops dead. "I swear, you must be thinking of someone else."

Believing that she detects a coy curl to his lip, she throws her arms about his neck—to the vast alarm of a passing matron unprepared for such a display. "Oh, Jacob! You are a great tease."

He peels her away and they resume their walk, in closer proximity now than before. "So you have made your decision, then?"

"I should say."

"And it is . . ."

"*Jacob!*"

"In the affirmative?"

"*Jacob!*"

"Or so I take it."

"You're impossible!"

"Not so. I only want you to be certain."

"You speak as if *you* are the uncertain one."

"Fan," he says. "Dearest Fan—I think only of you."

"You sound like my mother."

"I take that as a compliment."

"I did not mean it as one."

"Fan! You have changed."

"No."

"You have transformed in my absence."

"If I have, it is your fault. You didn't want me in America. You didn't want me with you at all."

"Now, Fan—"

"At best you were uncertain, and so you kept me on a string."

Marley makes no answer.

"You committed nothing, Jacob, while I committed everything."

"Oh, not *everything*," he says, a lascivious gleam stealing across his eye.

She tears herself free of his arm, and without an additional word she pivots and dashes off along a different path. Whether she has seen his look or fairly interpreted the intention behind it is impossible to know, but he has at least planted the seed. There will be more intrigue to be played out before their full relationship, whatever its contours are to be, is consummated.

Marley goes directly to Mrs. McCullough's bawdy house. The interior has the changeless quality of a diorama: the dusty furniture, the dead hearth, the drunkards. The lady in charge emerges at his knock, greeting him with a deep curtsey that very nearly permits some of her assets to spill free from her décolletage.

"We haven't seen ye around, Inspector."

"I have been occupied."

"Naturally." She nods her great head and anticipates his usual question. "Madeline's on this afternoon. You like Madeline."

"Madeline will do."

"Madeline will do plenty, or so I'm told."

"That's quite enough of your wit, Mrs. McCullough."

"No harm intended, sir."

Marley turns toward the stairs but pauses at the last moment, struck by an inspiration. "Chief among the issues that have occupied me, Mrs. McCullough, is the placation of a number of individuals within the legal community—powerful and relentless men who, if left to their own devices, would have your premises locked and yourself imprisoned in Newgate."

"I thank ye for that, Inspector."

"You may thank me by paying the fees which I have negotiated with these men on your behalf."

"Fees, sir?"

He names an amount calculated to give her a genuine but tolerable level of pain.

She draws breath. "I suppose I could scrape that much together, sir."

"Weekly, of course."

She winces.

"The alternative, sadly, is your destruction by powers beyond my control. I have done everything I can to forestall it, but matters are now in your hands." He turns and makes for the stairs, only to stop on the landing at the sound of her voice.

"I'll do it, sir."

"Very well," he says as he continues upward. "Have the funds ready when I am finished, and I shall collect them on my way out."

Thirteen

Scrooge, like his partner, finds his spirit awakened to the delights of London in the summer. With Marley home and the American business steaming ahead and the entire operation recommitted to disentangling itself from the slave trade, his soul is lightened to such a surprising degree that the return to his usual duties seems the veriest of holidays. At least twice and sometimes three times a week, he dallies with Belle over a picnic lunch in one of the many parks within convenient walking distance. Nay! *Convenient walking distance* be damned! He and his beloved shall go as far as they like, take as much time as they require! They shall even hire a carriage, should the spirit move them, and never mind the outlay!

In other words, Ebenezer Scrooge seems an entirely new man.

On the rare occasions that he encounters his partner he inquires as to the progress of divestment, and Marley reassures him that his efforts—although dauntingly, damnably, frustratingly complex—will show real progress any day now. Thus is the load on his mind and spirit eased even further. The subject of slaving disappears from his daily conversation with Belle, replaced by talk of the bright future they share.

Fan, however, is a different story. She comes to her brother on the day after her aborted walk with Marley, woeful and shaken and furious all at once. "The man is a beast," she says. "He willfully led me on before going to America, suggesting that we should be married upon his return, and now that he's come back he pretends not to remember. Or that it meant nothing. Or that I am mad."

"I warned you," he says.

"He's a monster."

"Perhaps. He is certainly changeable. *Protean* would be the word, I suppose."

"There is no adequate word for what he is, and there is no adequate word for what he has done."

"He has wounded you, and for that I am sorry."

"You warned me, as you said." By her tone, the idea seems to provide scant comfort.

"He can be very persuasive, our Mr. Marley."

"*Your* Mr. Marley. Not mine."

"Fair enough."

"I suppose you rely heavily upon his persuasive arts in this *business* of yours." On her tongue, the word has an evil sound.

"Oh, I must," says her brother. "I have very little ability in that department."

"All the better for you."

Scrooge smiles.

"I hope you do not trade away your soul in the process."

"Rest assured," says Scrooge, "I keep a careful accounting."

June becomes July, and word arrives from America that the *Betsy* is to set sail directly. Given that anything traveling from the New World to the docks of London must make more or less the same long and perilous journey—whether it is this sealed envelope or that anticipated fortune in beaver pelts—Marley calculates that the ship will arrive soon.

He scours the papers for any sign of her, and after a week has passed without news he takes to haunting the docks himself. He is widely known there, although each of his various associates tends to greet him with a look that caroms rapidly in some other direction. There has never been a percentage in advertising your connections to Mr. Marley, or Mr. Radford, or Colonel Diver, or whoever else this individual may be.

Before he sets out each morning he ensures that firmly tucked within his waistcoat is a letter signed by one Mr. Elijah Peleg of Nantucket, introducing him as Mr. Wilkins Micawber of Boston, said Peleg's legal representative in all matters pertaining to the acceptance of such goods as have been loaded upon the *Betsy* by the firm operated by Sr. Valentino Monteverdi. It is this precious forgery that he touches briefly, even talismanically, when word circulates that the *Betsy* has been spotted at the mouth of the Thames, where she now awaits a favorable tide. He checks the hour and runs a rapid mental calculation, and then he slips a handful of coins to a pair of idle longshoremen along with instructions to report back here in the company of a dozen able men at the stroke of noon.

He takes shelter from his own overwhelming anticipation within the confines of a grogshop, whose stools and tables are heavily occupied even at this time of the morning. He tosses off an uncharacteristic tot of gin to quiet his nerves, and then one more for good measure. Thus soothed, he experiences a moment's warm sentiment toward his absent partner—a feeling he acts upon by stepping outside, locating an eager boy, and pressing upon him a note to be delivered to Scrooge in exchange for a farthing.

She arrives, the note says. Just that and nothing more.

And surely enough she does, nosing into her berth as the last stroke of twelve rings out from every church bell in the city. Marley sizes up his crew of longshoremen and finds them tolerable if less than ideal, and then strides off amid the hubbub of tying up and making fast to introduce himself to the *Betsy*'s captain. He is called Crag, and he is known to be a hard master, both difficult to please and sharp in his dealings. Thus he has certainly proven himself in the management of that lost half load of slaves, and Marley is confident that they will get along like the oldest of comrades. He shall see to it.

The difficulty is that no one aboard seems acquainted with this Crag. Every crewman he consults gives back little more than a puzzled look and a tentative finger pointed at some other ship moored close by. "This here is the *Betsy*," they say, as if he is an idiot. "Perhaps you'll find your captain Crag aboard a different vessel."

"No," Marley reassures them until he is blue in the face. "I assure you that the *Betsy* is under the command of this selfsame Crag. She left Fort Albany seven weeks ago, laden with rum and molasses and beaver pelts. I care nothing for the rum or the molasses. They are no affair of mine. I offer them only as proof of my familiarity with this ship and her master. The pelts are my concern. The pelts only." On one or two occasions he comes near to presenting the letter from Peleg as evidence of a reality that is rapidly becoming questionable.

By and by he finds his way belowdecks, where Crag is nowhere to be found. The real captain, who goes by the name of Squelch, is a great ruin of a man, an avalanche of loose fat collapsed at the moment upon an unfortunate horsehair divan. He says that he has captained the *Betsy* for twenty-one years, before which time he served in antichronological order as her first mate, her carpenter, her caulker, and her cabin boy. Work aboard the *Betsy*, in other words, has been his entire life. Begging Mr. Micawber's pardon, he has never heard of any Captain Crag. Perhaps, he suggests, his visitor has been misinformed.

Marley names his various contacts in America. Squelch claims ignorance of them.

Marley invokes the respected Sr. Monteverdi. Squelch purports to know him not.

Marley describes the quantity of beaver pelts now occupying space in the hold. Squelch assures him that the *Betsy* carries only cotton, molasses, tobacco, and rats. He proves it by giving Marley complete license to inspect the hold, accompanied by his cabin boy, a child obviously too slow-witted to be duplicitous.

As they climb back into the sunlight of the main deck, Marley contemplates the fortune in pounds that he distributed in America—he sowed that precious seed with careless extravagance, now that he thinks of it—and something within his brain goes black. Enough with the *Betsy*. Enough with Squelch. Monteverdi is the man he must see, and he must see him now.

The longshoremen awaiting him on the quay seem tough enough, but they make no dispute when he sends them off without payment or explanation. They may not be sages, but they can see that Marley is not a man to be crossed.

Monteverdi's office lies in a district he knows well enough, a down-at-the-heels commercial area that has recently been reviving and revising itself courtesy of new money from elsewhere. Thus in both history and style it would seem to suit Monteverdi entirely. Marley hopes that he will find the moneyed little individual at his desk when he arrives, although the hour suggests otherwise. These Italians enjoy their food and drink, after all. So be it, then. He will wait if he must. He has waited this long.

He turns from a narrow boulevard onto a narrower street and then he turns again down the even narrower lane where Monteverdi has his business, and up ahead he spies a crew of day laborers. Masons and carpenters they are, just now returning from their own lunches, each picking up his tools and preparing to resume work. If Marley knows anything about laboring men he knows that the better part of the working day is behind them, and that whatever they accomplish this afternoon will be tainted by the strong drink they've just taken. Foundations will be tilted, walls will be askew, doors will refuse to latch. This is always the nature of work and the world. Small misjudgments ramify into networks of larger ones. He pities whoever is doomed to occupy the space upon which they are even now about to work their worst.

He clocks the numbers painted above each lintel as he goes along, counting down to Monteverdi's door, and he is astonished to discover that the laborers appear to be working inside the Italian's very place of business. Weren't these premises to be redone months ago? Wasn't everything to have been refurbished in gold leaf and marble? Absolutely. He is certain of it. He has seen workingmen drag their feet to extend a project before, but could these villains possibly still be at it? Poor, credulous Monteverdi! Surely they are doing their best to bleed him dry—an enterprise that Marley had thought until now was his and his exclusively.

He thrusts his head inside the door, and he despairs. The place is a shambles, and not a very large one. Even cleared of the workmen and their disarray, it would be less spacious than the tiny pair of chambers that he and Scrooge share. Further, there is neither a flake of gold leaf nor a chip of marble in sight. Quite the contrary, the carpenters are doing their best with crooked boards and straightened nails, and the masons are cursing their luck as they sort through secondhand bricks salvaged from some other ruin.

"Where is Monteverdi?" he asks, and for all the answer he gets he may as well be some disembodied spirit moaning into the ether.

"Monteverdi," he demands of the nearest workman, grasping him by the shirt collar and drawing him perilously near.

"No such figger here, guv'nor."

"But this is his office."

"Afraid not," says the workman, squirming within his grip and pointing to a dusty sign that hangs just inside the door. CARSTAIRS & SON, PROVISIONERS, it reads, EST. 1775.

Marley gawps.

"Old Mr. Carstairs is the one pays the bills," says the workman. "I should know, since I'm the son. Not the son went into the family business, though—the other one. The poor one. Although I do manage to make ends meet." With this last he smiles and raises a bent nail, demonstrating a happy willingness to shortchange even his own blood.

Marley releases him. "But what of Monteverdi?"

"Sorry, but like I said—I've never heard of the gentleman."

Fourteen

Blast and damn. Had he not weakened under the dual influences of gin and human kindness, he would never have sent that note to Scrooge, and he would now owe the man nothing in the way of explanation. He could make a show of awaiting the *Betsy* for a few more weeks, and then produce official-looking documentation of her tragic loss at sea. Later he could explain why Monteverdi, angered over the loss and perhaps a trifle superstitious (as foreigners so often are, especially papists from the warmer climes), had written off the notion of any further dealings with Scrooge & Marley. But no. He had to take a couple of drinks, and he had to get a little sentimental, and he had to go and tip his hand. Blast and damn.

How is he to suffer the indignity? He is ashamed enough of his gullibility and weakness without having to confess it all to his partner. And then there's the money. Fully one-third of all their capital, enough to yield a lifetime of comfort for both of them if invested properly, has vanished into the hands of those conspiratorial Americans. Were they employees of Monteverdi? Were they independent confidence men hired just for the moment? Were they merely clever opportunists?

Did they even exist at all?

Did Monteverdi himself?

Oh, wretched, wronged Marley!

He has never trusted banks and he has even less reason to trust them now, given the thoroughness and ease with which those duplicitous American financiers, with their fine stationery and their falsified imbecility, managed to swindle him clean. Yet if he is to recover his losses—the discarded riches, the ruined self-respect—he must make some adjustments to his methods. Those false fronts of his, arrayed one after another on the second and third floors of the house, can no longer be just depositories for appropriated cash and clearinghouses for phony paper. Krook & Flite and Squeers & Trotter and all the rest shall from this day forward possess actual accounts at actual institutions of finance. Scrooge, of course, does not need to know about them. With the three months that he's already had to rummage around in Marley's deepest secrets, he has seen more than his share.

Oh, wretched, wide-eyed Marley!

Scrooge knows where the treasure is and where the keys are kept. To move anything now would only raise suspicion. So he shall keep an eye fixed upon the future, and begin siphoning off forthcoming percentages into accounts to which he alone shall have access. It is his right, after all. He is the one doing the work and taking the risk. Scrooge is but a factotum, one step above a clerk. Good God, if he were any more than that, he would be able to detect malfeasance on Marley's part—particularly on the grand scale to which it is about to rise.

His new work will start, Marley decides, with recovering his share of the American investment. Painstakingly, methodically, one shilling at a time if necessary, he shall take it out of Scrooge's hide.

"So how did we fare?" asks Scrooge, roused by his partner's entry from a waking dream of endless wealth.

"Not half so well as expected," says Marley.

Scrooge sets down his pen.

"The Americans chose to tell neither Monteverdi nor myself," Marley says, papering over one lie with another, "that the trapping has been poor this season."

"Then prices shall be higher."

"They shall."

"So it will all come out in the end."

"It would, had our arrangements not been conditioned upon a fixed price."

"A fixed price? How unwise, Marley. How unlike you."

"So it would seem. But the markets have been stable for many years, and by acceding to a fixed value I assuaged Monteverdi's reservations regarding other, more complex, elements of our arrangement. It cost us nothing—or it should have."

"But now Monteverdi has come out on top."

Marley puts upon his face the look of a repentant old sinner, caught in the act. "So it appears."

"And we . . . we have *suffered a loss*?" Upon his tongue the phrase is poison.

"No, I assure you. We have simply not profited as we should have."

"And what of our investments? The original sums, and the additional sums you required?"

"They have been recovered. Entirely."

Scrooge permits himself to exhale. "And in the future?"

"In the future, we shall have no further dealings with Sr. Monteverdi and the fur trade. That I can promise you."

Scrooge smiles. "I never imagined that you would meet your match."

Even at second- or thirdhand, even based as it is upon a tissue of lies, the accusation stings. Monteverdi *did* best him, after all, even if Marley is not certain how the trick was accomplished. Every last element of his being wants to lash out in response to Scrooge's effrontery, but he does not dare.

"And think of all the effort you put into the project!" Scrooge says. "Such a waste!"

"Do not remind me." His look is abashed, but his brain is on fire.

"Ah, well," sighs Scrooge, picking up his pen as if it is now his place to dismiss Jacob Marley. "Let it be a lesson to you."

Marley nods and attempts an escape, but one more remark from his partner halts him.

"And let us continue divesting ourselves of those offensive businesses, shall we?"

"It will be more difficult now," says Marley. "In the absence of our profits from the fur trade, I mean."

"Oh," says Scrooge, "I trust that it is not beyond your abilities."

His tone strikes like a horsewhip, and Marley makes a wordless exit before his temper can get the better of him.

1807

Fifteen

Marley has spent months shuffling the deck, so when the new year arrives the cards are exactly where he wants them. The work has required long hours of careful planning, days of solitary labor in his workshop, and the more or less public assumption of several new identities, all of which has tested his limits and deepened his isolation. Each hour that he has spent reconfiguring his financial network—which now embraces the fictitious firms of Barnacle & Sons (maritime provisioners), Dodson & Fogg (solicitors), Honeythunder & Grimwig (general mercantile), and many others—each lonely hour that he has spent fleecing Scrooge instead of robbing some outsider seems to him a deep personal affront. An affront brought about by Scrooge himself, come to think of it. Which serves only to make him more intent upon punishing the man.

But grant Scrooge this: By demanding that his partner sell everything connected with the slaving business, he has given Marley full camouflage for his work. He has unwittingly opened the floodgates of change and let in a torrent of misdirection, of which he will be the principal victim.

Marley, to be certain, has not reduced their investment in the transportation of slaves by so much as a single iron chain. The business is too profitable. Nonetheless, he has seen to it that as far as Scrooge is concerned, it's all being obliterated. Such a change is not without consequence, of course, and Scrooge has not been surprised to see that the value of his share has plummeted as a result. "Very well," he says each time his partner presents him with further bad news. "With the help of the Almighty, we shall recover by and by! Besides, do they not say that good work should be its own reward?"

Scrooge's happy acquiescence to the picking of his own pocket does Marley's heart good. The single-minded bookkeeper has been reborn, and the great good cheer with which he meets every setback reminds his partner that his eye is on prizes even more elusive than financial gain: true love and Christian mercy.

From time to time, idly and without any real hope of return, Marley attempts to reestablish a connection with Monteverdi. In his books he has a dozen addresses for the miscreant's various contacts in the Americas, and he mines them one after another.

At first he writes as Micawber, cultivating a peevish tone of injured pride. When no response is forthcoming, he takes on one by one the identities of Micawber's various agents and representatives and solicitors, adding heat each time around. Demands for restitution are made. Lawsuits or at least their simulacra are filed in courts on both sides of the Atlantic. Arrest warrants are signed and sealed. Nothing helps, although the exercise does serve to maintain his skills in the duplicitous arts, now that the entire false-fronted enterprise of Marley Minus Scrooge is running without his daily intervention.

At length, an answer does come back from the Americas. It arrives within an ancient wooden crate, a swollen and misshapen thing whose seams are caulked with oakum and sealed with tar. Squatting there like a waterlogged demon on Marley's desk, it looks sturdy and stubborn enough to have journeyed across the Atlantic under its own power. The crate is directed to Mr. Micawber at these premises but bears no return address, which Marley takes for a sign. He fetches a crowbar from the warehouse and prizes the lid open in a shower of wood shavings. These he curses until Ebenezer arrives to sweep them up for kindling—and then he burrows down and down among them until his fingertips fall upon a tiny, crisp envelope in their depths.

"What have we here?" he says, holding it up to the light. There is a single small slip of paper inside, and he extracts it carefully. It seems to be an obituary, clipped from a New York newspaper. The subject, of course, is Sr. Valentino Monteverdi—merchant prince, philosopher, and world-renowned philanthropist. The praise it contains is effusive, imaginative, and would no doubt suffice to get Satan readmitted to Paradise. Marley smiles as he reads it, marveling at the excellence of the entire presentation—the ruined crate, the damnable shavings, the torn edges of the cheap paper upon which the obituary is printed. And then he turns it over at last and discovers upon the reverse a small portion of an advertisement for *The Finest Beaver Pelts in Canada*, and he laughs out loud.

"What is it?" inquires Scrooge from his chamber, for laughter is a thing rarely heard upon these premises.

"A fascinating development," says Marley. "Sr. Monteverdi would appear to be dead."

When Marley announces that the last traces of their slaving investments have been liquidated, Scrooge decides that a celebration is in order. He shall take Belle ice-skating. What's more, he shall surprise her with the invitation in person. He waits until the close of business, fortifies himself at home with a cup of hot tea, and troops off in the moonlight to her family's lodgings. At the top of the open staircase he knocks upon the door, and there he stands—his breath steaming and his eyes atwinkle—when she answers. He is dusted all over with snow, and in place of his customary top hat he wears a stocking cap that she knitted for him either last Christmas or the Christmas prior. It gives him a youthful air, and combined with the scarf wrapped doubly around his neck and the ice skates tucked beneath his arm with their curved elfin tips agleam in the moonlight it makes him seem an entirely new man.

"Come," he says. "Find your skates and let us have some fun."

Impetuous Ebenezer!

He waits until they are out on the ice, pottering along arm in arm, before he breaks the news. It has taken time and determination and a world of sacrifice, he says, but the firm of Scrooge & Marley is at last washed clean of the sin of slavery.

"How marvelous!" she says, letting go of his arm and gliding around into his path so as to coast for a moment face-to-face. "Why didn't you come in and tell Father?"

"I don't plan to marry your father," he says. "I plan to marry *you*."

She flings herself upon him, and in his startlement he loses his already precarious balance. Down they go, whooping. Belle loses a skate. Ebenezer loses his cap. The whole enterprise collapses into a merry mess, and by the time he has rebuckled her skate and she has refit his cap they are half-frozen and completely famished. Belle knows a restaurant not far from the pond, just a short walk down a dimly lit avenue, and so they take a few more celebratory turns and remove their skates and set out.

The night has grown colder, and they press ever so tentatively against each other as they proceed—so as to conserve warmth, Ebenezer would say if asked, and physical warmth is surely part of it. Thus joined together they move from lamp to lamp like a single earthbound moth, the sole creature out on this deserted street. A fog has come in that hangs in the air like particulate ice, collecting the lamplight that spills from an unshuttered window here and there. Moving from one pale glow to the next, their faces shine.

A shadow appears from the black mouth of a cross street. It moves powerfully, purposely, striding through the dappled fog toward some dark rendezvous.

"Jacob!" says Ebenezer. "Why, it's good old Jacob, who has done so much to extricate us from our weary chains. Jacob, the author of our happiness."

Belle smiles, feeling a warmth rise within her that this individual has never before induced.

"Jacob!" he calls.

Nothing. The shadow moves along, determined.

"Ho! Jacob Marley!"

The shadow stops, cocks its head, and steps forward into a little light of its own. "Why, Ebenezer, you old stick."

"He's not such an old stick," says Belle with a laugh.

Marley approaches. "As you say, Miss Fairchild."

"Are we now on such formal terms, *Mr. Marley*?"

"The nighttime enforces a decorum of its own, don't you think?"

She pulls Ebenezer's elbow closer to her breast. "And the cold does otherwise, in my experience."

"I understand," says Marley, with a smile that in daylight might reveal itself to be a shade lubricious. "So what are you doing out in this chill?"

Ebenezer rattles his skates. "We've been to the pond."

"How oblivious I am," says Marley, who in truth never misses a thing.

"And now we are off to supper," says Scrooge.

"Don't let me keep you." He shivers eloquently. "I must be going as well."

"But your lodgings are *that* way," indicates Scrooge.

"I have an errand."

"Be quick about it, then. 'Tis a most inhospitable night."

"Oh," says Marley, turning to continue along his way, "there are pockets of hospitality everywhere. Provided a man knows where to look."

"Very well," says Ebenezer, freezing and hungry and hoping that the next lamplit window will mark the source of their supper. He and Belle resume their walk, but let us leave them to their happiness and follow Marley instead.

His track takes him down one shadowed lane after another, wending and winding into the nautilus of London's underside, until he comes to the door of a place that is not Mrs. McCullough's but may as well be. It possesses the same disreputable air, the same ruined paint and spider-webbed glass, the same hand-lettered indication of Rooms to Let. In the darkness within a single lamp burns, and through the filthy, frosty window he can make out a covey of women gathered on couches around a small table. Upon the table is a bottle, and within each woman's hand is a glass, and they commune with great seriousness—both with one another and with the gin—until he springs the latch and opens the door and they arise like so many doves upon the blast.

"Inspector Bucket," they cry in chorus, for he maintains the same identity and extracts the same toll with regard to all enterprises of this sort.

"Ladies," he says, pressing the door shut behind him and turning the lock.

"Ain't a fit night," says one, with professional sympathy.

"I should say not."

"For man nor beast," she goes on.

"Can you always tell one from the other?" he asks. "Man from beast, I mean?"

"There's none here for me to judge," she says, with a coy toss of her head. "Save yourself."

"And saving myself is precisely what I mean to do," says he, hanging his hat and coat on a peg. "With your assistance."

"Me, sir?" asks the one.

"*All of you*," says the lascivious and insatiable Inspector Bucket. "The night is young, and I am terribly cold."

The fires are banked in the grates upstairs, so with the door locked and the lamp guttering they set to their pleasure down here upon the couches. Marley directs the proceedings with a peculiar and avid authority, as if he has done exactly this a thousand times before. Perhaps he has. Whatever the women may think of the acts that they are called upon to perform, they carry them out with the required urgency and to such a satisfactory degree that their apparent pleasure at length removes Marley from the prison of his own body and mind. Through their senses he seems to feel something. And when at last he can endure no more of it, he finishes with a small and stifled cry: "*Fan*."

Sixteen

She is a missed opportunity, and Marley hates a missed opportunity.

That good girl, that churchgoing girl, that naïve girl! Although she is not precisely a girl anymore, now that he thinks of it, or certainly not a girl for long. She must be what, twenty-four or twenty-five? Some would call that the very prime of life, although others—a desperate lady experiencing it herself, for example—would describe it as one step shy of spinsterhood.

That in itself could work to his advantage.

He curses his shortsightedness. He has been blinded by his work, that's all. Now that he has stabilized affairs at Scrooge & Marley, and now that three-quarters of the firm's profit goes straight into his private accounts, he possesses the leisure for something that might resemble a conventional romance. He has, of course, no interest in focusing all of his sexual energies upon her. The very idea! But surely an innocent girl would not have the power to limit his activities in that area. She would never hear of them, to begin with. And if she were to hear, he would have no difficulty redirecting her attention. He has concealed a thousand secrets larger than a midnight dalliance with some whore. He has concealed financial malfeasance on the grandest of scales. Contrast that against a little faithlessness in love, and you will find that there is simply no comparison.

Scrooge certainly is happy with that inconsequential girl of his, although Marley would wager that the two of them have never come within a league of the procreative act. They have no doubt barely dreamed of it, and its execution is at this point surely two or three years distant. Good God, what people will do in the name of romance. They will deprive themselves of the very thing they seek, to begin with. It's positively unnatural. And yet there must be something to the whole business, or why would so many commit to it?

He resolves that he will find out. If he can possess the best of both worlds—romance with Fan and continued free exercise of his manly rights—he would be remiss not to make the attempt. And so it is that he begins the full and brutal siege of courtship.

He begins inquiring after her by way of Scrooge, at first only once a week or so, and usually in the context of a question about the well-being of the family. But as the weeks go by he begins to focus his curiosity on Fan alone—not only on her health but on her interests. He makes note of the books she has read and the plays she has seen and the lectures she has attended, aiming to familiarize himself with whatever ideas might now be furnishing her mind. By January he has asked Scrooge to remember him to the girl at least three times, and by February he has begun sending her not just his kindest wishes but the occasional little gift: a book by some author whose work he knows she has enjoyed, tickets for her and her mother to attend a play she might like.

By the beginning of March he is prepared to commence the final assault.

"For Miss Scrooge, mum?" The boy holds out a small envelope inscribed in an elegant hand.

She thanks him and shuts the door and examines the face of the envelope, but there is nothing written upon it save her daughter's name and this very address. The ink dried across its creamy face could have been laid down by a machine built to ape the human hand at its most idealized and least personal. Whether it was put there by man or woman is impossible to tell, but Mother Scrooge has an idea—an idea confirmed at least in part by the deep impression of a signet ring on the reverse, sunken into a pool of bloodred wax: M.

She brings the envelope to the parlor, where Fan is reading today's *Morning Chronicle*, and she stands with arms crossed until her daughter has put down the newspaper and slit open the envelope.

"Mr. Marley desires the pleasure of my company—at the opera."

"How nice."

Her daughter frowns.

"I've seen an invitation like this on the horizon for some time now—haven't you?"

"Oh, I surely have, although I'd hoped that it would remain on the horizon rather than appear in the flesh." She sighs and slips the note back into the envelope. There is a stack of kindling on the hearth at her feet, and by dropping it there she signals its fate. "I should have known better."

"But Mr. Marley has been so very solicitous!"

"Mr. Marley solicits what he wants to solicit, when he desires to solicit it."

"Now, Fan."

"Now, Mother. Ebenezer warned me about him, and he was correct."

"Bah! What does Ebenezer know? Men can change."

"Mr. Marley changes too much and too often. He is erratic, mercurial—both in his interests and in his affections."

"But he has lavished such gifts upon you . . ."

"With the aim that I should find myself beholden to him."

"And you do not?"

"I do not."

"And still you accepted them."

"I did not ask for them."

"You could have refused."

"I chose not to."

"But . . ."

"He gave those gifts freely. I knew his mind from the start, and I chose to take the course that would frustrate him in the end."

"You are cruel, Fan."

"Mr. Marley is cruel."

"He will think ill of you."

"He will desire me the more."

"And what then?"

"He shall not possess me. He shall never possess me."

"Fan! This talk of possession. You speak as if you are some mere . . . commodity."

"Then I speak for Jacob Marley, in whose view the earth itself exists only to be bought and sold."

She blocks him at every turn. His invitations and entreaties vanish whole, lost in the well of her person as into a mineshaft. Nothing comes back, neither reply nor rebuff, not even an echo accidentally reflected in his direction by way of her brother.

He sends flowers. He sends sweets. He offers trips to museums, long walks, library visits, lakeside picnics, outings on the Thames. Nothing. He debases himself with the construction of letters that require him to assume within the crooked halls of his own brain the mental and emotional traits of a lovesick child. He finds the entire operation detestable and he wonders from time to time if she is worth it but in his heart he knows the answer. She is not, not by any means. Only the victory matters.

Regardless, she may as well be dead for all he hears. So he doubles and redoubles his efforts, his determined disposition growing cooler and cooler as the battle grows more heated.

On the rare moments when his attentions briefly falter, Mother Scrooge takes up the cause on his behalf. "I shan't be around forever," she says, and in those words her daughter hears, *With every passing day, you're less likely to find a match.*

Fan is careful not to rise to the bait. "Why, Mother," she says, setting down her needlework, "your health is splendid."

"Nonetheless . . ." She shakes her head as if she knows something no one else knows. The hour and manner of her own demise, perhaps. She coughs pathetically.

"It's not like you to dwell on such things."

Her mother sighs, and on the last wisp of air that her lungs expel she confesses, "I'm only thinking of you."

"And of how lonely I shall be when you are gone."

"Fan! I never suggested . . ."

"Of course you did."

"Perhaps a bit. But only because—"

"Because you're thinking of me."

"I am."

"I know." She does know, of course. So she takes up her needle and works quietly for a moment, considering. Then, softly but certainly: "While you're thinking of me, you must remember that I would rather go to my grave a spinster than consort for a moment with Jacob Marley."

And as difficult as it is, Mother Scrooge understands.

The turning point in Marley's assault upon her arrives by way of a newsboy on the evening of Wednesday, March 25. The Abolition of the Slave Trade Act has made its passage through the Houses of Parliament and is now the law of the land. Damn his eyes, he has forgotten about it altogether. In his enthusiasm over pillaging Scrooge's half of the firm, he has failed to insulate himself sufficiently from any number of more or less direct affiliations with the slaving business. In fact, in shielding himself from Scrooge's oversight he has in some cases made his own connections more vulnerable to public discovery.

According to the newspaper, the trade must cease entirely upon March 1, 1808. Thus he has precisely eleven months and four days to build an edifice of deceit sufficient to shelter his various enterprises against the full power of the government. He is up to the task, of course, but he cannot accomplish it while maintaining his assault upon Fan's stubborn heart.

Enough, then. First things first.

Seventeen

A three-year wait until the wedding will provide a decent and practical interval. Ebenezer has suffered some financial setbacks as of late, and he intends to recover before taking a wife. Belle, based upon the little that he has explained to her regarding the shifting balance of accounts at Scrooge & Marley, feels at least in part responsible for those setbacks, but there is also in her heart a kind of triumphal suffering, as if delaying the happiness of marriage to Ebenezer is the price she must pay for her abolitionist virtue.

By the end of May they have chosen a date. Belle is for announcing it right off, but Ebenezer fears that the news might overshadow the King's birthday—or so he says, that silly goose, and who is she to dispute so charming a notion?—and therefore they wait until July. The occasion is a formal supper in the Fairchilds' dining room, where the two families come together for what could only be the long-awaited announcement. Everyone goes along with the charade, for this sort of thing does not happen every day.

They make seven at a table for four. The Fairchild daughters, Belle and Daphne, have prepared the meal, and when the Scrooge family arrives Fan swoops in to help with the serving. Thus Mr. and Mrs. Fairchild, Mother Scrooge, and Ebenezer have only to make appreciative oohs and aahs as the dishes arrive one after another, and then to make room for the young ladies when the table is provisioned and the feast can begin. Fairchild provides the blessing, which notes the coming together of these two families in words direct enough to be suggestive yet vague enough to be denied should denial prove necessary. Belle is wildly blushing by the time he reaches *"Amen."*

After an hour, everyone present has been interrogated as to his health and the weather has been thoroughly analyzed and nary a bite has been swallowed. So many marvelous dishes, gone cold in the service of breathless anticipation. Mrs. Fairchild presses the boiled potatoes upon Ebenezer for the fourth or fifth time despite the presence on his plate of several untouched examples, and he finally resolves to proceed.

He rises to his feet and clears his throat and takes a sip of port that goes down the wrong way, requiring him to clear his throat again, although with even less success this time around. The eyes of both families rest upon him as he gasps for air and dabs at his lips and blushes—at least as fiercely as Belle had blushed before.

"What's on your mind, Ebenezer?" asks Fairchild.

Ebenezer puts down his napkin and takes up his glass once more. "It will come as no surprise," he says, "most surely not to *you*, Mr. Fairchild, with whom I have consulted in detail upon the matter . . ."

Eyebrows ratchet upward all around. This is most assuredly the moment.

". . . it will come as no surprise, as I was saying, that Belle . . ."

At the mention of her name she reaches out to take his hand, an action that unsteadies him to such a degree that a little wine spills from his glass onto the white linen tablecloth.

"Oh, goodness, Mrs. Fairchild, you must forgive my clumsiness . . ." The blood drains from his face and he stands transfixed, staring at the widening spill as he would stare at an adder coiled to strike.

"It's nothing, Ebenezer."

"It's claret, Mrs. Fairchild, and I fear that it will leave an intractable stain . . ."

Belle releases his hand and takes her own napkin to the spill.

"Please, Ebenezer," says her mother. "Go on."

He sets down his wineglass rather than risk further catastrophe. His hands shake as he folds his napkin and unfolds it and folds it again. He takes a deep breath and then another, and finally he speaks: "Belle and I have . . . *set a date for our marriage*." Amid joyous huzzahs from around the table—not the least from Mrs. Fairchild, whose linens and whose daughter both seem to be out of danger at last—he collapses back into his chair.

"I presume that I shall be your maid of honor?" says Daphne from across the table. Fan is of course her sole potential competitor for the prize, and she dares not so much as glance her way.

"I should say so," says Belle.

"Unless you find a husband in the meantime," Fairchild puts in.

"A husband who's in a bigger hurry to wed than Ebenezer has been," says his wife.

Belle comes to Scrooge's defense. "Ebenezer has his reasons," she says, giving his arm a squeeze. "And I assure you that they are excellent ones."

Scrooge lifts his hands and shows their palms, as if to fend off a storm of incoming praise.

"Perhaps I can clarify matters," says Fairchild, drawing out his pipe. "I can tell you, with some delight, that Ebenezer has recently over-seen his firm's divestment of all properties having to do with a certain distasteful—*and soon to be unlawful*—activity." He brings a flame to the bowl and puckers to nurse the tobacco's ignition, an aggrieved look upon his face that holds his listeners hostage to any such delay as he may choose to enforce. Once the tobacco is burning satisfactorily, he proceeds. "He and I were at first of different minds regarding the issue, but in the interest of pursuing marriage to our Belle, he saw the light." The irony of Fairchild's disappearing into a plume of tobacco smoke at that very instant is lost on no one, but it goes without remark. "As a result, our Mr. Scrooge still has a few small improvements to make in his affairs before he is entirely comfortable taking on the responsibilities of marriage. It does not alter his intentions or dim his enthusiasm or diminish his ability to carry forward the great project of supporting Belle when I am finally laid to my rest, I can assure you of that."

A look of alarm passes over Mother Scrooge's countenance, and she cannot keep herself from interrupting. "Are you quite well, Mr. Fairchild?"

"I shall be well when the fates of both of my daughters are settled," says he, with a pitying look at Daphne.

Belle, in the interest of rescuing her sister, raises her wineglass. "To Ebenezer!" she says.

"To Belle!" he counters.

"To Belle and Ebenezer!" say Mothers Scrooge and Fairchild, in one voice. It is almost as if they have rehearsed it. Quite possibly they have.

Mother Scrooge has a question for Fan on their walk home. "Do you see how Mr. Fairchild worries over the fate of his children?"

Her daughter laughs. "That has been his way forever and ever. The thought of his own absence from the world seems to fascinate him. Perhaps he believes the world will be a better place."

"Bah. There is no harm in planning for the future. A parent has a duty."

"Oh, Mother—it's not planning, it's an unhealthy fixation. Death was his theme when Belle and I were just children. It gave me nightmares."

"A child starving to death is *every* parent's nightmare. It certainly is mine—especially now that you have so thoroughly rebuffed Mr. Marley."

"The post has been quiet, hasn't it?"

"Very."

"Thank heavens."

"Be that as it may," says Mother Scrooge, "you would be wise to befriend Daphne, now that Belle is taken. You will look better against an older woman who remains unattached than against someone your own age who has already succeeded."

"*Succeeded.*"

"In making a match."

"I want more than a match."

"I don't mean just *any* match."

"You were in a hurry to pair me off with Mr. Marley."

"Mr. Marley has funds."

"Funds are more common than character."

"There's nothing common about either one."

"I suppose not, Mother. But God willing, I shall find a match with a fair supply of both."

1808

Eighteen

Years at sea have served not to roughen Captain Balfour but to smooth him, to soften his sharp edges, to polish his every surface until he has acquired the soft pale gleam of the carved whalebone knife that he carries in his pocket. He obtained the implement on some Polynesian adventure in the long-ago past when he was but a gunner's mate, and although it is useful only for opening envelopes or cutting pages as he reads one of his beloved naval histories, he keeps it with him always.

Stationed now in London, he misses the sea but not overmuch. His skills are required here at home, or such is the opinion of his superiors, and he is long-habituated to following orders. There are ships to be outfitted in yards on the Thames and in Portsmouth and elsewhere, there are men to be recruited and trained, there are missions to be plotted for the advancement of the latest national policies. If he can serve the crown better by overseeing such activities than by commanding his trusty old ship, the *Guardian*, then so be it. He only hopes that after he has served a reasonable landbound term he may once again be sent to sea, that he may finish his service in the place where he is happiest.

"Thy will be done," he accedes to the Almighty as he finishes uttering a prayer to that very effect—for in religious practice as in military life, he is accustomed to serving at the whim of some invisible superior. He opens his eyes and searches for a page in the hymnbook as the choir rises in the loft. Remote and enrobed and lit from above, they look to him like so many angels—especially the alto on the very right. (Is *alto* the term? Is that the lower of the two ladies' parts? Yes, he is quite certain. *Alto* it is.) The girl has about her an ethereal quality, something that elevates her not just above the choir but above the congregation and indeed above mankind in general. The passion carried by her voice and the devotion written upon her face stir not just his soul but also his heart. And surpassing all of that—although Balfour would like to think himself beyond such lowly considerations—is her beauty. A man is a man, though, there is no use denying it. And a man's passions are to be kept in check. In his years at sea he has often seen men succumb to their most bestial natures. He has witnessed and indeed punished iniquities so terrible that he is ashamed that the folds of his memory have carried them into this holy place. He of all people understands the vile lusts of men. But this is not that. Not by any means.

The hymn ends and a sermon follows and a freewill offering is taken. Balfour is still reassuring himself on the crucial point of his innocence when, prior to the benediction, the pastor invites the congregation to a reception for tea and cakes and good Christian fellowship. He makes a special point of welcoming visitors, and he does so with such warm feeling that Captain Balfour cannot help but follow orders.

By God, he'll be keelhauled if the angel isn't pouring tea. She is paired in the task with a yellow-haired girl of about her age who he recalls sat opposite her in the loft, the two of them brought together now in a contrasting pair of dark and light. They are making a game of their work and amusing themselves to no end, teasing with one parishioner after another, just as bright and merry as youth can make them. One particular gentleman—tall, bony, with a haunted look deep in his eye—attends to them both in a manner that suggests an attachment to one or the other, but Balfour cannot put his finger on the exact nature of it.

Puzzling over the possible connection he joins the line right behind the pastor, to whom he introduces himself. No, he explains by and by, he is new neither to the city nor to the faith, and although he has been long separated from both he intends to make the most of his return.

"How many years were you at sea?" says Reverend McPhail, a portly individual with a broad smile full of crooked teeth and an eager eye for the platter of cakes up ahead.

"Enough to miss it, and enough to be finished with it if that should be the King's will."

"Or God's."

"*Or God's*," says the captain, clapping the pastor on the back as if he has made a very fine joke. Should the Royal Navy's chain of command go higher than King George III, Balfour hasn't been informed of it. "We do as we're told, don't we, you and I?"

"True enough," says McPhail, craning his neck a bit and looking ahead to see if Fan has brought some of her justly famed ginger biscuits. Sighting confirmed, he points to them and says to the captain, "You, sir, are in for a treat."

"How so?" He looks where McPhail is pointing but can see only the girl.

"Miss Scrooge," says the pastor, "has brought along the delectable fruits of her kitchen."

"Miss Scrooge? Now, which would she be?"

"The one with the teapot. The dark one. To be frank, the biscuits she's brought will be the only items here worth eating."

"I'll have two, then." Balfour inclines his head. "Now, that long-boned fellow. Would he be her—"

"Her brother? Yes indeed. You have a sharp eye, Captain Balfour."

"Service on shipboard has honed my vision."

"His name's Ebenezer," says McPhail. "He is affianced to her friend, the fair-haired girl. Miss Fairchild."

"And who would Miss Scrooge be affianced to?"

"None yet."

"I am shocked."

"Surely you have seen more astonishing sights in your naval career?"

"Not that I can recall," says Balfour.

"Typhoons? Hurricanes?"

"None more remarkable," says Balfour.

"Pirates? Cannibal chieftains?"

"Never."

"Vast seas of ice? Lush equatorial Edens?"

"I assure you, nothing can compare to so marvelous a notion as that girl's being unattached."

McPhail picks up a small plate and offers it to the captain. "Then the world is still alive with the potential for miracle," he says, abundantly certain of his Lord and of himself.

He can be utterly charming, this Captain Balfour—warm as a tropical breeze and smooth as an unruffled lagoon at the first peep of sunrise. He is orderly in his habits, direct in his manner, sharp in his attire, and cleanly in his grooming. He possesses an easy smile that devastates the ladies, and he is handy with all of the current dances. (His repertoire further includes steps from societies as remote and exotic as those of Tahiti, the Canaries, and the Isle of Skye.)

Fan finds herself enchanted from the moment he compliments her ginger biscuits. From well before then, really. From the moment he came into view behind Reverend McPhail. She spilled his tea in pouring it, and in apologizing she spilled it again.

"On shipboard," he says, "spilling twice from the same cup is said to bring bad luck."

"Really?"

"Something like that."

"What's the cure?"

"My dear"—he fixes her with a concerned look—"there is no cure. There never is."

"Who will it affect, then—me, or you?"

"We shall have to see for ourselves."

"But how?"

"By remaining in close communication."

He winks and takes his tea and biscuits and moves off, but not far. Then again, no distance would be quite far enough to discourage Fan, not after so captivating an introduction. He could retreat to the Azores and she would still find him.

"My goodness," he says when she appears with a cup and saucer of her own, "perhaps I was mistaken about that bad luck business."

"Do you think?"

"I may have gotten it backwards," he says, setting down his cup and saucer on a nearby table. "To judge by the signs, my fortune seems to be improving by the moment."

But Fan is not to be so easily had. She teases, "Then perhaps the ill luck is to be mine?"

Balfour looks stricken—truly and deeply stricken—by the notion that crossing paths with him should be anything but the most positive development for her.

"I'm only teasing, of course."

He flattens a hand upon his chest. "Oh, thank God, Miss—"

"Scrooge. My friends call me Fan."

"Then I shall aspire to the right to call you that myself."

"And you are—"

He draws himself even straighter than usual, bringing his heels together and offering her a little bow. "Captain Harry Balfour, former master of the HMS *Guardian*, now stationed at Greenwich."

"Not Portsmouth?" A girl both beautiful and bright, she knows a little about the Royal Navy.

"Portsmouth, Devonport, London—I come and go, depending upon my various duties." That would seem to be the limit of what he will say on the matter, at least for now.

"And how are you finding life on dry land?"

"A bit cramped, if I may say." With one finger he tugs at his collar. "It's a large empire, but a terribly small country."

"And will you be trapped here for long?"

"I shall stay as long as it suits King George," he says, "although I fear that it shall be for quite a little while." He takes the last biscuit from his plate and bites it in half. "And you? What about you, Miss Scrooge?"

"Fan."

"Fan, then."

"I'm afraid that my story compares poorly to the romance of a life at sea."

"Let me be the judge."

She does just that, offering up for him the plain facts of her plain life here in London. Her mother, her brother, her father long gone. Her reading and her needlework. Her fondness for singing in the choir in this church. She leaves out nothing but Marley, for Marley is no longer part of any life she knows. He is only the despised past. He is but a repeated mistake, not to be committed again.

"That all sounds perfectly homely," says Balfour with a dreamy look, "particularly to a rootless old tramp like myself."

"Perhaps we have expanded each other's horizons, then."

Balfour peers into his teacup, making certain that there is at least a single sip remaining, and then raises it in a toast. "To broader horizons!"

Fan clinks her cup against his, wondering if toasting to anything at all is appropriate here in the church parlor, but already forgiving him for his worldliness.

Nineteen

"What's more," says Fan, "he's doing God's work."

"Forgive me," Belle laughs. 'Did you say '*Chaplain* Balfour'? I thought it was '*Captain*.' Although I must admit that for a man of the cloth, he cuts a dashing figure."

"You heard me, silly. Harry is no chaplain. He *is*, though, laboring at a cause very near to your heart."

"And that would be?"

"Enforcement of the Slave Trade Act. The navy is terribly serious about it. They've two ships already in what they're calling the West Africa Squadron—the *Derwent* and the *Solebay*. Harry has told me all about them. He only wishes he could be in charge of one and see some real action, instead of running things from behind a desk."

"And you? What do you wish?"

"The desk suits me fine. What would you think if Ebenezer were out gallivanting along the African coast, confiscating ships, rounding up slavers, risking life and limb?"

"It sounds romantic."

"It sounds perilous. And terribly solitary."

"But Ebenezer is my betrothed, and Harry is . . . what?"

Fan wrings her hands. "Harry is important," she says at last.

"You sound serious."

"I am."

Balfour's charm has worked its magic, then, with little active interven-tion on his part. His life has been characterized by hard labor and intense focus and methodical accomplishment, and so along the way he has grown wary of good fortune—yet he finds himself fortunate now. Per-haps the universe has been saving up a store of good luck on his behalf, and has chosen to deliver it all at once. Anything is possible.

Lucky or otherwise, he is to meet Fan this evening at her brother's place of business so as to join Ebenezer and Belle, those two famous lovebirds, for supper and a new drama at Covent Garden. He arrives early—he is forever arriving early—and he enters through the half-open warehouse door under the sign reading SCROOGE & MARLEY. He sees right away that this is clearly a place not meant for public visitation. The shelves are haphazardly arranged, poorly kept, dusty. Perhaps there is some system to be discovered beneath the disarray, but it escapes him.

Give me two days here with a proper crew, he thinks, *and we'd establish order.*

He has spied the office doorway—a darker blot in the lightless warehouse—and he is making for it when a figure appears from the mouth of an intersecting aisle. It is too tall and too broad to be Scrooge, and with a curiously threatening tilt of its head it introduces itself.

"Marley," says the figure. "My name is over the door. And you would be?"

Balfour introduces himself, although such persuasive power as his charm and authority have over most people does not seem to affect Mar-ley in the least. Perhaps it is a function of the darkness.

The figure may nod or may not. "The entrance is that way," it says, thrusting a hand in the direction from which Balfour has come, back toward the half-open warehouse door and the street beyond. Having come this close, he is to exit and try again. "Private property, you see."

"Of course," says Balfour. "Understood." Rules, after all, are rules.

When he's made his way out and located the office entrance around the corner, he finds Scrooge waiting in the alcove.

"Forgive Marley," he whispers.

"He hasn't offended."

"You're too kind, Balfour. He has been . . . *preoccupied*."

Preoccupied or not, the offender emerges now to welcome Balfour aboard according to his own particular lights. That is to say he ignores him utterly, pressing past the pair of them and onward into the depths of Scrooge's cell. "May we have a word?" he asks his partner, crooking a finger.

Whatever transpires behind that closed door will remain a mystery to Balfour, but it goes on for several minutes. Enough time for Fan and Belle to arrive via carriage, and for the three of them to decide upon their dinner venue. Fan has heard about an intriguing new spot in the City— it's called the Grasshopper, she believes—which she is eager to try. Any choice she might make in this line is perfectly fine with Balfour, who wants only for her to be happy.

The door finally swings open to reveal a tableau in which a smiling Scrooge stands holding the iron knob while his partner lingers in the shadows, slouched in a wooden chair with an aggrieved look etched upon his face.

"Perhaps Mr. Marley would care to join us!" Balfour offers. "We may not be able to obtain another ticket for the theater, but I'm certain that the Grasshopper could provide an additional chair for dinner."

Nothing from Marley.

"What say you, old man?"

Marley flinches at what he takes for a barb. Pleasantries aside, the very truth is that he does seem an old man, at least to himself. He shifts in his chair just enough to prove that he still lives. "Oh," he says with a cruel smile, "I'm sure these ladies have seen enough of *me*—Miss Scrooge in particular. Isn't that correct, Fan?"

Before she can answer, Balfour grins and barks out a jolly "Cheerio, then!" He thrusts an elbow toward Fan, which she seems relieved to grasp. And yet a seed has been planted, a question posed.

Balfour's mind is racing as they gain the carriage. He certainly cannot ask Fan what the fellow might have intended by such a remark. He cannot ask any of them. Perhaps it is nothing at all, or close to nothing. Perhaps Marley has merely offended her—spoken coarsely, lost his temper, Heaven knows what—at some time in the past, and over the intervening period this subtle wrong has festered into a sore spot for both of them. He definitely seems the type to nurse a grudge of that sort. Marley lurching about in the darkness with his "Private property!" Marley charging wordless through the hallway and heaving the door shut against a visitor. He's the type, most assuredly. The type that a wary individual would not want to anger, for Marley would never forget it.

In the end, before the moment is irretrievable, he finds a way to ask without quite asking. "For my part," he says as the carriage turns onto the street wherein their destination lies, "I'm delighted that it's just the four of us. For even if no one else has had enough of Mr. Marley, I for one certainly have."

"Having enough of Mr. Marley is easily done," laughs Fan, pointedly searching beyond the window for the sign of the Grasshopper.

"I wouldn't say that," counters Scrooge. "He is usually far more agreeable."

Fan glares at him, but only briefly and beyond Balfour's line of sight.

"As a rule, butter wouldn't melt in his mouth," says Belle.

Scrooge sighs. "I can't say what's gotten into him. As I told you, Harry, he's been preoccupied. Overworked, I suppose, although exactly how I cannot tell. Our duties, you see, are quite separate."

The carriage shudders and slows.

"In some ways," he goes on, "Marley and I are mysteries to each other. As are all men, I suppose you could say."

The carriage halts.

Balfour must ask now, or never. "Then why do you find him so distasteful, Fan? Is it that selfsame agreeableness? Do you perceive something feigned about it?"

"I perceive something feigned about every aspect of Mr. Marley," she says, reaching for the latch.

Scrooge leans conspiratorially toward Balfour. "He has been known to pursue the lady, from time to time."

" 'From time to time,' you say?"

"Mm-hmm."

"How odd."

"Mr. Marley is odd," says Fan, "and inconstant."

Balfour shakes his head and addresses Scrooge with a smile. "Between you and me, Ebenezer, I should no more pursue your sister *from time to time* than I should elect to *breathe* from time to time."

Fan's grip pauses on the latch. "Am I being pursued, then, Captain Balfour?"

"Would I have a rival in the cause, Miss Scrooge?"

"I should say not."

"Mr. Marley might think otherwise."

"Mr. Marley would be incorrect."

"Poor old chap," he sighs. "Perhaps he has a heart after all. I believe you've broken it."

"Good," says Fan, as if the word is the vilest of curses. She turns the latch, and Balfour presses open the carriage door, and out they all tumble toward the waiting delights of the Grasshopper.

1810

Twenty

Fan's wedding is to be in the high summer, Ebenezer's in the fall. Hers will be crowded, his intimate. Hers will take place in the ornate chapel at the Royal Navy's Greenwich Hospital, his in the lowly family church.

Two weddings in a single year. Mother Scrooge fears that the excitement will be her undoing. Ever philosophical, however, she consoles herself that should she fail to survive both, she will die having witnessed the superior one.

Ebenezer and Belle produce a surprisingly long guest list, considering. The entire membership of the church shall be invited, naturally, although which party any given parishioner may choose to align himself with—the Fairchilds or the Scrooges—is a matter not to be examined too closely. Beyond the church family, though, is where the surprises lie. Judging by the quantity of envelopes his mother must address in her slow, painstaking hand, Ebenezer would seem to be intimate with half of London's population. She wonders if the church will hold so many souls.

A notable percentage of the invitations return unopened, however, and more still vanish into the mists and vagaries of the city and its environs without generating so much as a proper answer. "Your associates

155

could profit from a lesson in the social graces," she tells her son as she sorts through it all one Friday before supper.

"My associates?"

"Certain of them, at least." She taps a judgmental finger on the list of delinquents, and then pulls open a drawer to produce the bundle of dead letters. "As for these, perhaps you could provide improved addresses."

Ebenezer riffles through the lot of them. *Badger & Son. Plummer & Snagsby. Merdle, Jaggers, Slumkey & Lightwood, Counselors at Law.* These and the rest of the errant invitees would all seem to be Jacob's contacts, one way or another. He shall look into them first thing on Monday, and issue fresh invitations right away. Heaven knows he would hate for anyone to miss the celebration on account of a clerical error.

But Jacob is nowhere to be found on Monday, as is more or less his usual habit. How silly and hopeful of Ebenezer to have thought otherwise. At midmorning he wraps his muffler around his neck and steps out into the icy winter street and locates a willing boy, a poor ragged thing needful of whatever kindness might be on offer, and for a shilling he sends him around to his partner's known haunts. A whole bob, with the promise of another to keep it company if he is quick about it. Such is the outsized generosity of the groom in waiting.

"Bob, sir? That's my name, sir."

"Bob, is it? Just Bob and no more?"

"Bob Cratchit, sir."

"Then we'll make it two bob and then some. A half crown for the prompt recovery of the missing Mr. Marley." And off the boy scampers, warm with hope on this cold winter morning.

The clock in the high church tower is tolling out a fogbound noon when he returns, abashed and disappointed, offering up his unearned coin in token of his uselessness. "Bah," says Ebenezer, closing the boy's filthy fist around the treasure and its fresh mate, two bob for young Bob. "You did your best."

"Thank you, sir. You're very kind." Nonetheless he backs away with the timidity of a dog accustomed to the lash.

"You are certain that you knocked upon his door."

"I did, sir."

"And there was no answer."

"There was none, sir."

"You used the knocker, not your fist."

"Oh, yes, sir. And 'twas a great grand knocker, too. I could barely lift it." He mimes the struggle.

Ebenezer frowns to imagine him straining so, and fishes deep in the pocket of his waistcoat. "Then have another shilling for your trouble, child. And make certain you spend it on provisions."

"For myself or for my brothers and sisters, sir? Or for my mum? My da is in Marshalsea, last I heard."

"For every one of you," says Ebenezer, emptying his pocket. The child could be pulling his leg, or so Jacob might insist, but generosity reflects positively upon the giver nonetheless. "God bless you all."

"You are too kind, sir."

"Not by half. But if you truly believe so, you can return the favor by keeping an eye on the premises while I go and seek Mr. Marley myself."

"Do you mean it, sir?" The child looks as if he has been invited to preside over affairs of state at Buckingham Palace.

"Absolutely." Ebenezer takes the hard chair and drags it closer to the little grate, in whose depths a pile of ruddy coals hisses merrily away. "Have a seat right here," he says, "and should any visitors arrive, advise them that I shall return directly."

The boy hops into the chair, luxuriates for a moment in the radiant warmth of the stove, and promptly commences to snore. Ebenezer locks his desk and his cabinets, just in case, and then he takes to the street.

➤➤

The knocker is indeed a ponderous thing, but Ebenezer does not require the use of it. He admits himself as his partner prefers him to do—through the basement entrance employed by the wine merchants, from which he makes his way through a series of narrow passages and back stairways to Marley's chambers. He commits a wrong turn now and then—running square into a closet from which there seems to be no other exit, finding himself high atop a windblown turret he has never noticed before—for the layout of the place seems even more devilishly twisted now than he remembers. One could almost be persuaded that its complexities have multiplied under their own power, with the implacability of some fatal disease.

Nonetheless, with time and persistence he gains his destination. He knocks upon the door and finds it not quite fully latched, as if his partner has vacated his quarters in haste. He takes advantage of the condition, gingerly edging the door open. "Jacob?" he calls through the crack. And again, pressing it the slightest bit wider, "Jacob?" Nothing. The air coming from the place smells musty, disused, as if the apartments are the long-abandoned den of some beast, and he pulls the door to rather than breathe it in.

My partner wouldn't go off and leave his quarters unlocked, thinks Scrooge. *We have far too many secrets for that.* Thus Marley may be somewhere in the house after all. He holds his breath and has another go at the door and enters for a quick sweep of the airless apartment—kitchen, parlor, bedroom with a tall four-poster bed hung about with curtains whose brass rings make a shimmering sound as he draws them open—to confirm that the man is indeed absent and not merely dead. Satisfied, he latches the door behind him and sets out into the mapless warrens of the great house.

Thanks to Scrooge's love of order, what begins as a lark soon becomes a challenge. Each corner he turns without locating Marley serves as an impulse to investigate two more. He goes methodically, intently, calling his partner's name down every hall and into every crack and through every grate he encounters. Suspecting that any wall may be false and any panel may operate at the touch of a secret mechanism, he raps every vertical surface with his knuckles, tests every squeaky floorboard with his toe. No bit of carpet goes unmoved, no threadbare tapestry hangs unmolested.

As he proceeds he keeps his turnings always to the right, on the theory that strict regularity must render any maze negotiable. He does have the keys to certain doors—the one to Mr. Pecksniff's on the third floor, for example, wherein he knows that a compartment hidden behind an etching of a pastoral scene (sheep, maidens) will yield the key to the offices of Honeythunder & Grimwig on the next floor down, behind whose baseboard the key to Pecksniff's lockbox is kept. And so on, and so on. His impulse is to follow such links, but he stops himself upon realizing that to do so would be to subvert his method. And yet how is he to proceed, with half the doors locked against him and the rest invisible?

Regularly, of course. Obsessively.

In Pecksniff's office is a writing desk, and within it Scrooge finds a moldy ledger and a bit of crayon. Thus armed he returns to his starting place at Marley's door. He makes some estimates as to the dimensions of the house, calculates what seems a reasonable correspondence between the length of his pace and the width of each inked row, and sets off again, cautious as any cartographer.

Other than his careful footsteps and his inquisitive rapping upon the walls—along with an occasional rumble or crash from the wine merchants in the dungeon below—the house is dead silent. An ordinary man would look elsewhere for his missing partner, but Scrooge is no ordinary man. He perseveres, marking the ledger as he goes, plotting the interlocking shapes of rooms and alcoves and passageways. By the time he is done mapping the second floor, the daylight beyond the windows is beginning to fade. By the time he is halfway finished with the third, the sun has set. He filches a lantern from Marley's rooms and completes his work by the light of it, puzzling over the schematic taking shape on the page and tugging at his lip in frustration.

Significant portions of the house would seem to be *missing*. He checks his work, pacing off relevant stretches a second and even a third time, but to no avail. The gaps that show up here and there—a broad section along the rear wall of the upper story, overlapping segments of the two stories beneath that, a number of narrow vertical channels that indicate either shafts or narrow staircases—are as incontrovertibly genuine as Scrooge himself. Careless as to whether he leaves any trace of his passage, he returns to the third-floor offices of Krook & Flite, a spot where the broad missing section of the rear wall meets with the largest of the narrow vertical channels. Armed with the lantern, he inspects every inch of the corner in question until he finds what he seeks: a mechanism, concealed in the base of a verdigris-encrusted wall sconce, that releases a sliding panel. He shines the lantern into the void beyond it, revealing a great long chamber filled to the roof beams with cartons, sacks, and strongboxes. To one side, exactly where he knew he would find it, is a precipitous staircase. He ignores the treasure that Marley has stored here—the entire premises is jammed with the stuff, it's just more inventory to be accounted for one of these days—and heads down the stairs.

"Are you quite well, Inspector?" The girl asks because a fierce convulsion has passed over the gentleman's body, and not a convulsion of the desired sort. The paroxysm was accompanied by a wounded howl suggesting that it is he, not she, who has been rudely violated. If memory serves, the last time such an incident took place it was only seconds before the ancient member of Parliament in question lay dead upon her bedsheets.

They have procedures for handling such things here at Mrs. McCullough's, for they are professionals. A physician by the name of George Peppercorn, discredited and impoverished though he may be, lives nearby and can supply any number of likely but unprovable diagnoses as to cause of death. A carriage driver who goes by Richard Camphor haunts the district as well, offering transport of the questionably deceased to other, more appropriate precincts. And then there is of course the able Mr. Wegg, whose access to his employer's wagon and ash pile simplify the complete disposal of the more troublesome cases. It is Wegg's good fortune that his services are not required in this instance, however, for he would go mad deciding whether the corpse involved belonged to the reported Inspector Bucket or to his own longtime business associate, Mr. Krook.

There is no corpse, however. Not yet. There is only Inspector Bucket, heaved now onto his back with one hand pressed flat to his hammering chest.

The girl—her name is Madeline, and she is chief among his favorites—asks again. "Are you quite well, Inspector?"

His eyes are peeled back wide and their anxious gaze darts about, searching the low smoke-grimed ceiling and perhaps the vaulted heavens above it for something that remains beyond his vision. Some evil revenant, perhaps, bent on doing him wrong. Or else some friendly spirit who has sent him this alarm before dematerializing into the ether.

He draws a calm breath at last. "I must go," he says. And so he does.

The unlit stairway plunges downward like a mineshaft, and at its sudden bottom a narrow panel opens onto the mysteries of Marley's workshop. No alchemist of old ever dreamed of such a place as this, for alchemists were men of theory and dream. Marley is no dreamer, and he is practical if he is anything. His workshop is a place where deception becomes truth, where loss becomes gain, where ideas become men—men who rise up and step out into the world and empty the pockets of such individuals as have had the misfortune to be born mere flesh and blood.

Scrooge is not much interested in the tools of his partner's malefactions, for he has neither the brain nor the hands nor even the stomach for using them on his own account. What does interest him is the extent and complexity of his partner's deceit—and within a tall cabinet located in the dustiest corner he finds the first indications.

There are names—individuals, offices, entire commercial empires—described in Marley's notes that he has never heard before, mingled with others that he has. Some—Badger & Son; Plummer & Snagsby; Merdle, Jaggers, Slumkey & Lightwood—are among the missing respondents to his wedding invitation. Others, many others, are utterly confounding to him. A Josiah Bounderby, Esq. A Sampson Brass, Ltd. The firm of Dawkins, Dawkins, Dawkins, & Drood. Here among the records of the real and unreal companies that he knows—or *believes* he knows—are records of other entities altogether. They seem entwined, interwoven, the cunning work of a mind even more devious than he has understood it to be.

There are older names and entities entangled here as well, names from the abandoned past, and in the web of them lies the greatest dismay for poor Ebenezer. His eye falls upon them in the lantern's gleam as upon a palimpsest of sin that lingers on through the ages, and he hangs his head. They are slavers and affiliates of slavers. He has believed himself shut of all such connections.

The Cratchit boy could happily sleep in Scrooge's chair all night, for even though the fire in the grate has died the room is still warmer than his family's quarters. More peaceful, too, in the absence of his many sisters and brothers. But such a kind fate is not to be his, not with the arrival at the door of this sudden fierce specter, charging in from the darkness and calling out for Scrooge.

"He's gone in search of Mr. Marley, sir," says the boy.

"I'm Marley. He's left you in charge?"

"Yes, sir."

"Just like him, leaving a boy to do a man's work."

"I done it as a favor to him, sir. He was kind to me."

"I'll bet," says Marley. "Kinder than I'd have been."

"Just leaving I was, Mr. Marley." Muttering thus, the boy makes for the door.

"Take your coat, then. Dare to come back for it, and I'll skin you alive."

"Don't worry, sir," says the boy, opening the door into a wind that nearly tears it from his hands. "I don't *have* a coat." With that the winter night sweeps him away.

Marley lights a candle and spends a few minutes scouring his office, trying locks and checking drawers and generally determining whether anything might possibly be other than the way he left it. He finds nothing, and yet he is not satisfied. Although the shocking pain in his chest has passed, the memory of it has him unbalanced, wary. He's halfway prepared for a sign that everything he's built in the world is about to collapse around him. For a moment he'd thought that the child might be the bearer of such a message, but no.

So Scrooge has been looking for him, has he? *Whereabouts*, he wonders. He surely knows some of Marley's usual haunts, although the list to which he has access is highly redacted. Even still, most of those locales are spots where old Scrooge would not be caught lingering. So where might he be instead? Where could he go, should the idea occur to him, to do damage worthy of that infernal clutching at Marley's chest and vitals? With a swallow that nearly resurrects the pain, he realizes. And off he goes to his own residence, his private lair, his palace of secrets, to see what mischief his partner may have gotten up to.

Young Cratchit's footprints—of no more consequence to Marley than the traces of some game animal—are visible in the snow just outside the door, but soon they're lost among half a hundred others. Were he paying attention, he would note that the child seems to have turned down a narrow alleyway, a grimy passage employed mainly by pickpockets, beggars, and other practitioners of the more larcenous and tawdry arts. But he is not paying attention, for his mind is occupied with thoughts of his house and his partner. Businesses along the street are closing up, their lamps going dark and their doors swinging wide to empty their prisoners into the freedom of the street. They are a lively and good-humored lot, he thinks, considering that moments before they were surely yawning over their desks, complaining of exhaustion and low wages.

The thicker the crowds the slower his progress, and the slower his progress the more tangled his thoughts, and the more tangled his thoughts the greater his impatience. He shall never get home. By the time these infernal crowds have let him pass, Scrooge will have learned all of his secrets, grasped how thoroughly he has been cheating him all these years, and had a constable brought around for his arrest.

While Marley's mind races, Scrooge's plods ahead like an old draft horse. Back and forth it goes, slow but implacable, dragging understanding like a plow. And like a plow, the path it traces across the thicket of Marley's deceit is both narrow and exact. He cares nothing for his own finances. He cares nothing for the illegality of anything that Marley may have done. Indications of these things he dismisses without so much as registering them, for there is but one principle driving him on, one realization to which every discovery worth making must adhere: that the firm of Scrooge & Marley, unimaginable as it may be, is still very much in the slaving business.

The facts are incontrovertible. All of the firm's historic holdings and investments are still in place, although Marley has hidden them beneath clever new accretions of falsity and fraud. The old agreements remain in force. The old contractors remain employed. Entire vessels—the *Marie*, the *Dauntless*, the *Mercator*, the *Seahawk*—have been reported lost, collected upon, secretly rechristened, and falsely registered under foreign flags so as to go about their business undisturbed by British law. It is nearly inconceivable, and yet here it is before him.

So lost is Scrooge in his thoughts that when a snowball strikes the window above the workbench, the sound of it fails to register. Register the second one does, though, and straight to the window he goes to spy the boy, standing alone in the yard below.

He swings wide the window and thrusts his head out into the cold. "Cratchit?"

"I saw your light, sir."

"What of it?"

"Mr. Marley's on his way."

"I should think he might be. He does live here, after all."

"He don't look happy, sir."

"He'll be less happy when I finish with him."

"You were kind to me, sir. I thought I owed you."

"Owed me what?"

"A warning, sir. Mr. Marley don't seem like a fellow to cross."

"You're a wise boy. You'll go far."

"Thank you, sir. I should think there's wisdom in choosing when to do battle with one such as Marley."

"And you're a clever boy as well."

"Thank you, sir. Does that mean you'll go, then?" He casts a desperate look back over his shoulder, down the hill toward the torchlit street. "I took a shortcut. He'll be right along."

"Perhaps you're correct," says Scrooge.

"Live to fight another day."

"Come see me in ten or fifteen years. I'll put you to work."

"Then you'll go?"

"I will."

"Now?"

"Yes."

"Goodbye, sir."

But Scrooge is already gone and the window is shut and the light is vanishing into the depths of the house.

When Marley arrives, there is nothing to see. The entire premises, so far as he can tell, is just as he left it. The child was lying, no doubt. He saw Scrooge leave on some errand, sprang the lock, and let himself in. Thank heavens the negotiables were locked away, or he'd have to hunt the urchin down and take the loss out of his skin. It's bad enough that the little bastard gave himself the run of the stove.

Twenty-One

Scrooge has no time for despair, no time for fury, no time for anything but work.

He does not even go home. He returns to his office instead, plants himself behind his desk, and transcribes the web of Marley's deceit into a fresh ledger. The facts of it are etched into his brain right now—it is as if he's tracing them onto the page—but rather than risk the loss of a single incriminating detail to time and memory he spends the night getting it down complete. He does not stir from his chair, and his pen flies as fast as his mind can race. He blots errors and corrections and desperate stray splashes of ink with sand, with blotting paper, with the linen of his sleeves and the flesh of his fists. By dawn he is nearly as black as his partner's heart, tattooed all over with the inverse image of every error he has made and corrected in the process of charting the wickedness that he must now undo if he is to keep his promise to Belle and to her father and to God Himself. He douses his candle as the first pale light of day strikes the frost on his window. The room is frigid, his fingers stiff, his feet blocks of ice—but what of it? A man with work to keep him warm does not require a stove.

He rises and locks the ledger away and goes home to bathe and breakfast. He is resolved that so far as Marley is concerned, he must behave as if nothing in the world has changed. So on the chance that the man should appear at his desk this morning—and he probably will, given the events of the evening past—Scrooge must now collect himself, remove all signs of his long night's labor, and be back in ordinary form before the start of business.

With the exception of certain traceries of ink still embedded in the palms of his hands, he succeeds. He reappears at Scrooge & Marley a minute or two ahead of schedule, and as he unlocks the door he is overwhelmed by a sudden gust of uncertainty. What if the project before him is too great? It is certainly daunting in its complexity—doubly so, since he will have to undo Marley's work without Marley discovering it. Additionally, there is the fact that he is but imperfectly suited to the job. His strength is in calculation, not strategy. Standing there between the outer cold of the street and the inner cold of his office, he feels his heart sink. Perhaps he should confront Marley after all, tell him what he knows, and insist he make it right. But no. Even if he could explain how he came to be ransacking his partner's residence last evening, even if Marley put a good face upon it all and agreed to correct his wrongdoing, how could he be sure in the end that he did so? He can rely only upon himself. He must go stealthily, methodically, and above all righteously about keeping every single promise he has made to his beloved Belle and by extension to her fathers both on earth and in Heaven. Such is his duty.

On the other hand, he could lie.

He could lie to Belle and to her father and to God Himself. Plenty of other men would, automatically and without qualm. Society is full of them: Duplicitous men ready to take the easy route clear of whatever trouble they may have brought into the world. They and their fathers and grandfathers make up a considerable portion of the human race, if his business partner is any indication. They recede into the past, generation by generation, terrible ordinary men with terrible ordinary failings and terrible ordinary secrets that they have learned to keep even from themselves—burdens fated to accompany them to their graves and beyond. Scrooge is not an especially religious man and he has no particular ideas about Heaven and Hell, but he does not like to imagine himself a restless ghost, weighted down by the bloody iron chains of innocent men made chattel.

So ends his crisis of conscience. So begins the labor that will warp his spirit and consume his future. He crosses the threshold and closes the door and sets about his great work.

Twenty-Two

Ebenezer is to have come along on a scouting trip to the chapel at Greenwich Hospital, but at the last moment he declares himself overburdened. He hardly looks at Belle when he says it, although he does glance up from his desk and let his gaze veer over her shoulder and out the grimy window. "Needs washing," he says, before he looks back down.

"What?"

"The window," he mutters. "It needs washing." The entire office is much in need of a cleaning that it will never receive, should history be any indication. "So much has escaped me," he sighs, as if that explains everything.

From the doorway, Harry sees Belle's disappointment. "I'll find a boy to clean your windows," he says. "By God, I'll do it myself if it'll free your schedule. You're needed on an important mission, my friend."

Belle, unmoored in the center of the room, smiles a fragile smile.

Balfour takes Fan's elbow. "This sister of yours will get married only once, after all—or so I should hope. Ha-ha!"

But Scrooge is having none of his good cheer. "Fear not," he says, dipping his pen. "The wedding is on my calendar. It is only these preliminaries of yours that I shall have to miss."

"*Preliminaries?*" says Balfour. "Why, what a perverse idea. Is all of life but one preliminary after another?"

"You could say that. All of it leading unto death, I suppose."

"He doesn't mean it, Harry," says Fan. "But when he's decided to be stubborn, there's no changing his mind. We should leave him alone."

"Alone indeed," says Belle.

But Balfour makes one last attempt. "You have to eat," he says. "We'll be having a nice luncheon afterward."

"I most certainly lack the time for that."

"In the officers' dining room." He dangles the notion like bait. "On my account."

"And that pleasure too I must forfeit," says Scrooge, looking up at last. "Now, if you will forgive me, I am falling further and further behind."

To Harry Balfour's delight, his bride-to-be gasps as the sexton swings wide the chapel doors. She believes the odd little man to be a sexton, anyhow, although he could easily possess some other title, a military one whose precise meaning would no doubt evade her. But never mind that, and never mind her friend Belle who can't see inside from where she stands, and never mind her husband-to-be as he waits beaming behind her, smiling a toothy smile that she glimpses only for an instant before gathering herself and daring to step with mingled hesitation and joy into the magnificent chapel of Greenwich Hospital.

Light enters from high arched windows on either side, suffusing the great chamber with a gleaming warmth that seems stolen from Heaven itself. Her vision rises upward with it, drawn to the elaborately decorated ceiling. There is no rampant popish mob scene painted up there to unsettle the eye and confuse the soul, not by a mile. The broad arched vault is divided and subdivided according to geometric principles worthy of the staid old Church of England, cut up into rows and columns of squares and octagons and circles carved out of plaster and painted in gold, cream, umber, and heavenly delft blue.

Her eye cannot settle there, though, for the geometry of the place draws her gaze back downward toward the altarpiece, an enormous painting of what at first seems merely the aftermath of a cautionary ship-wreck, but—according to the sexton or whoever he is, and he seems quite intimate with the details—proves to illustrate the story of how St. Paul, imprisoned by the Romans and wrecked upon the isle of Malta, miraculously survived the bite of a poisonous snake. The image comes alive for her once she knows its meaning, and she believes that by study-ing it she could worship here for a month without having to hear a word of scripture or a scrap of a sermon.

High up at the other end of the chapel, cased in mahogany and sup-ported by six marble columns that seem barely up to the task, is the pro-digious pipe organ. In its patient silence she senses a promise akin to that of the resurrection. "Will we hear it on our wedding day?" she asks Harry.

"Oh, of course. We could hear it now, if you like."

The sexton swallows.

"My rank does carry privileges. I'm certain that an organist could be located, along with a man to provide the wind."

"A *calcant*, Captain Balfour."

"Hmm? Oh, yes. Well. Do you suppose you could find one?"

"Skilled men are quite rare, I'm afraid."

"I should think that treading upon the handle of a bellows wouldn't call for as much skill as all that . . ."

"The music relies upon it, sir. Perhaps in a lesser sanctuary, with a lesser instrument, for a listener of less importance . . ." He lets the thought trail off, indicating Fan with a delicate wave of his hand.

"Please don't go to any trouble," she says, as much to Balfour as to him. "Besides, I would rather wait and hear it first on the occasion."

"Very wise," says her Harry. "And very romantic."

They take a moment to admire the altar and the elevated pulpit, and as they drift back down the aisle they come upon Belle, her face cast downward, deep in contemplation of an image set into the black-and-white tiles of the marble floor. It is a rope and anchor done up in gold, representative of both the Son of God and the Royal Navy.

"Beautifully executed," says Balfour.

"But it's fouled," says Belle. "The anchor, I mean. The rope is tangled all around it. Wouldn't that make things difficult?"

Harry laughs. "How insightful! As many times as I've looked at it, I've never noticed. Perhaps the navy should consider recruiting you, Miss Fairchild."

Belle laughs, and the others laugh too, but there remains in her heart a dark foreboding as to what particular entanglements—and disentanglements—may lie in Fan's future and her own.

The spring comes into full blossom, and preparations for Fan's wedding proceed—although Belle cannot say the same for hers. Ebenezer seems to grow more remote, more preoccupied, with the passing of each week. He has no interest in the wedding, and, in fact, he seems to shy from the subject if she raises it. He seems to care little for Belle or her companionship. She begins to fear that his affections have been compromised.

One solitary evening, when she can endure no more uncertainty, she goes to his office. He remains there these days until midnight or later, toiling in the glow of a single candle until exhaustion sends him home. When she finds him in his usual withdrawn state she takes immediate steps. She relocates the candle to a shelf in a corner of the room, pulls up a chair next to his, and takes the pen from his hand with the caution a man would use to pull the tooth of an African lion. He gives it up, and she puts it away and takes his freed hand in both of hers. His gaze is bereft, and his hand is cold.

"Ebenezer," she says.

He starts, like a man waking from a terrible dream.

"Ebenezer—how long has it been since we've talked?"

He looks to consult his daybook, but between the darkness and the teetering piles of unfinished work upon his desk he cannot find it. The frustration warps his expression, drawing down the corners of his mouth and pushing out his lower lip and furrowing his brow. He looks old, she thinks, a good deal older than the man to whom she pledged her future three years ago.

"I believe it was yesterday," he says, "but I cannot prove it."

"We saw each other yesterday, but we didn't talk. Not really."

"I'm afraid I don't know what you mean." His hands rove reassuringly, even tenderly, over the papers on his desk. She reaches and takes firm hold of one so as to focus his attention again.

"We haven't talked, really talked—about something important, I mean—in months."

He blinks, purses his lips.

"Now, I don't have a record of it in my diary," she says with a smile, although there is a barb in it, "but I'd say you've been difficult to reach since sometime in the winter."

"*Difficult to reach?* Why, I am right here. My hand is in yours."

She looks him in the eye by the dim light of that one remote candle. "What has happened, Ebenezer?"

"I've—I've been working."

"I know."

"I've been keeping the promise I made you and your father."

"But that was done with long ago."

"There were . . . setbacks. Unexpected complications."

"I appreciate that. But it's consuming you, Ebenezer. Can't you see that?"

"I've been struggling to restore my financial position."

"Never mind your financial position."

"You see, the freer I get of that evil business, the more impoverished I become."

"I don't care."

"With each passing day I grow more desperate. *We* grow more desperate."

That one crucial word would seem to mark the restoration of her old Ebenezer—the beloved friend whom she has lost to worry and work—and on hearing it she grasps his hand all the more tightly. "Do you need more time?" She hates to propose it, but if delaying the wedding will ease his mind and restore him to himself then she will make the sacrifice. "Another six months? Another year, if you require it?"

He is dumbstruck, his mind no doubt racing ahead to the quantity of good work he could accomplish in that interval. The mask of woe upon his face has begun to slip away, and she knows what his answer will be.

"A year, then," she says.

"It would be a kindness."

"Oh, Ebenezer," she says, "I would do anything to make you happy."

"I do not deserve you, Belle." Tears in his eyes give back the candlelight.

"You deserve an opportunity to set things right," she says. With that she reaches out and closes the ledgers open upon his desk—he makes no protest—and they seal their fresh promise with an embrace.

Twenty-Three

Marley would seem to be the only citizen of London not present at the wedding of Miss Fan Scrooge and Captain Harry Balfour. His absence goes unnoted.

The wedding takes place on the hottest day of the year, and only the lingering chill provided by the chapel's massive stone walls keeps the temperature inside from rising toward the intolerable—particularly given the number of people present. Between family and friends of both the bride and the groom and Balfour's extensive military connections, every pew is full. The balconies would groan if they weren't built to withstand the assault of the ages.

Not a breath stirs—until somewhere in the depths of the building a pair of men begin working the great leather bellows, and the concealed wind box takes on its burden of pressurized air, and the mighty organ roars to life. A full symphony orchestra, a military band on parade, and an airborne chorus of trumpeting angels could not match the glorious din. It might be Bach or it might be Mozart or it might be Scarlatti for all anyone knows, but it has unmitigated power.

The groom enters after a moment, clad in his full naval regalia, and once he has taken his place at the altar the organist begins the strains of "Jesu, Joy of Man's Desiring." Upon this cue the bride makes her appearance in a gown of the finest watered silk, a gift from the Huguenot Antoine Bernière. Only the deafening clamor of the organ covers up the delighted gasps of the ladies as, accompanied by her brother, she glides up the aisle.

The chaplain attends to the preliminaries (prayer, scripture, homily) with just the right blend of solemnity and speed, and then, in the presence of God and Man and in the shadow of shipwrecked St. Paul (to say nothing of that cast-out viper), the deed is accomplished.

Mother Scrooge teeters and nearly swoons during the recessional, overcome with joy and relief and the separate recurring fear that she shall not live to see her son so well matched now that he and Belle have put things off, but Ebenezer notes her distress and rushes to her side. Together they go down the aisle and out into the heat of the summer day, where they are the first to embrace Fan and Harry.

"I suppose you'll be next, old chap," says Balfour.

A nod from Scrooge.

"That is," he goes on, having spied Belle exiting the chapel, "unless your bride-to-be wearies of seeing you escort other women down the aisle."

"Oh my," says Scrooge as she approaches, and "Can you forgive me?" as she draws close. For he was indeed to have accompanied her out of the church—until his mother's spell, anyhow.

Belle is far from put out. "Never mind," she says. "I found one of the ushers—a fine, upright, and terribly handsome navy man—to escort me."

Crisis averted, they turn to Mother Scrooge, whose health seems nicely restored by the fresh air and sunny weather. The crowd is streaming from the chapel doors now, and the good humor and merriment is so contagious that they can barely remove her for the family reception at home. Yet remove her they do, to a carriage provided by the navy for the occasion, and off they go.

1811

Twenty-Four

Every pound that Scrooge withdraws from the slaving business is doomed by the laws of economics and morality to lose value the moment he invests it in a more cleanly enterprise, and thus keeping one of his promises must in the end prevent him from keeping the other. He will never restore both his honor and his fortune, and he falls further behind with each passing day. He knows this, certainly—he sees that his goal is an illusion and his methods are a trap—but he has given Belle his word and he soldiers on. The ability to focus on detail to the exclusion of consequence is both his gift and his curse. And so he loses himself, almost literally, in beautiful minutiae.

He rarely leaves his cramped little chamber, emerging only for nourishment and sleep. Marley's general absence from the premises simplifies certain elements of his work, particularly the handling of correspondence. Rather than let letters collect unopened on his partner's desk, he unseals them and acts upon their contents as necessary and then either burns them or seals them again for Marley to read later. Many times he intercepts communications from men in the slaving business—inked expressions of shock and dismay at the termination of some agreement by that meddling Mr. Scrooge—which, if seen by Marley, would bring his hopes to ruin.

Occasionally, when he is sure that Marley is elsewhere, he makes a stealthy visit to his partner's house with the aim of collecting portions of the riches hidden there. The secret chamber under the roof is his favorite for its remoteness and capacity. Only once is he nearly caught in his work. He has loaded up a valise with as many Spanish dollars as he can lift and is about to let himself out when he hears the man's footsteps below. He steadies his breathing and listens as his partner mutters and curses in the room at the bottom of the stairs, busy at his worktable with some project. The hour grows late. Scrooge hears him exit the workshop, whistling an airy tune. The whistling keeps up, almost inaudible now, and soon the smells of cooking rise to Scrooge's nose. His stomach growls. He lowers the valise carefully, fearful of making some noise—the clank of coins, the groan of a plank—that might betray his presence. Marley is decidedly in for the night and so Scrooge has no choice but to remain, the pair of them haunting each other until dawn. Only when his partner slips out after breakfast does Scrooge dare to make his escape.

As often as he visits, and as crammed with riches as the house is, he never takes a full inventory. He does, however, begin to understand that even with as much wealth as his partner has cached away here, the available stores are not limitless. One day he will slip up, or withdraw too much, and Marley will take note. There will be the Devil to pay.

Fan and Harry have taken spacious rooms in Greenwich, on the top floor of an imposing house with splendid views of the river. "Were you to go to sea," she says to him one morning over breakfast, "I should sit in that chair by the window and pine away until you returned."

"How romantic," says Harry. "And how boring. Also, thank God, how unnecessary."

"I should like to have a spyglass before you go, so that I could spot you at the very earliest moment."

"I could requisition a spyglass now, if you like."

"You'd just use it to keep an eye on the docks."

"I might."

"And I don't want you distracted."

"You," he says, pushing back his chair, "are the only distraction I permit myself."

"Oh, Harry."

"Besides, if I were to vanish tomorrow, you would move straight back in with your mother."

"Or she could come here, and keep me company while I pine."

"I'm certain she'd enjoy that."

"Knowing Mother, she just might." She does worry about Mother Scrooge, however. The poor thing is alone now, without a child to comfort her in her widowhood. Ebenezer doesn't even attend their usual Friday night suppers anymore. "When I meet Belle for lunch," Fan says, "I'll ask her to see if Ebenezer could look after Mother a little more closely."

"Ask him yourself, as long as you're traveling into the city."

"He never has time for me. I suspect that Belle would have better luck."

Thanks to intelligence gained through the seafaring grapevine, the loss of various undocumented cargoes, and paperwork obtained through assumed names at false addresses, Marley has already discovered where the money is going. And he has no intention of taking the matter up with Scrooge.

May the scoundrel bleed himself dry, he thinks. If Scrooge is determined to send himself to the workhouse, then he shall secretly divorce his financial interests from those of his partner and let the bastard sink of his own weight.

He begins by leasing any number of rooms in any number of boardinghouses and private residences and commercial enterprises around the city, and with the help of the amenable Mr. Wegg he transfers portions of his wealth—little by little—to their safety. He reestablishes connections and agreements with his old slaving partners, sometimes using false identities and sometimes using his own, always directing the proceeds straight into his own pockets. He hears of Scrooge's visits to his house from the wine merchants below, and rather than raise suspicion he changes no locks and alters no hiding places. Let Scrooge believe that he is undetected, and that the shrinking of their mutual fortune is entirely his own doing.

And let the firm of Scrooge & Marley be damned.

To Belle's surprise she encounters Ebenezer on the street, struggling along in the mud and snow beneath the weight of a heavy valise. She catches up with him easily, for his steps are slow and labored, and she surprises him without meaning to, for his breath is loud and his concentration is fierce. Her touch on his shoulder startles him into dropping the valise, which lands with both a wet thud and a metallic jangle.

"Are you now in the chain-making business, Ebenezer?"

"Oho! Nothing of the sort." His face is pink, his tall forehead damp.

"Have you gone into silversmithing, then?" Her eyes twinkle.

"Never," he says. Then he leans in close and in a whisper that's half-conspiratorial, half-aggravated, he adds, "If you must know, I am on my way to the bank."

"It's not that I *must* know—"

"I have affairs to attend to," he says. "Business affairs of an important nature."

"Shall I walk with you?"

"Where?"

"To the bank."

"Oh, that." His gaze flickers down to the dropped valise and then goes anxiously to the crowded street, as if he is on the lookout for highwaymen. "No. I believe I ought to concentrate on my business. I have a terrible lot of work to do this afternoon. I fall further behind with each moment that passes. You understand."

She does understand. She understands that the additional year she granted him has wrought a change for the worse. She would say so if she could, but she cannot. Not now. Instead, she pursues Fan's request and asks if she might join him and his mother for supper on Friday. That would be a start.

"Oh," he says, "I haven't dined with Mother for the longest time. I suppose I've rather given it up, actually. You may go if you like. No doubt she would enjoy the company." With a grunt he heaves the valise from the ground and starts off down the busy street, utterly alone.

Twenty-Five

The dire occasion that Belle's father has spent the better part of his life anticipating finally comes to pass. In the springtime he falls ill with a lung ailment and rather unceremoniously dies, leaving his wife and two daughters at the mercy of his unwilling landlord, Mr. Liveright.

The funeral is poorly attended, the church cold, the bereaved desolate in their pitiful number. Scrooge, sitting dutifully in the front alongside Belle, turns around at one point to assess the number of mourners present. In a blink he can count them all. Once the service begins he closes his eyes as if in prayer, although he is actually testing himself to see if he can recall some detail about each one of them—a name if he knows it, or a hat, or the color of a dress—and he is happy to confirm that he can. The image is not just burned into his retina but engraved upon his brain.

His eyes have snapped open and he is smiling a satisfied smile when Belle looks his way. The heat of her gaze upon his cheek is sufficient to draw his attention. Her skin is pale, her cheeks wet with tears, her face an agonized mask. Such eye contact as he makes with her does not ease her sorrow or diminish her pain, although he does have the presence of mind—late though it comes—to put his smile away.

➻

At the reception that follows, she can neither speak to Scrooge nor glance in his direction. Her betrothed may as well be in the ground alongside her father, for she has lost the two of them. Surrounded now by those who love her—her mother and her sister, Fan and Harry, ladies from the church—she sinks into their consoling affection as into a feather bed from which she knows she must one day rise alone.

By and by he intrudes. Mrs. Fairchild swarms upon him and takes him in an embrace under which he stiffens, murmuring and patting her gingerly on the back. With a single look Belle communicates to her sister that contact with Scrooge is not a thing to be encouraged, and so Daphne drifts away to the kitchen.

When Scrooge has extricated himself from the mother's grasp he approaches Belle, who presents a frigid shoulder.

"I am sorry," he says. It is a beginning, but no more than that. Whether he is sorry for the loss of her father or sorry for the coldness he displayed during the funeral is impossible to gauge, and he makes no effort to clarify.

"Think nothing of it," she says. She turns her back and silently retreats to a narrow settee beneath an overhang in a dim corner. Scrooge follows, only to find that she has positioned herself at the center of the bench so as to exclude him, and that if he means to remain he must stand, looming over her in the confined space. A disinterested party would think he means her harm.

"Your father . . ." he begins.

"My father placed a great many demands upon you."

"He had every right."

"No." She shakes her head, her eyes downcast. "He had no right whatsoever, and neither did I."

"You speak as if I have resisted! On the contrary—I've done my best. I continue to do so."

"But your heart isn't in it."

"My heart belongs to you."

"No, Ebenezer. No. It does not. My father and I asked you to change your nature, or at the very least to defy it, and for that I'm sorry. It's too late to forgive Father, but you can still forgive me."

Scrooge wrings his hands. "My dear," he says, "I have impoverished myself for you."

"You've done it against your will."

"On your behalf, nonetheless."

"But not on *our* behalf, Ebenezer."

Here ensues a pause from Scrooge, as if the calculating engine within his head has suffered some failure.

"I thought not," she says. "And so I release you."

"Release me? From . . . ?" Scrooge is pure puzzlement.

"From your vow, Ebenezer. From our engagement."

"No."

"Yes."

"But *I* would never release *you*."

"You already have," she assures him. "You've exchanged your pursuit of me for the pursuit of wealth."

"In my mind, the two are linked so closely as to be one and the same."

"Think of how you have ignored me over these months. Over these *years*. It wasn't always so, but the truth is that when we agreed to be married we were very different people. We were poor and content to be so."

"Not content."

"Content to make our way together."

"And we shall."

"No." The word comes out upon a little sob. In response, Ebenezer drops partway to his knees and moves to embrace her. She takes a handkerchief from her sleeve and holds it up between them like a rampart. "No," she says once more. "If even the slightest warmth remains within your heart—for my father or for me—then leave me to my grief. Begone."

Stunned, Ebenezer Scrooge roams the muddy streets of London. Anything is better than going home, home to the shabby little rooms he has lately so neglected, home to a future emptied of everything he has counted upon in this life.

Why has she said not a word of this before? Why has she chosen this day to drive a stake into his heart? He thinks back upon the happy times they have shared—distant now, yes, but undeniable—and in the shadow of her rejection they seem to be turning incorporeal, fading like dreams at the cock's crow. He curses her for ruining them. No, for stealing them! Yes! That's more in the order of things. She has come like a robber in the night and spoiled his future by pillaging his past.

Perhaps she has found another. That would explain it. She has taken on some secret paramour. The individual was likely present at the funeral, lurking around the periphery with a song in his heart. Yes. That must be it. The woman has been untrue to him, unfaithful in her way as Marley has been in his. They are united against him, as are the economic and moral powers of the universe. No question of it. All while he has remained true as true can be—both to her and to his promise. The indecency of her behavior in return, the duplicity of it and the secrecy as well, brings him low.

Night falls. He walks on. With his long legs clacking out a furious gait he stalks from street to lane to alleyway, from gaslight to lamplight to torchlight, wending farther and farther outward through the maze of the city. He does not know what he shall do when morning comes, should it come at all.

As the hours pass, his walking works its magic. He wearies, and he falters, and he slows. His fury cools and his reason returns to him out of the mist. He has wronged Belle. He has wronged her in the past and he has wronged her now. How absurd of him to think that she could be unfaithful! She is an angel, the gentlest and kindest and truest soul in all the world, and it is he who has cast her aside. He with his fanatical obsessions. He with his ledgers and his labor. He with his numbers and his numbers and his numbers.

He returns to his office at dawn, disheveled and humbled and inspired. He cannot go back to her now. He cannot apologize and swear that if she gives him sufficient time he will set things right. He has failed to keep that promise too often. She would be a fool to have him. What he must do is continue his work—not ploddingly, not dully, not as if his world somehow goes on unchanged, but with renewed commitment and redoubled vigor. He will grow rich and he will grow righteous and he will grow into the man Belle deserves. Let it commence this very morning.

1814—1817

Twenty-Six

Now that Scrooge and Marley are fully occupied with ruining each other, their personal relations have grown more friendly than at any time before. Neither of them would benefit from any other arrangement, of course. And so it comes to pass that for two gentlemen bent upon taking food from each other's mouths, they rub along with remarkable congeniality.

From time to time Scrooge worries that he has become a trifle too friendly with his partner, that Marley will note the change and divine that he is up to something. He does not, on the other hand, attribute Marley's behavior to any suspicious cause. The man has always been unpredictable. If he is behaving in a familiar way toward Scrooge, then he must believe that it will work to his advantage. Marley, for his part—being in the last and thus most profitable position in their ongoing double- or even triple-cross—knows exactly why Scrooge has softened. He also knows that it will do him no earthly good.

So they work at cross-purposes, but they work—tirelessly and endlessly. As time passes they each gain ground and lose it and gain it once more. Thus even in their nefarious ways do they find themselves riding the more or less predictable tides of ordinary business.

—✦—

While they are buried and oblivious, the rest of the world goes on.

Fan and Harry have a child—a rosy-cheeked little villain named Frederick in honor of his grandfather Scrooge. Her mother weeps with joy whenever she sees or even thinks about the child. "Oh, wouldn't your grandfather just love you to death," she says, cuddling little Freddy and kissing him as the tears stream down her cheeks. Fan does not disagree with her, although she knows her claim to be preposterous. Her father was a flinty old character, cold as the Thames in February, the last or next-to-last man on earth to go softhearted over a baby—even one bearing his name. But let Mother Scrooge have her fancies. They harm no one.

The old woman comes to help when Freddy arrives. The two of them—the family's eldest and youngest—share a bright and airy upper chamber with windows all around. The glass is soon smeared all over with Freddy's fingerprints, a good portion of them laid down while they watch his father marching off to work or trudging back home. She cannot bring herself to banish them with a cleaning rag, and so they build up week after week into a sentimental impasto of milk residue, saliva, and Heaven knows what else.

As the spring ends and the high summer takes hold, Fan and her mother settle into a comfortable routine, re-creating here along the riverfront many of the customs that characterized their lives back in the lanes of London—with the addition, of course, of the baby. In fact, two or three nights a week little Freddy is the only male in the household, for his father often travels to London and Liverpool and elsewhere on missions that keep him away overnight. As the ships of the West Africa Squadron have found their way out of the wharves of England and into the great wide treacherous world—and as they have begun to register triumph after triumph over the piratical miscreants who are the squadron's sworn enemies—Harry's duties have expanded. No longer is he focused mainly on the outfitting and manning of ships. With the maturation of the squadron he is called upon to oversee an expanding roster of investigations, court proceedings, and so forth. Having come to his maturity in a life of action on the high seas, he was at first uncomfortable with the change. But with the passage of time he has come to see that all the hard and dangerous work done by the men of his fleet can bear fruit only under careful oversight here at home. Beneath that weight he has grown ever more serious, although the only sign of it visible during his happy moments with Fan and Freddy is a somber shadow behind his eyes.

Conditions have also changed for Belle, thanks to a gentleman named Arthur Cope. Upon Fairchild's death, Cope was the solicitor employed by Liveright to oversee the family's eviction from the rooms above his stables. An unprepossessing little man, compact in his person and plain in his speech, he at first struck Belle as a mere implement of Liveright's, a thing with no more humanity than a quill pen. But as the proceedings went along he proved himself compassionate—or as compassionate as possible, given the circumstances. Among his kindnesses was an unstated but genuine effort to delay their eviction for as long as possible, and the discovery of some inexpensive but charming alternative rooms which, though a trifle small, suited the displaced family well enough.

He arrived at the door early on the morning of their departure, wearing a workman's rough clothes and volunteering to help in any way he could. Belle leapt upon him and kissed him through tears, with a startling passion that very nearly launched the little man off the high porch. She hardly knew herself why she did it, but it made all the difference.

Those rooms so jealously coveted by Liveright, by the way, were to remain empty and cold for the rest of the old man's life. God knows he must have gone to the grave contented.

Belle and Arthur marry in a year's time, freeing space in the lodgings kept by her mother and sister and making conditions there more comfortable. Daphne will always tease Belle that Cope recommended such cramped rooms as part of a long and subtle plot to wrest her away from them and into marriage, but Belle prefers to believe that if there was any plot at all it was her doing.

Arthur has always wanted children, and although Belle has not actively considered the possibility she warms to it right away. Motherhood—first the notion of it and then the reality—suits her completely. When she and Arthur have been married for just a year she begins meeting Fan and Freddy in the park with her own little Annabelle. In another year it will be Annabelle and Rebecca. In one more, Annabelle and Rebecca and George. And so on, and so on. Arthur rises in his firm and money is no object and the children bring them nothing but delight.

Arthur suggests they name their fourth after his favorite uncle, a merry old Scot on his mother's side with a fine arm for the fiddle and a high, powerful singing voice. His name, he says, is Ebenezer J. MacTaggart.

Belle asks what the *J* stands for.

"James," he says.

"I will grant you *James*," she says, her eyes flashing, "but not Ebenezer."

Which marks the first time he has seen a hint that his bride and Fan's brother may have crossed paths. Their betrothal has certainly gone unmentioned all these years, not from a desire on anyone's part to keep it a secret but because the person of Ebenezer Scrooge has all but vanished from the haunts of his relations. Rarely have Belle and Arthur and their brood visited the waterside Balfour residence upon some family occasion (Harry and Fan bought the house a few years ago) and encountered Ebenezer in the flesh. No matter what feast is being celebrated, he has been mostly an absence, a mystery, a minor embarrassment.

"Not *Ebenezer*, you say?"

"Never."

"What could you have against the name?"

"It has . . . bad associations."

Light dawns. "Surely not with Fan's brother."

"Yes. With her brother."

"Oh, he's a bit of an old stiff, I'll grant you that. Not the sort you'd aspire to have your son emulate, I suppose."

"He once courted me. Long ago."

Arthur is dumbfounded. "Courted? You? Ebenezer?"

"At the time, it didn't seem so strange."

"Why not? Did he have a heart then? Was he made of flesh and bone like an ordinary man?"

"We were in fact to be married."

"No."

"He was a different man then. But he changed, and I released him."

"Thank God for that."

"It was difficult, Arthur."

"Difficult? Did he do something to make it so?"

"Oh, no. Sentiment is what made it difficult. Ebenezer only made it necessary."

"I see." He gives himself a little shake. "Then in the future we shall banish his name as you have banished his person."

"Thank you."

"And with apologies for shortchanging my dear old uncle Ebenezer, we shall make do with James."

1818

Twenty-Seven

Captain Balfour faces a conundrum. It has been creeping up on him for a good long while, and he cannot delay acting upon it forever.

The difficulty began with the arrest of the crew of the slave ship *Mariel*. Nothing unusual about that—the West Africa Squadron has seized dozens of ships and freed hundreds of captive men, women, and children in the years that they have operated along Africa's western coast. What makes the case of the *Mariel* unusual is that while her crew was arrested and her cargo freed, the ship herself was not impounded. Because although the crew was British, the vessel was American.

Balfour has heard rumors about such arrangements, but he has not seen an actual instance until now. The very fact of it puzzles him. The occasional American ship will still smuggle slaves, to be sure, but he can think of no reason one should look abroad for a crew. Experience and character would of course be factors, and the disreputable men of the *Mariel* are definitely well suited to their trade. They are the saltiest old dogs a person could imagine, and judging by the content of the affidavits they have filed they possess not an ounce of moral fiber to be shared among them. Their testimony is a tissue of contradictions, evasions, and outright lies.

And yet Balfour sees a pattern within it. Many patterns, in truth, with threads that cross and recross one another like the product of a loom.

The *Mariel* herself holds the key, he thinks. She lies moored now along the Slave Coast, abandoned and empty and utterly unclaimed. She would seem to have no identifiable ownership whatsoever, but Balfour knows that to be impossible. Someone holds her papers and someone profits from her crimes. Exactly what American or Americans this may prove to be is of course no concern of his. He lacks any jurisdiction that would permit him access to such records as the American authorities may have on the subject. Besides, returning the *Mariel* to her rightful owner is their problem, not his. Still, his curiosity has been aroused.

It was one peculiarity about the first mate's testimony that did it. The gentleman in question, a Mr. Flee, had a habit of referring to the ship not as the *Mariel* but as the *Marie*. His captain, one Jeremiah Grommet, never made the same mistake—nor did any of the other officers or crewmen whose testimony was recorded. The same clerk transcribed all the records, too, in the same hand and in the same volume and over the same period of time. So Flee's mistake stands out, if a mistake it was.

Perhaps, Balfour thinks, *he is the only one calling the ship by her proper name.*

Records show that once upon a time there was indeed a British cargo ship called the *Marie*, and that she was by all signs employed in the Triangular Trade—at least until the autumn of 1807, when she vanished somewhere off the Antilles. Her insurers contested payment, as insurers will, but in the end a settlement was agreed upon with her owners, the firm of Nemo & Hawdon, based in London. She had gone down with a hold full of rum, and all hands were tragically lost.

Crew rosters are largely missing, however. And what's worse, the firm of Nemo & Hawdon closed its doors shortly after the settlement was paid out. The cities and towns and villages of England have their share of Nemos and their share of Hawdons as well, but Balfour's agents cannot find a single one willing to admit the slightest connection with the failed partnership.

One autumn day, on a lunchtime constitutional along the byways of London, Balfour decides to seek out the address of the old firm. It is lodged indelibly in his mind, for he has gone over the details in the case of the *Mariel* so often as to have learned them by heart. The address is an unlikely one, as it turns out, set in a residential neighborhood that does not promise much in the way of commerce. And yet there it is, a great house set back on a little knoll behind a rotted iron fence. A wagon belonging to a wine merchant is making its way up the dusty approach, and its driver has left the gates open. Balfour will thus be free to draw near to the house without introduction or interference. What a stroke of luck! Perhaps he is on the verge of meeting someone who recollects those two mysterious figures, Nemo and Hawdon. Perhaps the entire matter is about to throw itself as wide open as these iron gates. But as he draws near he takes note of a plaque—just a little slip of tarnished brass, really—set alongside the latch. J. S. MARLEY, it says.

It cannot be. And yet.

He dares not ask him outright, for if the man does possess some connection with the firm in question, it might be a matter that he would prefer to leave undisclosed. If there is one thing Balfour has learned through his years in the naval service, as a seaman and as an officer and now as a student of the particulars of maritime law, it is never to ask a question whose true answer you do not already know.

So he sets his agents to work pursuing other angles and avenues. He sends orders to the captain of a ship now cruising the Slave Coast that the *Mariel* is to be boarded in secret and examined—her records, her hold, her superstructure, her appointments of every kind—for any irregularity. He sends men to every bank and customs house and courthouse in all of England, with orders to search every ledger and cabinet and scrap of paper for a record of any transaction having to do with the firm of Nemo & Hawdon.

And then he waits.

Twenty-Eight

Madeline hazards an observation from beneath the bedclothes, this being the sort of moment that might pass for tender despite the police inspector's hard nature. "I appreciate being your favorite," she says, "but do you know that Mrs. McCullough gives me nothing for my time?"

"Are not my attentions sufficient in themselves?"

"There are attentions, sir, and there are *attentions*."

"My attentions shield you from the law," he says, rising up in the bed to loom over her.

"And that's a kindness, no mistake."

"So long as Mrs. McCullough obliges, I shield every denizen of this filthy knocking-shop. Why, in my absence . . ."

"I know, sir."

He eases a bit. "Good. The freedom to pursue your work unmolested by the law is a gift beyond price."

"Yes."

"And still you would require more."

"No, sir. Not require. Never *require*."

He settles back under the linens. "Good girl."

She waits. Around them the house is alive with the sounds of love-making in a dozen varieties and perversions and simulacra. Bedframes creak and headboards hammer against thin walls hollowed out by the passage of vermin. Women sigh and men groan, and the occasional shout of ecstasy or surprise or agony, feigned or otherwise, lays bare the night.

"Forgive me, sir," she says at last. "I wasn't thinking of you."

He grunts.

"I was thinking of my two little babes."

"Babes?" He throws back the bedclothes. "They have no place in this discussion."

She endures the sudden cold. "I know that, sir. I know it now."

"Mentioning children within these walls is an atrocity," he says, rising and lurching toward the chair upon which his clothing is draped. "Have you no matronly instincts whatsoever?"

"I'm sorry, Inspector."

He shivers, not entirely from the chill in the room. "Your own off-spring, soiled so utterly . . ."

Madeline wraps herself tight and whimpers into the stinking linens while he dresses in silence and takes his leave. Once downstairs, he dons his coat, extracts his fees from Mrs. McCullough—"Count that out again, my good lady, and more slowly this time"—and slips invisibly into the street. *The nerve of that girl*, he fumes. *Believing I might owe her something.*

The archives that Balfour's agents are busy ransacking all around England are chaotic and vast, so it's no surprise that the first results arrive from the coast of Africa. The boarding and search of the *Mariel* required only a single night's time, and although there was little to be discovered in the way of credible logbooks—or any other record-keeping, for that matter—one isolated detail about the ship herself proved not only remarkable but revelatory.

The officer leading the boarding party noted it in the torchlight as their dinghy rounded her stern. *'Tis but a trick of the shadows*, he thought, for it seemed a strange shifting in the way the torchlight played across the quarterdeck rail—more precisely, across the weatherworn and half-rotted wooden panel mounted directly beneath that rail. The panel was carved in relief with the ship's name, *Mariel*, the word surrounded by shabbily artful clusters of flowers. But as the men drew near, the shadows cast by their torches seemed to crawl weirdly, uncannily, over the letters.

The officer called for them to cease rowing, and they drifted to an unsteady halt on the rolling tide.

He thrust out his hand. "Do you see it, boys?"

"See what, sir?" Each man cocked his head as the mystery expressed itself to him in a slightly different way, depending upon his angle and his distance and his acuity of vision.

"I do, sir," said one of them at last. "I see it."

One by one the rest agreed, although not a man could say exactly what it was that he was looking at. The terminal letter of the ship's name, and the flowers to its starboard side, were apparently not carved into the panel at all—but painted upon it instead. The shadows they cast were fixed and solid in the moving light. It was unnatural. It was a fraud.

"Let's go, boys," said the officer. "We have work to do—aboard the *Marie*."

So the sunken *Marie* has returned—and not as some rum-drunk tar's tale of a ghost ship, but as a genuine working slaver caught in the act and subsequently abandoned to the mercies of wind and water. Balfour has a fair idea as to why no one has dared claim her. She is a British vessel after all, sailing these years under a false flag, and subject to immediate confiscation should her true owners come to light.

The very idea. He might expect this kind of chicanery from the Americans, but not from his fellow Englishmen.

He issues orders that his agents here at home are to complete their work by year-end, and by the middle of November the results have begun to filter in. They are complex, incomplete, seemingly unconnected. The defunct firm of Nemo & Hawdon left a scattered trail of transactions having to do with a number of ships, not just the *Marie*. They variously purchased and owned and conveyed shares in several other vessels that also vanished mysteriously in the period just before the government began enforcing the Slave Trade Act. Unlike the *Marie*, however, the rest of these ships had no troublesome or traceable insurance claims on their records. They simply disappeared.

Balfour thinks he knows where they went.

In addition to buying and selling ships, Nemo & Hawdon also dealt in the raw cargoes of the Triangular Trade—not just men but rum, sugarcane, molasses, and manufactured goods. They transacted business with a wide range of firms, some of which are still in good standing here in London and some of which are as long vanished as Nemo & Hawdon themselves. Among these last he notes a Barnacle & Sons, maritime provisioners; a Honeythunder & Grimwig, engaged in general mercantile; and a Sampson Brass, Ltd., shipfitters. All of these entities are gone, gone, gone, leaving behind only a few records processed by the law firm of Dodson & Fogg—also now defunct—to tie them all together.

Well, there is something else.

All of them, like Nemo & Hawdon, share Jacob Marley's address.

Moreover, Marley's own name makes appearances within the collected documents—upon the records of certain transactions (deeds, transfers of property, contracts) handled by that selfsame Dodson & Fogg. The curious aspect is that it's always Marley himself, always just plain Jacob Marley, and never the firm in which he is allied with Scrooge. The man would appear to be either shielding his partner or defrauding him. Balfour's money is on the latter.

➤

He hopes to brave the beast in his lair, but when he goes he finds only the beast's business partner. He cannot interrogate Scrooge, for if his instincts are correct, the poor fellow knows nothing. Ebenezer hardly looks up from his work when his brother-in-law blows in on the wintry gale. The chamber is frigid despite the single coal dying in the stove, dark despite the single candle burning on the desk.

"Ho, ho, old man!" Harry shouts from the doorway. He strips off his gloves and steps in and thrusts out a hand for Scrooge to ignore. "I keep meaning to bring Freddy around," he says, "so as to let him spend a few moments with you."

"No time," says Scrooge. And then, "Freddy who? Is he by any chance a creditor?"

"He's your nephew."

Scrooge's face is the picture of irritated befuddlement.

"Fan's son. And mine, of course."

"Ah," says Scrooge. "Just so."

"Then again, you'll come by the house next week, won't you? On Christmas Eve? You'll see him then."

"If I must."

"You must. It will do you good to escape this place for a little while."

"Hmmph. It will just mean more work on the morrow."

"Not on Christmas, surely."

"Why not? Does interest not accrue on Christmas? Do naval ships not rust on Christmas? Why should I be the exception? Why should you?"

"Come for your mother," says Balfour. "Come for little Freddy. He will not be four years old again."

"And I will not be forty-three years old again—more reason to conserve my time."

"We shall look forward to your presence." He shuffles his feet and fusses with his gloves, casting about in his mind for an angle regarding his interest in Marley. In the end, he comes out with it directly. "Before I go," he says, "do you happen to know where your partner is?"

"Elsewhere." Scrooge has picked up his pen once more, and his mind is engaged in other matters.

"So I noted. When do you suppose he might return?"

"I have no idea."

"I see."

"The man can read. Leave him a message if you must."

"I shall," says Balfour. "By God, I shall. Consider it done."

Later, when he reads the note for himself, Scrooge learns but little. *Please call at your convenience*, it says in a surprisingly diminutive hand, over Balfour's signature, naval rank, and office address. There might be something to be made of those details—the mention of his rank, the use of his office address instead of his home—but Scrooge refolds the note and lets it vanish into the storehouse of things he knows but does not need.

What could *Captain Harrison T. Balfour*—that's how Marley's nemesis signed his cryptic note, not with a familiar *Harry*, not with a simple *Balfour*, not even with a terse but nonetheless businesslike *Capt. Balfour*—what could the man possibly want with him? Between his role in the West Africa Squadron and his success in the battle for Fan's heart, Marley has at least two perfectly valid reasons to bear him unending malice. Thanks to Balfour's efforts—thanks to his mere preening presence, damn his eyes—he can neither make an honest living nor pursue the object of his affections.

He puts off the errand as long as he dares, and in the end makes the trip to Greenwich on the afternoon before Christmas. The old pensioners who reside in Greenwich Hospital are preparing for a feast, so the place is alive with music and laughter. Marley passes from hallway to hallway unacknowledged, in no hurry to ask directions from these toothless old veterans with their sunken cheeks and their rheumy eyes and their fixed expressions of dull-witted glee.

Balfour's office proves to be located in a separate building altogether, and even with that discovery under his belt Marley has trouble locating it. The building is poorly staffed on this day of all days. He succeeds at last, however, and strides past the empty desk of some absent clerk in an outer chamber to knock at the door of Balfour's sanctum.

"Enter!" calls Captain Harrison T. Balfour.

Marley steps in. The room is vast and its furnishings have an understated elegance—everything is polished mahogany, fluted plaster, artfully tarnished gold leaf. It's all calculated to intimidate, of course, but Marley is immune to such influences. Over the course of his career he has communed with the wealthiest magnates and the lowest slip-gibbets, and in the end he has turned each of them to his use. Let Balfour have his uniform and his accoutrements. None of it will either serve or save him.

"Captain," he says.

"Jacob."

"Harry."

Balfour smiles grandly and rises to his feet. His massive desk is set upon a pedestal, an arrangement that gives him the advantage of elevation. "Sit," he says, indicating a pair of small hard chairs placed before the desk. "Please."

The geometry suggests that this is to be an interrogation, so Marley succumbs or seems to. He chooses one of the chairs and settles into it, arranging upon his face a look of meek expectation.

Balfour, however, does not return to his spot behind the desk. To Marley's surprise he sacrifices his tactical advantage, steps down, and comes around to take the other chair. He angles it to face more toward his visitor, and Marley—his hand being forced—does the same.

"That's better," says Balfour.

"Much," says Marley.

"This office, you know. This rank of mine. It comes with trappings."

"I understand."

"Trappings and expectations."

"No need to explain." So this, he decides, is Balfour's game. Establish your power, and then augment it by pretending to throw it away. The man bears watching.

"Thank you so much for coming by," says Balfour. "I realize now that my request may have been a bit . . . *mysterious*."

"It was indefinite."

"I did not mean it to be. I assure you of that."

Of course you did, thinks Marley.

"When Ebenezer suggested that I should leave you a note, I just . . ."

"You were in a hurry. You didn't think."

"Precisely," says Balfour. "Thank you for your understanding. At any rate . . ."

And here, Marley knows, is where it will begin.

"Recently, in the course of my work, I have come upon some information that I believe you'll find of great interest."

"Is that so?"

"Oh, yes."

"Great interest, you say?"

"Very great."

"Would this information be related to my *business* affairs?"

"Closely related."

Which in truth comes as a relief to Marley. Although he has been as cautious as possible, his personal affairs—complex and colorful as they are—might bear up even less well to scrutiny. "I'm surprised you didn't take this up with Ebenezer."

"Well, yes. That is a fair question. As it happens, the matters at hand do not touch on the firm of Scrooge & Marley. They concern you only."

"I don't understand. My affairs are tightly bound with those of your brother-in-law."

"Which is why I come to you, Jacob, as I would come to a member of my own family."

"*I* am the one who has come to *you*, Harry."

"Of course," says Balfour, flustered right on cue. "The important part . . . what I meant was—"

"You intend to behave toward me as if I were family."

"Yes."

"And I thank you for it."

Balfour flashes a smile then stands to retrieve an expanding leather case from a nearby bookshelf. "I'm sure there are good reasons for everything I've discovered. Perfectly sound explanations for all of it."

"Certainly."

Balfour opens the case. "I never let this collection out of my sight," he says. "I'd hate to have it fall into the wrong hands."

Marley nods.

He withdraws several documents, by no means the entire contents of the case. "I wanted to discuss this evidence with you before any . . . *action* might be taken."

"Evidence? Action?"

"In good time." He hands the documents to Marley.

They prove to be a varied lot of ordinary commercial paper—deeds, contracts, transfers, bills of sale. They are executed in any number of hands and inks, and they are signed and stamped and sealed as custom and law require. Their condition and apparent age vary greatly. They are forgeries, of course, forgeries one and all, of such high quality that at first glance Marley does not recognize them as the work of his own hands.

"What have these to do with me?"

"The firms, man! The firms!" He puts down the case and leans in to show Marley exactly what he is talking about, an indicative finger leaping eagerly from page to page. "Squeers & Trotter! Barnacle & Sons! Honeythunder & Grimwig!"

Marley purses his lips and marvels. "Why, these gentlemen are all my tenants," he says.

"As are Dodson & Fogg, the solicitors behind *every single one* of these transactions!"

"But what of it? What have they done? Have they perpetrated some crime?"

"There is only one crime that interests the West Africa Squadron," says Balfour. "You know very well what it is."

"You don't think . . ."

"I do."

"Then I shall have a word with them. I can hardly be providing accommodations for a cabal of slavers and thieves."

"In due time, Jacob, in due time. I shall send men around for them at the proper moment. Meanwhile, we must keep this between ourselves."

"Of course."

"Not a whisper."

"No."

"Not even to Scrooge."

"No."

"And stay on the lookout."

"I will."

"Watch for any irregularity."

"Irregularity?"

"Some alteration of business practices, perhaps. A change of owner-ship. Worst of all, the closing of one of these businesses entirely." Here he reaches into the case again, and withdraws a single document. "That's what happened to *these* fellows."

The document is a genuine one, recording the settlement of an insur-ance claim filed by Nemo & Hawdon against their lost cargo ship, the *Marie*. Marley takes it in both hands and with effort holds it steady.

"The ship sank, the claim was settled, and they closed their doors," says Balfour. "They simply vanished without a trace. You do recall them, of course—these fellows Nemo and Hawdon?"

"I do."

"I suspected as much. For in addition to acting as their landlord, you entered with them into certain other business dealings. According to the records."

"I did."

"Not unlike the additional dealings you had with these other disreputables. Honeythunder, Grimwig, and the rest."

Only the smallest and most hesitant of nods from Marley.

"That said, might you recall exactly where the two principals—Mr. Nemo, Mr. Hawdon—went after they quit business?"

"I fear that I never knew."

"Hmm. That's a shame, really. Their trail has gone quite cold. I had hoped you might produce something that could set us on them again."

"I am sorry."

"Think nothing of it. My agents are unearthing new information all the time. Slowly, quietly, I am putting the picture together." He takes the settlement paper and returns it to the leather case. "We have just learned, for example, that the *Marie* was never wrecked at all." He gives Marley a hard look. "Quite the contrary. She was rechristened in secret and sold to an America firm. The entire business was a fraud from start to finish."

"A fraud, was it? Hence your interest in Nemo and Hawdon."

"Heavens, no. Fraud is a matter for the police, not for the West Africa Squadron."

"I see."

"Our aim is far larger, and our means are equal to it. I can tell you in confidence that the *Marie*—now the *Mariel*—is at this very moment moored off the Slave Coast, giving up her secrets one by one."

"Best of luck to you, then," says Marley, as if he means it. The room seems to have gone cold around him.

Balfour tucks the case beneath his arm, stands up, and returns to his desk. "One more thing before you go," he says.

Marley rises too. "And that would be?"

"The investigation will take its course in the months ahead. Such connections as exist among these villains—and others like them—will be revealed. The business will end, I assure you, with exposure and disgrace and imprisonment."

"I should hope that you are correct."

"I am," says Balfour. "And with that in mind, I counsel you as I would counsel a brother seated at my own hearth. Look to your affairs, Jacob. Clean your house. It's time."

The halls are empty when Marley makes his exit. Empty and cold and echoing.

He lingers in an abandoned square as the sun goes down and the lights go up. Clinging to the shadows, he watches the building and he waits. At last Balfour appears, bundled against the cold, that leather case gripped tight beneath his arm. He was telling the truth about that—how he guards it with his person. As for the rest of his tale, who knows how much was gospel and how much was guesswork? Marley cannot say.

He follows Balfour as he makes his way home along the riverfront, trailing along the street behind him in the scattered darkness, and when the man is safely behind his own door—there are signs of gaiety within, piano music, the shout of a happy child, a surprising glimpse of the profile of Ebenezer himself—he turns away into the darkness, for work awaits him yet.

Supposing that Balfour is telling the truth and that the *Marie* does indeed lie in irons off the coast of Africa, what then has become of her crew? They've been arrested, no doubt. Arrested and brought home to stand trial and face their punishment. This surely won't be the first time some of them have seen the inside of a prison. All the same, it's unlikely that the courts will find reason to charge them all. As captain and first mate, Grommet and Flee will certainly be held. But the rest of the *Marie*'s crew—from her laudanum-addled surgeon and her one-eyed carpenter down to the ruined run of her common seamen—will likely be let go. Some of those individuals may have even bought themselves clemency by testifying against one another, or against Bildad and Peleg, their fictitious employers. Fictitious Americans, at that. Marley congratulates himself that having made them so was a stroke of brilliance. Letting Balfour chase them for a while will buy him time.

Going over these things in his mind, Marley passes a house or two where he could find shelter for the night and even a kind of commercial comfort, but he strides on. At an intersection he encounters a carriage spilling out its burden of high-spirited celebrants onto the frozen street, and he inquires of the driver as to his availability for hire. Soon enough, his mind racing far faster than the carriage, he is at his own gate. He pays the man to wait—overpays, really, out of necessity and a manufactured semblance of the Christmas spirit—and admits himself. Once inside the house, he makes for his secret workshop without delay.

The time has come for Bildad and Peleg, his two imaginary Quakers, to commit their final act.

It is to take the form of a letter—a letter he has been composing in his mind all the ride home. He settles upon his stool, chooses a sheet of the highest-quality vellum, and uncorks a pot of his customary disappearing ink. The message he has in mind uses elevated language and a bit more of it than most businessmen would find necessary, and it employs the biblical *thee* and *thou* so beloved by individuals of Bildad and Peleg's sect. It is worded so as to be doubly and triply clear to even the most ignorant reader, and it concludes with an assurance of payment sufficient to get the attention of any man in London.

When the ink is dry he folds the sheet and seals it within an envelope addressed using ordinary ink in that same careful hand, and then he addresses a second, larger envelope into which he inserts the first. This he directs to himself—not *himself*, of course, but the individual whose role he shall play in the hours to come—and then, after he has given it signs of wear and transit, he returns to the carriage.

The denizens of this dockside tavern are in a boisterous mood as Christmas Eve ebbs away into Christmas morning. The arrival among their number of a tall, slender, and anonymous gentleman goes unnoticed until he makes his way to the bar and quite loudly orders drinks all around.

"To what do we owe your generosity?" asks the barkeep in the silence that ensues.

"Credit the Christmas spirit!" says Marley. "That, and instructions from certain wealthy Americans."

"*Wealthy Americans*," sneers some ingrate. "What sort of wealthy Americans would buy a round for the likes of us?"

"The sort with an interest in locating the crew of the *Mariel*."

A gasp or two.

"Now, would any of those gentlemen be among us this evening?"

"*Gentlemen*," scoffs the barkeep.

"I'm being kind," says Marley. "Generosity is the soul of the season, is it not?"

The barkeep occupies himself.

"By disputing their gentlemanly character, sir, are you suggesting that these persons are known to you?"

"The crew of the *Mariel*? By God, yes."

"And have you an idea where I might find them?"

"One or two might be upstairs, sleeping it off," he says with a thrust of his head. "First room on the left."

Marley goes. In the room he finds a bed and in the bed he finds an ancient skeleton clad only in ragged trousers and a moth-eaten stocking cap. He locates a candle and lights it and positions it so as to ascertain whether the skeleton is yet breathing. Why yes, yes it is. He taps it upon the shoulder and steps back.

The skeleton sits up, blinking against the candlelight.

"You've served aboard the *Mariel*?"

"I have, sir." The skeleton stretches its long jaws in a shuddering yawn.

"Name?"

"Stitch, sir. Edgar." The skeleton squints.

"Duties?"

"Cabin boy, sir." The skeleton adjusts its old bones.

"Cabin boy. Seems unlikely."

"Many aspects of the *Mariel* was unlikely, sir."

Marley sets the candle on a rickety table alongside the bed and draws up a chair. He places upon his knee the set of envelopes he has prepared. "Are you in contact with your shipmates, Mr. Stitch?"

"Them as remains in the vicinity."

"I assume that some have hired on with other ships?"

"Some. Work is terrible hard to find, sir." Stitch fastens his hollow-eyed glare upon the envelope, his lips moving as he reads what is written there. "You'd be Mr. Micawber, then?"

"The very same."

"I know you. Leastways I know your name."

"Then you know of my connection with Mr. Bildad and Mr. Peleg."

"I do. Captain Grommet cursed you as regular as he cursed them."

An apologetic smile from the amiable Mr. Micawber.

"The captain'll be off to Newgate soon enough. I suppose you know."

"I do."

"Flee as well. Some others." A tear seems to be coalescing in Stitch's eye. "Them old bastards'll die in the nick."

"I can do nothing for them," says Marley. "However, I have a fair proposition for you, and for any of your shipmates whose purses may seem a bit light at the moment."

Stitch dabs at his eyes with the wretched bed linens.

Marley opens the outer envelope and withdraws the inner. "For the veterans of the *Mariel*," he reads from its face. "That would be you."

Stitch takes the envelope and draws out its contents into the candle-light. The vellum is blank, bearing here and there only the faintest imprint of a quill's touch. "You're a cruel man," says Stitch, his hopes dashed. "A cruel man working for men who are crueler still."

"Despair not, friend. For reasons of confidentiality, my employers make a practice of sending their most sensitive orders in this way." He commandeers the paper by one corner and draws it toward the flame. "'Tis disappearing ink, you see." Stitch's eyes go wide as the letters appear, and when the sheet seems ready to erupt into flame Marley pulls it away. He peruses it quickly before handing it over.

Stitch reads the message once, twice, and then once again for good measure. His eyes go wide. "That'd be a heap of money for such a job, Mr. Micawber."

"I should say—and the same pay for every man who has a hand in it. The owners must quite desire the thing done."

"Not a pound up front, though?"

Marley takes the letter, turns it his way, and studies it. He shakes his head. "No, not a pound, and I must say that I'm not surprised. You know how these affairs go. The funds change hands when the matter is accomplished."

"That sort of arrangement is what keeps ones such as me in a state such as this."

"Very well," says Marley. "If you choose not to take the job . . ." He holds the page over the candle again, more closely this time, and it vanishes in a burst of smoke and soot.

"I didn't say that."

"Then you vow that you'll do it?"

"I do. I will. And I'll have no trouble finding help—not for that pay."

"Excellent," says Marley, rising and preparing to make his exit. "I shall advise Mr. Bildad and Mr. Peleg that the good ship *Mariel* shall be burnt to the waterline with all practical haste."

He leaves Stitch alone to his plotting and his dreams, and he creeps silently down the stairs. At the bottom he steals a glance into the tavern, where the men are just now finishing his earlier round. He could slip away now, abscond unseen, but instead he has another go.

"One more for every man!" he calls out to the barkeep, and when the fellow turns to his work Marley vanishes into the night. It's Christmas, after all. Let them have their fill, so long as it is not at his expense.

1819

Twenty-Nine

The year has turned and the seasons have changed and Marley has been awaiting word of the *Mariel*'s fate with mingled anxiety and sorrow. Her loss shall be very nearly incalculable. She has been his private property for a long while now, and over those years she has provided the steadiest and purest of profits, costing him nothing in the way of fees or licenses or, God forbid, upkeep. And now, thanks to that accursed Balfour, she is lost. She was lost to him before he ordered her set afire—moored thousands of miles away on the Slave Coast, utterly beyond hope of recovery.

At least now she will tell no tales to Balfour and his men.

Marley sets down the newspaper. Her destruction cost him nothing, of course. He must take comfort in that. Besides, the simple fact that Stitch or Snitch or whoever he was could even locate her serves to confirm that at least a significant portion of Balfour's story was true. Marley must take all of it seriously, then. He must presume that Balfour believes himself close to discovering the remainder of his slaving connections and then throwing him straight into Newgate with Grommet and Flee and the rest.

No doubt he plans to do so in the kindly manner he would employ if Marley were an actual member of the family.

On the other hand, Balfour did seem sincere in promising a means of escape. *Clean your house*, he said. It was an opportunity couched in a warning. All Marley needs to do is wash his hands of the slaving business, and Balfour will see that he does not suffer for his criminal history. No doubt that was why he made it clear that he carries those documents upon his person at all times. He is keeping them out of the general investigation, giving Marley the time he needs to make amends.

But he will not wait forever. That was clear.

And Marley has never been in a hurry to divest himself of a profitable enterprise.

Suspecting that Balfour will detect his hand in the burning of the *Mariel*, Marley goes to him directly. Not at his office this time, but at home, in that grand house along the riverfront into which he saw him disappear on Christmas Eve. He goes on a Friday evening, around suppertime, trusting that he will find him there with Fan and the child and that their conversation will thus be conveniently limited to generalities and coded signifiers. It's best not to go too deeply into the details. It's best not to make or accept or even suggest any promises, however vague they may be in outline.

When he arrives, however, he finds his quarry alone.

"Come in, come in!" shouts the captain, as if Marley's surprise visit is exactly the delight he has been dreaming of. He has a fire roaring in the hearth and a glass in his big right fist and an open bottle on the kitchen table. He takes Marley's cloak and finds him a glass. "You'll permit an old sailor his ration of gin, won't you?"

"How could I do otherwise?"

"And you'll accept one of your own?"

"Aye, aye, Captain," says the dutiful Marley.

As he pours, the twinkle in Balfour's eye suggests that the ration presently dwindling in his glass is his second or third of the evening.

"At the close of the week," he says, "I like to indulge in a little taste of shore leave."

"Your wife doesn't mind?"

"My wife doesn't *know*." He clinks his glass against Marley's and they both sit. The room is warm and Marley's forehead is damp and Balfour's cheeks are pink. "She dines on Friday evenings with her mother, now that the old woman finally trusts her to raise the child without her assistance. Between you and me, I thought she'd never go home."

Marley raises his glass. "Then here's to your mother-in-law. May she ever know her place."

"Amen."

"How old is he, now, the child?"

Balfour narrows his eyes. He is an experienced drinker, a seasoned Royal Navy man through and through, and if Marley thinks he will work some cozy angle upon him with the help of the gin he is mistaken. "You didn't come here to talk about Freddy."

"No. No, I didn't. Not at all."

"You came to talk about that burned ship."

Marley smiles. "I see that you've consulted the newspapers."

"Quite the opposite. The newspapers have consulted me."

"I see. And you have told them . . . ?"

"Considerably less than I know."

"They say the Americans are conducting an investigation."

"So they are. The Americans have jurisdiction, of course. The ship is theirs."

"*Was* theirs."

"Was."

"So—the Americans have jurisdiction, and the British have . . . what?"

"Information."

"Information which you are keeping from the Americans?"

"Information which I am keeping from everyone."

"From me? From a man who is like family to you?"

"Do not press me, Jacob." He coughs into his fist. "More gin?"

Marley shakes his head. "The truth is, I did not come here to interrogate you—"

"A wise decision."

Marley grins like the friendliest dog in the district. "I came to make a confession."

"That you burnt the *Mariel*. Or, more correctly, that you hired the work done."

"Precisely."

"By certain gentlemen who are now awaiting trial in Newgate."

"They are?"

"They are." Balfour stands and goes to pour himself another drop. "A trial will bring everything out," he says when he returns. "Including your connections."

"Not so long as I *have* no connections."

"Might it only be so, Jacob. Might it only be so. As I said, I possess information that I am doing my best to keep from everyone."

"I remember well. That case you keep with you at all times. Those documents."

"You have not aided your cause by committing a grievous international crime, or by endangering the lives of my men and yours . . ."

"I regret it."

". . . or by sending your hirelings off to prison for life."

"Should you choose to press the charges."

"Jacob, you are testing me."

"That was never my intention. You advised me to clean my house—"

"To make things right, not to make them *look* right. You've been doing far too much of that all along, I'm afraid."

Marley manages a look that's regretful, apologetic, and more or less endearing at the same time. "Forgive me," he says.

Balfour slams down his glass. "God may forgive you. As for me, I will merely provide a bit more time to clear up your affairs. The men of the *Mariel* are to be tried in four weeks. Upon that occasion I shall either find you clear of your interests in these matters or see you in court."

"And how shall I prove my newfound innocence?"

"Documentation," says Balfour. "Preferably of the genuine variety."

Only four weeks, thinks Marley as he regains the street. *It is impossible.*

Only four weeks to bring down the efforts of a lifetime, untangling a vast webwork of commercial ties both real and convenient.

Only four weeks to pauperize himself utterly by trading in the slaving business for lowly rum, sugar, and cotton.

Only four weeks to sacrifice his rank, his security, and his very future at the feet of that great grinning *Captain Harry Balfour*, who has already stolen his one true love.

The man is heartless.

If only, he thinks, *if only it were possible to tie the whole business back to Scrooge.* Such an arrangement would serve Harry and the inconstant Fan and even old Ebenezer himself properly. Let Balfour pursue charges against Stitch and any such disreputables as he may have brought on to assist in burning the ship, only to discover in the end that the trail leads not to Marley but to his own brother-in-law! There would be poetry in it. But no. Tying the slaving business to Scrooge would require truly parting with it himself. He would lose everything in the process, and he has no intention of taking matters that far.

He shakes his head and plunges along the night-lit streets of London, his mind churning. He tries reconstructing his conversation with Balfour, and each time he goes over it the implications grow worse. It is possible, after all, that Balfour has had until now little or nothing to tie him to the *Mariel*—much less to her destruction. If he was bluffing all along, working strictly on suspicion and conjecture, has Marley just confirmed everything?

Dear God, that could be the case. He has been most poorly used, tricked and cheated and manipulated into confessing crimes perhaps even greater than Balfour suspected at the outset.

The man is a devil. His promise is not to be relied upon, and his word is not to be trusted.

Marley must devise some means to subvert him. He has four weeks.

"Madeline ain't in tonight," says Mrs. McCullough.

"That's fine," says Inspector Bucket.

"She's been poorly."

"I'm not here for Madeline."

Mrs. McCullough looks a little crestfallen. Madeline *does* seem to be his favorite, after all.

"I'm here for Mr. McCullough."

She lifts an eyebrow.

"Where will I find him?"

She smiles her feline smile. "That would depend on the contents of his purse. If he has a penny to spend, he'll be at the Fox and Hare. If he hasn't, he'll be at the graveyard. He's been pursuing the resurrection business of late."

"An ugly trade, stealing bodies."

"He's only making the best of that for which the deceased lacks further use, I'd say."

"Say what you like."

"It's better work than some he's taken." She moves close and whispers into the inspector's ear, her breath stinking of tobacco and poor dentition. "Seeing as them involved is already dead, I mean."

The inspector cares little for the difference. "Which way to the graveyard?" he asks, and she advises him, and he goes.

McCullough proves to be there indeed, and the instant he detects movement at the gate he drops his shovel and draws a flintlock navy pistol. It gleams in the moonlight, an untrustworthy thing of French origin no doubt purloined from the corpse of some veteran of that country's revolution. It's possible that he has just this minute acquired it from the grave at his feet, and that it is therefore rusted tight or at least empty-chambered, but Marley doesn't risk either possibility.

"McCullough!" he calls, making himself visible in that same pale light. "Fire on me, and your wife loses her protector. As do you."

The resurrection man gives a nervous laugh and tucks the pistol into his belt. "Forgive me, Inspector. I thought you was the law."

"Don't test me."

"Ach," says McCullough. "No harm done."

Marley opens the gate and enters and draws near. McCullough has raised an impressive pile of earth, his work filling the air with the scents of dampness and decay. Down in the hole a roughly made coffin is peeking through, and the grave robber works at one end with the tip of his shovel to begin prizing it open.

"Leave that one where he lies for now," says the inspector.

"*She*," corrects McCullough, laying down his shovel. "Poor thing died in childbirth."

Marley scoffs. "Man or woman," he says, "it makes little difference to me."

"I suppose not. Seeing's she's dead and all." For he knows the habits of Inspector Bucket.

"Come," says Marley. "Sit." He leads the way to a pair of upright gravestones, side by side, upon which they settle like a couple of gargoyles.

McCullough takes out his pipe and fires it up. The stink of it is appalling.

Marley sneezes, recovers, sneezes again. "Mrs. McCullough seems quite pleased with your new line of work."

"Oh, she is. Most definitely. It's less risky, for one thing. And always cash on the nail."

"I see."

"There's nothing like a cash business," he goes on. "I tell me customers, *If you can't pay for the body, I'll find someone who will.*"

"An excellent principle."

Smug and self-satisfied, McCullough sucks upon his pipestem.

"All the same, do you ever miss the old trade?"

McCullough gazes dreamily through the smoke. "It *was* a trifle more exciting, I'll grant you. It really got the old heart pumping."

"No doubt."

"Made a man feel alive."

"It would, that kind of thing." Marley permits the idea to suspend itself there in the graveyard miasma for a moment. "Perhaps," he says after a while, "you would consider one last commission."

"I might," says McCullough. "If the terms was right."

"Cash on the nail, of course."

"Of course."

"You're no fool."

"I ain't."

Marley takes from his pocket a handful of gleaming Spanish dollars. McCullough's eyes go wide.

"Do you suppose you might be at liberty next Friday evening?"

He waits until the woman and child have made their exit. The inspector was imperative on that subject. There must be no witnesses, least of all these.

Once they are gone, whisked away by a hired carriage bound in the direction of central London, he approaches the house as bold as you please. He is no picklock, this McCullough, but his employer possesses a broad knowledge of criminal activity and has instructed him in the basics of the trade. The work goes easily enough. Perhaps he has discovered the makings of a new career, should the resurrection business take a turn for the worse.

Within the house he waits again. The inspector, who seems to know everything, is acquainted with the arrangement of the downstairs rooms and has instructed him as to where he should station himself—just beyond the kitchen, in the shadows of the dining room—so as to surprise the gentleman when he arrives. The gentleman in question is known to take a drink or two of gin on a Friday evening, and McCullough is left to his own judgment as to whether or not the man shall be permitted to do so now. Any gin not drunk by the gentleman, of course, shall belong to McCullough when his work is done.

An hour ticks by, according to his repeater. He is to wait no more than two hours altogether, abandoning the work at that point and exiting through a rear passageway rather than risk meeting the woman and child upon their return. Soon enough, however, the gentleman arrives. He admits himself through the front door—McCullough has forgotten to turn the lock but the gentleman in his urgency seems not to notice—and hangs up his hat and coat on a peg in the front hallway before stepping into the kitchen.

McCullough generously permits the gentleman a single tot of gin, which he takes at the kitchen table. Twice he turns to peer into the dining room as if he has detected some unknown presence there, as if he has felt the weight of McCullough's very gaze upon his neck, and twice he returns to his drink.

Rather than risk discovery upon a third such occasion, McCullough rises from the shadows with his revolver drawn and places a ball in the nape of the gentleman's neck from close range. The inspector has called for the use of a knife so as to lessen suspicion—no powder blast, no evidentiary ball—but he seems to know little about the difficulty of killing a man up close. Willing nonetheless to meet the inspector halfway, and fully satisfied that the gentleman is indeed dead, McCullough excavates the flattened ball with a spoon and places it in his pocket. When his work is accomplished and he has a moment's leisure, he will flat-arm it across the Thames and count how many times it skips. The spoon he will keep, for it seems the purest silver.

Right now, though, with the gentleman's leather case securely tucked beneath his arm, he draws a carton of lucifers from his waistcoat and fulfills the last of his obligations by setting the place on fire.

Thirty

Marley hates a funeral, but attending Balfour's is the least he can do.

As he makes his solitary way along the wet streets to Greenwich, he ponders the contents of the coffin. There can't have been much left of Balfour but scorched bone, identifiable amid the wreckage only by its sad presence. The place went up like a tinderbox and burned straight to the ground with little in the way of interference by either God or man.

He enters the chapel like a condemned prisoner, his shoulders hunched and his downcast face set in a credible mask of misery. Clad in his customary black he blends with the other mourners on this rainy afternoon—a sluggish and damp and ashy lot pooling in this glorious place like something that has failed to find the drain.

The music is somber, the atmosphere is chilly, and in the vast chamber Balfour's coffin seems inconsequential, dwarfed beneath the grand tableau of the shipwrecked St. Paul. The contents of the box, thinks Marley, must be very nearly weightless, a dusty, disarticulated, and horrifyingly gape-jawed monstrosity that would shock these grieving naïfs and send them shuddering into the street. Pity the pallbearers. They will need to exercise caution in making their way down the aisle and out the chapel door, lest the bones get to rattling and unnerve the mourners. *Ashes to ashes.*

Marley endures the obsequies and then lingers in his pew, head bowed as if in prayer, while the others begin to file out. He desires to place himself just so within the slow-moving river of them—not too early and not too late but somewhere in the middle. He must make himself unremarkable, just one more sympathetic soul come to mourn the tragic loss of a good man. He shall not have many such opportunities to persuade Fan that he has changed.

Ebenezer is first in the receiving line, a breakwater against the assault of too much emotion, followed by a gray-visaged brother of Balfour's and then by Mother Scrooge and finally by the widow herself. The widow Fan and her five-year-old Freddy, erect at her side as a steadfast tin soldier. The boy seems drained of all emotion, borne up to his full height by sheer will, while his mother seems on the brittle edge of every kind of collapse.

Marley practices on Scrooge, exercising upon him the look he will give the rest of the family, a look that says he has hollowed himself out so as to accept into his own voided soul the overflow of their desolation. *I am wholly at your service*, his steadfast gaze and his shuddering exhalations say. *Let dear old Jacob help.*

He actually flings himself upon Balfour's unsuspecting brother, clapping the fellow powerfully and repeatedly upon the back like an ancient companion reduced to wordless grief. The brother stiffens at first but weakens as Marley persists. Ultimately he gives in, his cheeks bathed in tears drawn forth by the assault of counterfeit sympathy.

Mother Scrooge is an easy mark, for she has considerable history, right or wrong, as a partisan of Marley's. He permits himself to call her by that very name—"*Mother Scrooge*," he whispers in her powdered ear—in a manner that asserts his right to do so not via Fan or Ebenezer but by dint of his own long and almost filial connection to the woman herself. As a result she nearly refuses to let him go, and yields him up only when the individual preceding him in line, a high-ranking naval officer apparently accustomed to delivering bad news (his consolation has about it a professional quality), has finished with Fan.

As the officer moves away, Marley takes a scant half step toward her so as to maintain a decent and respectful distance. He stands bereft and alone, shaking his head in stunned amazement, wringing his hands as if to cleanse them of every wrong he has ever committed. "Dear, dear child," he says.

"Jacob." Her face crumples, and she extends to him her innocent arms—for that is what convention requires, that is what ordinary people do under circumstances as terrible as these. Thus, and thus compromised, she unwittingly invites him in.

The wreckage of the house is barely a stone's throw from the chapel, and on this damp and sunless day the smell of burning penetrates the air. Everything stinks of ash and ruin.

Marley lingers in the chapel yard, damp and cold and inadequately sheltered by an overhang. He breathes and he coughs and he sniffs at the fabric of his coat, savoring the smell of fire. He shall bear it upon his person into the days and months ahead, and it will serve as a reminder of the great transformative work by which he has granted himself the liberty to pursue all such business and personal interests as might please him.

The mourners file out and filter away down the streets and lanes, and when they are gone the family leaves the chapel in the company of the pastor. Leaning upon one another they creep toward a hired carriage and a curtained hearse hitched to a mare as black and wild-eyed as Death. Only little Freddy seems fully under his own motive power, and he breaks away and skips ahead to admire the horse. She has no patience for him, and with a snort and a shudder and a stamp of one great hoof she sends him on his way.

Marley peels himself from the shadow of the chapel and aims his gaze downward and starts toward the street, plotting a course that should permit at least one member of the party to catch sight of him.

Surely enough: "Mr. Marley!" comes Mother Scrooge's voice, clotted thick with emotion.

He lifts toward her a look both abstracted and disconsolate.

"Oh, Mr. Marley!" She waves a handkerchief in the direction of the carriage. "Won't you accompany us to the cemetery?"

"I should be honored," he says, as if this is the first time he has thought of it.

The pastor joins the driver on the box, and the others arrange themselves within the carriage. As they shudder away from the curb, Marley takes a moment to embroider his position. "I hardly deserve a place with the family," he says, "but it is my honor to support you all as best I can in this painful time."

"Just this past week," says Fan, marveling, "Harry mentioned something about wanting to treat you—*yes, Jacob, you*—as if you were in fact a member of the family. And to think that I balked."

"Now, now," says Marley. "Harry was a fine man. One of a kind, really—a naval hero and an upright leader of men and a Christian of the highest order. There is no reason to curse ourselves for not living up to his standard."

Sighs and murmurs all around. The carriage bounces, sways, rights itself.

Marley goes on. "Nonetheless each of us—you and I included, Fan—must permit ourselves to be led by his example in the future."

"And may God strengthen us for the effort," says the brother.

"Amen," says Marley.

"Amen," say one and all.

The carriage rounds a corner and rattles on toward the graveyard.

1820—1825

Thirty-One

"Mr. McCullough's been arrested," she says, "but ye'd know all about that." The lady arches her eyebrows and gives Inspector Bucket a smile that has within it no trace of the sweet or the seductive or even the sincere.

"I've heard," extemporizes the ready inspector.

"Ye'll be springing him soon, I expect?"

"Oh, very soon," says the inspector. "You can rely upon that."

She winks. "I should hope there'll be some restitution in it for the poor dear."

"Restitution?"

"For time spent. He's been off the resurrection trade since they hauled him in."

"It's not my business that he got caught."

She leans in. "What *is* your business is that he ain't confessed. Nor named the man what hired him."

"Would you be threatening me, Mrs. McCullough?"

"I'd be reminding you, Inspector Bucket. Reminding you, is all. That we're in this nasty business together."

"Do you suppose he'll be believed if he says that I of all people hired him for such wicked work? Do you further suppose that even if he *were* believed, my fellows in the constabulary would not protect me?"

"*Honor among thieves* is it, Inspector?"

"Honor? Never. These matters have to do with power—and if not power, then leverage. I happen to have great quantities of both, as you can imagine."

"So there'll be nothing in it for Mr. McCullough?"

"I didn't say that. He shall be fairly compensated, I assure you. He shall receive everything he deserves."

"But not a penny more, Inspector." She laughs her troubling laugh. "Not if I know you!"

"You might not know me as well as you think."

Mrs. McCullough's look suggests otherwise.

"Now," he reconfigures. "Is Madeline occupied?"

"Madeline?" says the lady, with a pathetic tilt of her head. "Why, Madeline's gone to join the angels."

Marley gives her a look that's doubtful and disappointed at once.

"Cupid's Disease," she explains. "Runs in the trade, you know."

"Understood. But—"

"I do my best for my girls, Inspector. And for my customers likewise. You know that."

"I do."

"I run a clean house . . ."

"But Madeline? I had no idea."

"She'd been poorly. You knew that."

"I did."

"Not so many good days, toward the end."

"I should think not."

"A pity, really."

"Yes," says the stymied inspector. "A pity."

"There's other girls, though," offers Mrs. McCullough. "Plenty of other girls."

"No, thank you," says the inspector. "Not today."

An individual as competent and versatile as rough Reagh McCullough—petty thief, snatcher of corpses, steady hand for bloody work of all varieties—deserves better treatment than this. But justice is hard to find within the great cruel crucible of London, and thus in the courts and in the newspapers and in the arena of public opinion the gentleman is being reduced to a laughingstock.

"Inspector Bucket?" cries the magistrate in a most unseemly display. "*Inspector Bucket?*" he cries again, hammering upon the bench with the flat of his hand and laughing until jolly tears roll down his cheeks. "If you are going to invent a story, Mr. McCullough, you will have to do better than that. I am well-acquainted with the brave and true gentlemen of the London police, and I can assure you that there is no such individual in their employ."

A quick general polling of the courtroom confirms the magistrate's opinion.

"But I swear," says McCullough. "It was Bucket put me up to it. Paid me well enough, too. In advance."

"You are doing yourself no kindness . . ." says the magistrate.

"Great powerful bloke he is, sir. Smooth in his way but a ruffian underneath. He ain't the sort to be trifled with."

The magistrate rolls his eyes.

"Not that murder's his usual trade, mind you. Generally he's concerned more with your knocking-shops and such."

The magistrate shows interest. "That would be his specialty then, this Bucket? Prostitution?"

"Oh, yes, sir. He's keen on the subject. And not strictly from the legal point of view, neither."

"I see. How, then, did this knocking-shop expert come to hire you for murder and arson?"

McCullough swallows.

"That seems a bit removed from his usual, does it not?"

"It does, sir."

"Well, then?"

"We have friends in common, sir."

"*Friends.*"

"Friends. Yes, sir."

"Would you care to elaborate? Perhaps those *friends* could help us track down this elusive inspector of yours."

"I'd rather not say, sir. Not if I ain't required."

"You've said quite enough," says the magistrate, nodding. "You've said enough to guarantee your hanging, in fact."

And so he has.

Marley observes the trial from a safe distance, and it is with mingled anticipation and delight that he scans the news each day for the latest report. He takes a private and professional satisfaction in how beautifully his masquerade as a member of the constabulary has isolated him from this most grievous crime. *Inspector Bucket* indeed. The name itself is an absurdity. He can no longer recall how he came up with it or why in the world he imagined that it would succeed. Credit a rich imagination.

He is, however, saddened that he must abandon the role for good. What a useful, flexible, and profitable creation the inspector was! Although at first nothing more than a device for obtaining the services of expensive women at no charge, the gentleman brilliantly expanded his horizons as need and opportunity required. Imagine, making off with both pleasure and money upon each visit to the bawdy house! No one could do it! Not even Marley himself! And yet the inspector managed the feat. Marley can no more recall the inspiration for the fellow's sham financial arrangements—alleged payments to other authorities, assurances of protection from their lawful predations—than he can recall the source of that ridiculous name, but the profits were genuine and reliable. And never mind extortion! Before he was through, dear old Bucket had not only facilitated the murder of that meddling Balfour but kept Marley's own name clear of the transaction.

Jolly old Bucket! Useful old Bucket! Delightful old Bucket! Marley wonders how he shall ever get along without him.

In fact, he despairs at the prospect. So well known is the inspector to the denizens of every knocking-shop in London that he dares not show his face in a single one of them. He could of course go farther afield in search of his sport, but the girls get around. It would be just his luck to invent some new identity and travel as far as Gravesend or Brighton only to find himself fingered as the long-lost inspector, brought back to pay the price for McCullough's wrongful conviction.

Such a fate would never do. He shall have to get by without, unless he can chart some other course. In the meantime he keeps his own company and heaps up his wealth and confines his pleasures to the port wine he steals from the tenant in his basement. The solitude is good for his peace of mind and the acquisition is good for his soul and the tawny port is good for dulling the pain of a certain sore spot he's been developing on the inside of his lower lip. He holds the rich red liquid there until it burns away the sting. No doctor or apothecary could devise a superior treatment.

Thirty-Two

How like the old days it is, back home in her mother's small but tidy apartments, back home in the poky little bedroom where she spent her youth and young womanhood, back home with the only alteration in circumstance the exchange of her brother for her son.

She detests it.

The world has stalled. The dependable clockwork universe, which gave a stutter when Ebenezer and Belle went their separate ways, ground utterly to a halt when fate took her beloved Harry. *He was drunk*, people whispered. Drunk and alone and bent over a bottle, oblivious to the fire erupting around him. Such is the way with navy men, or so the world believes. She knows it to be an errant lie, yet she cannot dispute it. And even if she could, what would be the use? Harry is in the ground. Belle is wed to Arthur. Her brother and she are alone once more, Ebenezer with his ledgers and she with her fatherless son.

It could be worse. Minus Harry's small pension and Ebenezer's occasional begrudging contributions to the family purse, they would be in the poorhouse—the whole wretched lot of them thrown into Marshalsea for debts they could never repay, with only poor young Freddy released each morning to spend his hours blacking the boots of more fortunate individuals.

Mother Scrooge advises her that she ought to be happy. They have each other. She has indelible memories of Harry. The time has come to cease living in the past. Why, even Freddy, may God bless him, is finding new playmates and taking a little pleasure in his altered circumstances.

"Freddy has his entire life ahead of him," says Fan. "It's only right that he should."

"You have yours ahead of you as well."

"No."

"Fan."

"I do not."

"*Fan.*"

"I did, though. Once I did."

"Yes. And you were happy then, my dear. Even before Harry, I mean."

"I don't remember."

"I do."

"I didn't know what happiness was."

"And you still don't know what happiness might lie ahead."

"*Happiness*," says Fan. "Happiness is humbug, and I've had my fill of it."

For all he stirs from his desk, Scrooge may as well be a mushroom in the shape of a man. He lurks there hour after hour in the comfortable dark and the customary damp, scratching away at his ledgers, consuming ink by the potful as an ordinary man might consume tea.

Visitors he bars outright unless they bear money or offer profitable terms. Merely raising his head to acknowledge a man's presence gives him pain, for pushing his eyeglasses up the slope of his nose and refocusing

his vision away from his work costs precious seconds that could otherwise be spent upon calculation. His watery eyes are dim with strain
and his long hands are spattered with ink and his tight pigtail is pre-
maturely salted with worry, yet each day he advances, moving forward
and accruing additional wealth bit by bit. Perhaps it is only a shilling or
two, perhaps it is a hundred or even a thousand times that, but it is all
progress and it is all for the better.

Precisely what goal he may be inching toward is now unnamable,
since Belle is pursuing life without him and the God of Christianity has
not shone His countenance upon Scrooge since the day she broke off their
engagement. He has not so much as seen her in the ten years since her
father's death. Fan mentions her in his presence now and again, generally
in a tone of voice that suggests a lingering jealousy over her friend pos-
sessing a husband who continues to dwell among the living. Arthur Cope
is no Harry Balfour, not by Fan's lights, but he does have the advantage
of remaining above the ground.

"I couldn't," says Mother Scrooge.

"You must," says Marley.

"Ebenezer does his part," the old woman reassures him.

"I'm certain that he does. He's a kindly soul."

She stifles a laugh.

"Be that as it may," says Marley, "even Ebenezer can't desire to see
his mother and sister in the poorhouse."

"No."

"Or innocent little Freddy, for that matter."

"Oh, definitely not. Definitely not Freddy."

"What a cruel fate that would be!" says Marley, perhaps imagining it.
"And yet, even now, the poor child could do with an additional pleasure
or two."

"Well . . ." hesitates Mother Scrooge.

Marley extracts an envelope from his waistcoat and leans it against Mother Scrooge's teapot. The envelope is fat, fatter by far than Freddy, and the old woman looks upon it in the flesh as she would look upon the gift of another grandchild.

"You are altogether too kind," she says.

"Fan doesn't need to know," he says as he rises to leave, certain that Mother Scrooge will tell her anyhow, and at the earliest opportunity.

Surely enough, Mother Scrooge does exactly that. And the very next morning Fan arrives at the offices of Scrooge & Marley, powered by a full head of steam, looking for her benefactor and learning that he is elsewhere as usual. She very nearly leaves the money with her brother, but the light that rises in his eye at the prospect puts her off.

She seeks Marley at home instead. She passes through the gates and climbs the rough path to his door and employs the knocker with a vengeance. For a few moments the house yields up no more than distant sounds of hammering from the wine merchants in the cellar, but she persists until Marley himself finally creeps down the stair and opens the latch and tugs the great stubborn door open the slightest crack. The action seems to leave him winded.

"Fan!" he says, a trifle unmanned by the weight of the door and uncharacteristically self-conscious. He leans against the frame and, despite the hour, gathers the folds of a dressing gown around his neck. The dank atmosphere of the stairwell seems to have cast a chill over him.

"*Mr. Marley.*" She makes no move to come in, but stands gazing upon him as if she has never truly seen him before. He looks to her diminished.

"To what do I owe . . . ?"

"*You owe nothing,*" she spits back, "*at least not to me,*" for the pathways of her brain have been firing at a furious pace all morning and there is not a thing in all the world that he could have said that would not have provoked a similarly cutting answer. She thrusts the fat envelope through the crack and when he does not take it she lets it fall, spilling out notes as it tumbles toward his feet.

He does not bend to collect them. He does not so much as acknowledge that they have fallen. Money, says the look upon his face, means nothing to him. She, by contrast, means everything.

There is something more in his look, too: a hollowed-out longing, a soul-wrenching pain, a wordless depth of regret and rue. She sees it as his dry lips part to whisper "Forgive me," and she sees it as he removes his hand from the neck of his garment and begins to press the door shut.

"Wait," she says.

"I would not make you unhappy for the world."

She puts her own hand on the door, not pushing back but just resting it there as a sign. "Jacob," she says. "You and I were doomed at the start. We remain so."

"You misjudge me."

"No."

His voice cracks. "You underestimate me."

"We have done all this before."

He shrugs. "Very well," he says, in the tones of a condemned man. He turns and looks off up the dim stairway. "Should you require me at some future date . . ." But his thought turns into a mumble and the mumble turns into a cough and the cough dies a long slow death.

"Jacob."

He waves her off, leaving the door ajar, and shuffles toward the stair. She follows, pushing the door wide in a burst of light.

He half turns and squints into the sun, both revealed by it and reduced. "Do you remember what Harry said at the last?" he says. "He said that we were all one family. The two of you and Ebenezer and myself. Mother Scrooge and Freddy. All one. He was in the midst of doing me a kindness, you see, and those were the terms in which he explained his reasons."

"What sort of kindness was it?" For although she still dreams of Harry each night and thinks of him every waking moment, she has heard no new report of his good character in ages, and she hungers for it.

"The nature of the kindness is of no account now. It is lost with him, and I must fend for myself."

"If I could help you in his stead, I would."

Marley laughs, a sad and shocking thing. "Can't you see?" he says. "You feel that very same family impulse."

She stands abashed.

"Harry was right."

She weeps.

A little wind picks up and shuffles the scattered notes like leaves. One lodges itself beneath his bare foot and he stoops to retrieve it. "Let us help each other," he says. And wordlessly, she acquiesces.

By and by the connection will do them both good. Jacob is too old and ill to be a credible suitor, and Fan is too heartbroken to be credibly sought. Months will pass, and Balfour's words will become flesh as Jacob insinuates himself as part of the family. That old table for three—first Mother Scrooge, Fan, and Ebenezer, and then Mother Scrooge, Fan, and Freddy—will expand so often to four that they will give off borrowing the neighbor's chair and buy one outright. Marley will pay the bill, of course. No one will think anything of it.

Thirty-Three

Marley has more good days than bad. So many good days, in fact, that the bad ones seem negligible, aberrant, perhaps even meaningless. He is half a century old now and he feels his age everywhere from time to time—in his bones and in his skin and in his liver. Perhaps, he tells himself when he is felled by one symptom or another, he has always felt this way and has just forgotten. No one can remember everything. Not even Jacob Marley.

The rash that blooms upon his torso and limbs is tolerable for the most part. Pink and flat and painless, it is mainly a private annoyance that he can hide beneath his clothing, particularly during the cooler seasons. Only when it invades the soles of his feet and the palms of his hands does it present difficulty, and then chiefly when it erupts into warts and pustules. The sores upon his feet pain him and hinder his movement, bending his gait into a hesitant limp that he hopes is not too noticeable. Those upon his palms are a shade more troublesome, for they make him reluctant to shake hands upon the closing of a business deal. That sets an unfortunate tone. He takes to wearing gloves in public, although his wounds' persistent weeping means that he must don a fresh pair several times a day. They prove to be more dressing than dress.

The doctor counsels mercury and patience. He is a grave old man, an expert at every kind of collapse and decay, and upon completing a thorough examination he prescribes a double dose of the medicine—both a pill and a topical salve. "A night with Venus," he says with a little twinkle in his eye, "and a lifetime with Mercury."

"A lifetime, is it?" asks Marley.

"This is a treatment, not a cure."

"But I will live."

"You will live, and the syphilis will live as well. In the end, you shall go to the grave together."

"If you mean that as a comfort . . ."

"I am not in the business of comfort, Mr. Marley. I am in the business of medicine."

"Then I was misled. I understood you to be in the business of *cures*."

The doctor proceeds undaunted. "We shall need to wait and watch, of course. The symptoms may diminish for a time. Vision troubles, or pain in the joints, or loss of weight may suggest that the disease has gotten its second wind and is progressing. You can expect fevers, night sweats, a sore throat."

"I don't expect them. I have them."

"They may pass."

"I may pass," says Marley.

"You shall," says the doctor. "But in the meantime, cheer up. Unlike many of my patients, you're still upright."

There is upright and there is upright, and Marley finds himself pressing toward both. It is something of a surprise.

The handicaps that his condition has set before his various business activities, frustrating at first, have enforced upon him a slower and more thoughtful pace. He divides his time more or less equally between his bed and his workshop and his previously underutilized office at Scrooge & Marley. Scrooge, growing more accustomed to his presence, begins to think of him more as partner than adversary. Oh, he still chisels away at the man's private fortune whenever he can, but he takes significantly less pleasure in it. He wonders now and then if his partner is playing some new game, working some new angle. Marley has told him a little about his condition, no more than is required to explain his various shortcomings and absences, and as a result Scrooge, not ordinarily given to pity, feels a tenderness toward the old felon. *Perhaps*, he thinks, *the disease has softened his mind*.

Back at home, Marley turns his artistic gifts toward a new avenue. He has taken his talents as far as he can in the area of counterfeiting— there is nothing he cannot do by way of forgery, and there is even less that he *desires* to do these days—and so in periods when his rash subsides and the tender skin of his hands permits, he takes up the delicate and deceitful art of trompe l'oeil. It suits him perfectly. Before long the apron hanging on a peg inside the door is not an apron at all, but a painting of one. The brushes and scrapers hung upon the walls are not brushes and scrapers, but their perfect likenesses. He even decorates the workbench itself, adding reflective spills of varnish and curly wisps of torn paper and artfully scattered pencil shavings, their every curve and shadow painstakingly executed in oil.

1830—1832

Thirty-Four

Marley doesn't give much thought to his illness anymore, for over the years his symptoms have faded and gone largely to rest. Perhaps he is free of it, he thinks. Perhaps the doctor was wrong about its course. Perhaps some quality of his constitution has let him fight off the wretched disease entirely, while less robust individuals—poor Madeline, for example, may God rest her immortal soul—are doomed by their weakness to succumb.

Regardless, he continues the mercury treatments. He keeps up his modified habits, too. Most days he is in the office, keeping a patient eye on his accounts and a cautious eye on his partner. His holdings are still vast, sufficient to see him to the end of this life many times over, and although he luxuriates in the comfort of it all he pities his younger self for the price he paid in making it possible. He regrets the self-absorption and the cruelty and the blindness to the needs of others. Why, these days just having a quiet supper opposite that delightful young Freddy Balfour— *Fred*, he must remember, for the boy is all of sixteen years old now, nearly a man, and putting away childish things—just dining with the lad gives him happiness beyond imagining. The younger Jacob Marley, the Jacob

261

Marley who had no pleasures beyond those of the countinghouse and the knocking-shop, never knew such ordinary joys.

Sundays and afternoons and early evenings when the light is good he confines himself to his workshop, where he paints. He has turned his attention from trompe l'oeil to still life and at last to portraiture—he favors the faces of strangers he has passed on the streets and in the lanes, unknowable individuals who seem made entirely of secrets—and although he is dissatisfied with his efforts thus far he believes that he has promise. It is better to fail at a difficult thing than to succeed at the commonplace again and again.

Without once consulting his partner, Scrooge brings on a clerk. There was a time when such an action would have been unthinkable—the expense of it alone, never mind the audacity—but Marley raises no objection. He actually rather pities the fellow, this Bob Cratchit with his long face and his pinched nose and his air of a wretchedness beyond his years.

He is young, this Cratchit, terribly and pitiably so, as young as Marley and Scrooge were when they came of age and joined their fortunes together. But Cratchit has none of the nerve, none of the ambition, none of the drive that let them make something out of their partnership. He is quite good with calculations and has a fair tolerance for long hours, yet he brings to his work not a trace of the single-mindedness that made Scrooge *Scrooge* from the very beginning, not a particle of the imagination that made Marley *Marley*. There is, by contrast, an airiness about him, a lack of weight. If he were a ship he would be rudderless and light in the hold, doomed to be blown this way and that across an unforgiving sea. Marley foresees a family in his future, a suffering wife and hungry children, and he pities them their association.

He makes various charcoal studies of him, rough attempts to capture his gloomy look or his collapsing physique or his defeated bearing. He would get him entire if he could, bring him home and confine him in his workshop and execute his likeness down to the atom, for the man provokes within his breast unbridled curiosity and even sympathy. He no doubt possesses secrets and woes to which Marley would not dare seek access. So he watches him daily, safe behind the screen of his own busyness, and he speaks to him no more than is required, and he wonders about him as he has begun to wonder about the rest of mankind. Mysteries all.

He makes no effort to capture him in paint, however, for he has turned his attention to a different subject—one closer to his heart and better known to his eye, although mysteries still remain. Mysteries upon mysteries, in fact, for the years that he has spent in proximity to this individual have served only to compound the puzzles of personality and history and heart.

After six months, brushstroke by brushstroke, error by error, correction by correction, he is satisfied with the portrait. He is very nearly proud of it, and there are few things in his life that he is proud of now. As days and weeks go by the likeness lives on in his workshop, set upon a shelf where the light is good, but he will be damned if it does not cry out for something more. And so he opens his old cabinets and sharpens his old tools and returns to the old arts upon which he built his fortune.

He constructs a frame, an ornate thing carved of elm and beechwood. He perfects it first and then he brutalizes it, filing down its sharp edges and drilling wormholes in it with a brace and bit and abusing its full pristine expanse with a length of chain taken from one of his strongboxes. When he is satisfied he gilds it and rubs away the gilding in patches and gilds it all over again with materials of a slightly different shade. More battering with the chain and a quick dousing with some thinned black paint and at last a handful of powdered graphite burnished in with a ragged cloth, and it looks one hundred years old or more, an object stored in some attic or warehouse, the forgotten object of long neglect. It is a thing of softly gleaming beauty.

Into it he mounts the portrait. The completed work is too heavy to be returned to the shelf where the plain stretched canvas once stood, and so he leans it against the wall in a dim corner. There it will stand until he is ready to introduce it to the world beyond his workshop. A thousand other objects have made that transition prior to this, certificates and correspondence and licenses and more, but they have all been things of duplicity and deceit. They were frauds, created for gain. This portrait, despite the false luxury of its framing, is different. Revealing it fully will require some preparation.

Thirty-Five

It is a warm spring afternoon in London, just about suppertime, and no one would recognize Inspector Bucket or Mr. Nemo or any of Jacob Marley's other public personae in the gentleman who now makes his leisurely way along the streets. Those men kept to the shadows, strode with desperation, cloaked themselves more often than not in anonymous rags. Not Marley, not anymore, for he is well-fixed and will not live forever. Yet he has survived. He has survived his encounters with Professor Drabb and Ebenezer Scrooge and Harry Balfour and, thus far, syphilis. He has set aside the weary habits of greed and acquisition, and substituted in their place something more humane. And he is at this very moment on his way to dine with a woman who, if not the love of his life, is at least a refuge from the worst of its torments. He can almost forget that he once paid for the murder of her husband. But that was long ago. Those were other times. He has been reborn into himself.

Gathered about the table, the four of them make a homely little family, perhaps even more comfortable than the same gathering would have been with Balfour in his rightful place instead of Marley. Marley provides no friction, after all, because he has no standing beyond that of a guest;

he has no authority to exercise and no role to play. It hardly matters that he pays the rent and keeps the larder stocked. Given sufficient time and familiarity, particulars such as these may be reduced to nothing.

Fred's appetite has grown as rapidly as the rest of him, and their dinner has barely begun when he calls on Marley to pass the beets around again, please. Marley accedes, and as he hands off the bowl Mother Scrooge spies an unlikely stain upon his otherwise characteristically pristine cuff.

"Is that coal dust?" she asks. "What would you be doing messing about with coal at this time of year, Mr. Marley?"

He stretches out his arm, studies the spot.

Mother Scrooge flicks at it with her napkin, but that only smears it.

He winces, draws the spot nearer to his nose, gives an inquisitive sniff. "It would seem not to be coal," he says.

"What, then?"

He shrugs and smiles a coy smile and lowers his hand into his lap as if hiding the stain might end the discussion.

"Are you letting yourself go, Mr. Marley?"

"Never!"

"I believe that you might be."

Fan speaks up. "It's only a mark, Mother."

"He's letting himself go, he is."

"Honestly," says Marley, "I suppose it's most likely graphite."

"What?" says Mother Scrooge.

Fred comes up for air, calling for more mutton.

"Graphite," says Marley, passing the platter. "Most likely."

"Whatever it is, it's got under your nails as well," remarks the newly observant Mother Scrooge.

"I've been working on a little project," he says.

"You've been failing to take care of yourself. You require looking after."

"*Mother.*"

266

"If you won't—"

"Mother."

"It's nothing, really," says Marley. "A little artwork with which I've been amusing myself. I must have gotten distracted."

"I didn't know you had an artistic bent," says Fan.

And thus is the bait taken.

"Ever since childhood," he says.

"You must show us, one day."

"Perhaps I shall."

Exactly how long has she known him? All her life, it seems. He was there almost half a century ago, when she arrived at that dreadful boarding school to collect her brother. She was only a child then, sent by her father in the company of a gray-faced and taciturn driver, but Marley made an impression upon her. She remembers him extracting from Ebenezer a promise of regular correspondence—"Be sure I hear from you on the first of every month!" he said—although he did not look like the sentimental type. Perhaps, trapped in the clutches of Professor Drabb, the poor boy was simply starving for human kindness. A monthly note from someone, anyone, even dull old Ebenezer, could work wonders.

She did not know then and she does not know now that each of her brother's notes would include an additional note, a commercially negotiable one, in payment against a fictional debt. Marley kept the boy impoverished thereby but also kept him close, and when their schooling was finished and the false debt repaid their real work began.

From that day forward he was a fixture in her brother's life and generally nothing more than that, an unremarkable thing as ordinary as a coat hook or a gas lamp. They had moments, yes, but those moments were fleeting and ill-fated, because in any sort of relation that they might conceivably pursue he would forever wield the powers of age and masculinity and wealth, leaving her to fall back upon the one power she retained, which was that of withholding. Everything changed at the bottom of the stairway. She quit being the object of his pity. She took strength in his weakness. She understood that perhaps—*perhaps*—he possessed a heart after all.

And now they find themselves here once more, at the bottom of that same stairway.

The last of the day's light is dying as they go upward. The house is quiet, dead, with the wine merchants closed up and the rest of the tenants entirely mythical. Fan has never set foot beyond the foyer, and as they proceed down the hall the presence of those names on door after locked door—Plummer & Snagsby, Barnacle & Sons, Bildad & Peleg—strikes her as surpassingly queer. The rooms behind them might as well be prison cells as places of business. They could be magical chambers built to confine an army of ghosts.

"I thought you lived here all alone," she says.

"Oh, I do," says Marley. "These other fellows conduct their business during the day, when I am busy conspiring with your brother. It's been years since I've seen a single one of them."

"I had no idea," says she. "This grand old house. I just thought . . ."

"It's not so grand," says Marley. "Quite far from it, really."

"Large, then."

"It is that. Large enough for the whole lot of us. And as long as these fellows pay their rent, we mind our own affairs."

The door at the end of the hall leads to his apartments. The parlor beyond it is plain, spare, and not terribly clean. Its walls empty, its curtains threadbare, it is the nakedly private dwelling place of an ascetic spirit unused to human visitation. There is in fact only one chair to be seen, a very small and uncomfortable-looking one at that, drawn up hard by the cold fireplace. On a little table beside it is a teacup, its bottom filmed over with residue, left there one night before the weather turned warm. To one side is a poky little kitchen, more jumbled and lived-in by the look of it, and another room opposite where he no doubt takes his rest.

"Forgive me," he says. "I don't often receive visitors."

"Your apartments are just as I imagined they would be," says Fan.

He is still sly enough to know that she means it in a way that is kind but not complimentary.

"Well," she says. "Where did you hang it?"

"Oh!" says Marley. "The painting! Of course! Turn around!"

The windows all face to the west, and the last of the sun's rays are streaming through them just now, piercing the thin weave of the threadbare curtains. The light falls upon the far wall, burnishing the rough plaster with a golden haze, and the burnishing applies equally to Marley's hand-built frame and the painting within it. No museum could show it off to better advantage.

"This was the only wall large enough," he says, as if anything needs to be explained.

Fan clasps her cloak to her throat. "Oh my," she says. "Oh, Jacob."

"What do you think?"

"I think you have captured me."

He has. And not just the Fan of this moment but the Fan of every moment she has lived. There is childish Fan in the play of light upon her smile, desirable Fan in the secrets promised by her eyes, independent Fan in the frankness of her gaze, widowed fan in the faint hollows of her cheeks. In the painting she seems to be of no particular age, and the effect is devastating. She steps away, toward the fireplace, putting a hand upon the back of the empty chair to steady herself. The chair, old and ill made, tilts a little at her touch, and she lowers herself down onto the seat instead.

"I felt it was a fair likeness."

"Fair? It's *perfect*. So perfect that it saddens me to look upon it."

"Why should it sadden you?"

"Because you've caught the truth about me. About all of us. I look at once so hopeful and so doomed."

There is a lifetime in her sentiment. There are multiple lifetimes—not just her own but Harry Balfour's and her mother's and Ebenezer's, too. Even young Fred's, if the pattern established upon this earth for generation after generation holds.

"*Hopeful and doomed*," says Marley. "And here I mainly wanted to get the nose right."

Fan smiles, and her smile crumbles, and Marley comes to her side. He places a hand upon the chair and she places her hand upon his. "Poor dear," he says. "It's a painting. It's not mankind."

But it *is* mankind, isn't it? And her heart has been pierced through, hasn't it? And old familiar, difficult, harmless, hurtful, greedy, inconsequential, generous, impossible, omnipresent, unknowable Jacob Marley is the one behind it. She weeps, and he produces a handkerchief. She sags, and he kneels to lift her up. They embrace, and the sun sets over the springtime city, and when he rises he does not light a candle in the darkened rooms. Not from miserliness, but from decency.

1833

Thirty-Six

Scrooge orders Cratchit to write his sister, inviting her into the office for consultation upon a certain unsaid matter of import, but she makes no reply. *How very unlike her*, he thinks. Marley is surely to blame. No doubt he has hardened her heart against her brother's influence. So he has Cratchit write her once more—and more urgently this time, with hints that the peril afoot goes well beyond financial matters—but the result is the same. What an embarrassment, to be ignored by his own sister! He is certain that Cratchit is watching the calendar and privately relishing his master's humiliation, although nothing could be further from the truth. Bob has problems of his own.

In the end, because the matter at hand is indeed of the utmost consequence, he visits her. It is a rare occasion. He hardly goes anywhere these days. His office and his bank and his pitiable rented rooms. The coffee shop where he takes his meals. Occasionally, when his partner is enduring one of his weaker days, Marley's bedside for the transaction of some private business matter. How he hates to waste the time. How he resents the interruption of his work. How he despises the man for his weakness.

→→

He finds his sister looking well enough, although she seems to have taken up Marley's habit of lingering beneath the bed linens. His first impulse is to criticize her for it outright, but he holds his tongue. He has more sensitive sums to calculate, and he will touch on her lassitude in time.

"You have ignored my messages," he says, standing at the foot of her bed like doom, shoulders up and arms behind his back.

She offers him a quizzical look. "Perhaps Mother failed to—"

"Do not blame Mother." He presents his hands, one envelope in each. "These were on the hall table. In plain sight. Unopened."

"Forgive me," she says, for what else is there?

Scrooge pockets the letters, sniffs, steadies himself. "I understand that you are still keeping his company."

"Whose company?"

"Marley's."

"Have you come here to forbid it? Are you now my father as well as my brother?"

"Father or brother," says Scrooge, "if I may not forbid your misbehavior, then I may yet discourage it. As I have done since the beginning."

"What is it to you? What is it to you at this late date?"

"The man is a wretch. The notion of your associating with him makes my skin crawl."

"I care little for the condition of your skin."

"You have exposed our blessed mother to his society."

"Mother can look after herself in the little time she has left."

Scrooge clears his throat. "I have visited his apartments, Fan. I have set my eyes upon his painting of you. It is a vile thing."

"How could it be so?"

"It is too—*intimate*."

"It is affectionate."

Scrooge scoffs. "You have been compromised, my dear."

"And you have been perverted."

"Oho! '*Perverted*,' you say!"

"By a life spent in solitude."

"Perversion would be Marley's specialty."

Fan looks hurt, coughs, rubs her jaw. "Jacob cares for me, and he always has."

"Jacob desires you. The difference is significant."

"Either way, there is faithfulness in it."

"Bah. Jacob Marley is the most faithless man alive."

"That distinction would belong to you, Ebenezer."

He hesitates.

She darkens. "You envy me, don't you?"

"What?"

"You envy me his attentions."

Scrooge barks out a laugh. "His attentions! I would not give a shilling for his attentions!"

"Nor would you give a shilling for Belle's."

"You underestimate me, Fan."

"You overestimate yourself. I know you, brother. I know who you are and what you prize in this world."

"You have become cruel," says Scrooge, "just like your *friend*. I came here only to save you."

"I am well past saving," she says, coughing into a handkerchief already stained red. "And so are you, Ebenezer."

1836

Thirty-Seven

He awakens from dream into nightmare. The hand pressed upon his brow belongs not to his beloved but to his nurse. Her touch is chilly, but his beloved's touch would be chillier still—cold and raw as the grave in which she has lain for some months now, while he has only sickened further. Death seems bent on keeping its cold-hearted distance from Marley, and the notion that it came for her first is the purest punishment.

The nurse is a giant of a woman and he is a trace of himself. He does not know her name or where she comes from or how long she has been in his employ. She is in truth more keeper than nurse, for she fixes his meals and cleans his rooms and bathes his withered ruin of a body. She lifts him soiled from his bed now, handling him as gently as a wolf handles a rabbit, and as he groans and gasps she strips both him and his bed down to the essentials. She does not seem to mind the smell. A cauldron of water laced with ammonia simmers upon the grate where a fire burns day and night supplying ash for the making of lye. It is forever laundry day in these rooms. The parlor, draped with linens hung to dry, might be either a sailmaker's loft or the scene of a haunting.

"You're to have a visitor today," says the nurse once he is dressed again and sitting up. "'Tis Christmas Eve, after all."

"What visitor?" The words whistle as they come from between his cracked lips. His mouth is sore and his teeth are entirely gone although God has granted him a toothache nonetheless.

"Why, Mr. Scrooge, my dear." She disappears out the door bearing the linens, and he does not watch her go because the effort required to turn his head is too great. That and the pain. His every joint and muscle is on fire.

She returns in a few moments and he is surprised to see her because his brain is overwhelmed by the sensations inflicted upon it by his body. She brings tea, however, tea and laudanum, and the two compounds cheer him considerably. The tea is a comfort, the laudanum a necessity. It restores him.

He is surprised again when Scrooge arrives. He cannot tell if minutes have passed or hours, for he is floating upon an opiate fog and time is nothing to him. Scrooge raps at the bedroom door as if to raise the dead.

"Go in, go in," says the nurse. "He's decent."

"I shall be the judge of his decency," says Scrooge.

"Enter," mumbles Marley, better late than never.

"Toothache?" says Scrooge, emerging.

"You could say." His voice is muffled by the kerchief wrapped around his head and chin.

"Does that headscarf help?" says Scrooge, drawing up a chair.

"No. Nothing helps."

"Then remove it. It makes you look like a dead man."

"I am preparing for my fate."

"No," says Scrooge, opening his case and drawing out a document. "*This* is how we prepare for your fate." The document is Marley's last will and testament, drawn up by a flesh-and-blood lawyer known to both of them and presented now to be signed and witnessed.

"Fred is in it? As I insisted?"

"Fred is in it."

Marley smiles, an alarming sight. "After all, he must have a living."

"He could *earn* a living, like the rest of us. It would do him good."

"He ought to have something to remember me by. Show me the page, will you?"

Scrooge does.

The words swim in his vision, and so he scans the paragraph for what he believes is an acceptable interval, pronounces the language satisfactory, and asks for the quill. Scrooge goes to fetch the nurse, and the remainder is accomplished in a moment. Once she has witnessed his signature and returned to her laundry, Marley fixes his partner with a dull eye.

"Fred is the last of your family," he says. "Why have you so little feeling for him?"

"I have feeling enough," says Scrooge. "Feeling enough to believe that hard work improves a man's character. Feeling enough to know that a life of ease funded by another's ill-gotten gains will serve a man poorly."

"We must agree to disagree," says Marley.

But Scrooge is not finished. "You are a fine one to ask about my lack of feeling for Fred," he says. "You, who passed the French disease on to his mother."

"I cared for Fan."

"As did I."

"I had been so very well, Ebenezer. My condition. I didn't know . . ."

"Humbug. Everyone knows. The disease sleeps and then it awakens. It is a treacherous thing, and one not to be taken lightly."

"We cared for each other," says Marley, who understands treachery.

"Did you advise her? At the outset, I mean? Or even as you . . . went along?"

"I believed that she knew."

"*You believed*," hisses Scrooge. "Bah."

He thrusts the will into his case and removes from its depths another document, the record of some trumped-up transaction that he has found in the bowels of Marley's office. "On the subject of belief," he says, "I should like to present you with this."

Marley reaches for the document, grows dizzy, and asks Scrooge if he will do the reading on his behalf.

"No need," says Scrooge. "There is little here of import beyond the names of the solicitors who perpetrated this particular fraud."

"And those names would be?"

"Sweedlepipe and Steerforth. Memorable appellations, don't you think?"

"Names to conjure with."

"Names not to be forgotten," says Scrooge. "And for my part, I never have."

Marley is adrift. He requires either more laudanum or less. "I'm afraid I don't . . ."

"*Sweedlepipe and Steerforth*. Ridiculous names. Absurd names." He stabs at the paper with a lean finger. "You used them here, just twelve years ago—but you first employed them at Professor Drabb's. When we were boys."

Marley squeezes his eyes shut. "Drabb's," he says. "I remember."

"You've been taking advantage of me from the beginning. There was never an ounce of kindness in you. Never a trace of so-called *feeling*. And yet you accuse me."

"You wrong me, Ebenezer. I have possessed feeling. Perhaps not for you—at least not so often or as deeply as I should have—but most definitely for others."

Scrooge wrinkles his lip.

"For your sister."

"Bah."

"For her son."

"Humbug."

Marley falters, his supply of defensive materials having run low.

"Is that all, then, Jacob? Is that the sum of your so-called *feeling*?"

Marley casts about in his mind for some truth upon which to hang his defense. "The plain fact," he concludes, "is that regardless of feeling, you and I have always struggled for advantage. It is the way of the world."

Scrooge casts the telltale document into the grate. "Just so," he says with satisfaction. "We have indeed struggled, you and I. We have struggled mightily. And in the end, I have claimed the victory."

"Only because I relented and left you to have your way."

"No," says Scrooge. "It is far simpler than that. I am the victor because I shall live."

Marley makes no answer.

Scrooge bends and takes up his case and fastens it tight. "And once you are in the grave I shall be your sole executor, your sole administrator, your sole assign, your sole residuary legatee, and—I have no doubt—your sole mourner."

"Not sole. Not sole. There is always Fred."

"*Fred.*" Scrooge repeats the name with a dry chuckle. "Fred, I'm afraid, will be quite busy looking after himself."

A dark light dawns upon Marley.

"To deprive him of the privilege of toil would have been to ruin him," says Scrooge.

"But the will . . ." Marley turns in the bed, reaches out, spasms.

"Did you fail to read it closely? I would have expected better of you."

"But my wishes, Ebenezer."

"There are wishes, and then there are wills."

"Then shall I leave nothing to the boy?"

"A token. A token of your *feeling*, if you will. That is all."

"Have pity on him, Ebenezer."

"Pity is not in my line of business, nor was it ever in yours."

Something flares in the back of Marley's eyes, a smoldering trace of their old gleam. "How little you know me after all these years," he says. "Why, I pity you at this very moment." He gathers himself the slightest bit, straining in the bed as if he might yet make himself even a suggestion of the individual he used to be. "I pity you for loving money over men."

"Bah."

"I pity you for casting your nephew aside in order to gain a fortune you do not need."

"Humbug."

"You possess enough, Ebenezer."

"One might say so. But soon I shall possess everything. I shall take occupancy of these premises of yours, and I shall make a full inventory of the riches you have hidden here and elsewhere. I shall record every last farthing and ducat, marking it all down double-entered and cross-referenced in as many ledgers as may be required. In short, I shall devote myself as years go by to totaling up the sins of Jacob Marley. There will be justice in it, justice at last. For both of us."

"It's too late for justice," says Marley.

"Perhaps," says Scrooge, "but it is never too late for an accounting—and I shall have mine."

"May God have mercy upon your immortal soul," says Jacob.

He drifts off as the church bell strikes God knows what. Some hour more than twelve, by the sound of it, and whether the whole world or only Jacob Marley has spun off into uncharted chronological territory on this Christmas morning he cannot say.

Now that he considers it, the sound might be the clanging of a ship's bell. Ships' bells mark the watches, do they not? And how many watches are there? With how many hours to each? The questions ramify too quickly to ponder, but the sound of the bell as it rings out its last is surely not that which he has heard so often from the church steeple. It has a wilder clang to it, a weird and keening timbre that speaks of distance and movement and desperation.

There are men here. No, not men—at least not all of them.

Call them souls, then, for souls they are, and together they are bound in the belly of this ship, bound not only by manacles and chains but by strange, complex, and looping encrustations made from cashboxes, keys, padlocks, ledgers, and heavy purses wrought in steel. He can hear them as the ship tosses and their weight shifts like the weight of snakes, coil upon coil. His ears are filled with their brutal grinding.

No one calls out. No one speaks. No one dares breathe, for the air in this place is death.

He knows these souls. He knows Madeline the whore and he knows McCullough the murderer and he knows poor ancient Stitch who burned the *Mariel* for nothing. He knows a hundred others whom he has wronged directly in this world or the world prior. He knows a thousand more—slaves and children of slaves—whom he has wronged at great remove. He knows Fan. Here in this stinking hold, they are bound and they are bound.

Only one is missing. Balfour.

Perhaps his absence is a sign of hope. If there is mercy in the world, Captain Harry Balfour of the West Africa Squadron will spy this ship tossing upon whatever sea she sails and board her, set her captives free, right every wrong. It is not too much to ask. It is far too much to ask. It is not.

END

Acknowledgments

Few projects are as solitary as the making of a book. Yet there are always those, thank God, who help along the way—sometimes by helping to make the writing better, sometimes by helping to make the writer better. *Marley*, then, would not be the same without . . .

Marly "Without-an-E" Rusoff, who understood what I was up to from the get-go, and moved heaven and earth to see that it all came to fruition. It wasn't easy. She just made it look that way.

Peter Borland, Libby McGuire, Sean deLone, and James Iacobelli at Atria, who made my work better than I knew how to make it myself, dressed it up in a killer outfit, and sent it out properly into the great big world.

Bob Hill, David Lindgren, and Steve Kendra, early readers, of course, but mainly true friends and counselors and companions who have been with me from childhood and will be there when *Marley* is a memory.

Lauren Baratz-Logsted, Tasha Alexander, Danielle Younge-Ullman, Keith Cronin, Jessica Keener, Darcie Chan, Renee Rosen, Sachin Waikar,

and Karen Dionne, members all of a secret society that both grounds me
and lifts me up.

Charles Dickens, who left enough strategic holes in *A Christmas Carol* that I was able to cook up an entire novel out of the missing bits.

Emily and John and Sam and Ivy Bryk, who give me so much delight that nothing else really matters.

And Wendy, who for some reason always believes.